THE CORFE CASTLE MURDERS

DORSET CRIME BOOK 1

RACHEL MCLEAN

ACKROYD
PUBLISHING

Ackroyd Publishing

ackroyd-publishing.com

THE CORFE CASTLE MURDERS

CHAPTER ONE

LAILA STOPPED HALFWAY up the stairs, her senses pricking.

There was someone in her room.

She could hear drawers being pulled out, doors being opened. Footsteps; no matter how hard the intruder tried to be stealthy, this was an old, creaky house.

Was Archie back?

No. Archie wasn't coming back till Monday. He had a meeting in London, something to do with securing extra funding for the dig. Now they'd uncovered evidence of 12th century occupation, they were all hopeful.

Holding her breath, she took one step up, as carefully as she could. She could see into the room she shared with Archie, over the top step.

It would be Crystal. The woman liked to poke her nose into other people's business. As the dig leader, she seemed to think she had the right. But their bedrooms had locks, and were supposed to be private.

She'd become complacent. She should remember to lock her door every morning.

The intruder came into view, facing away from Laila. She gritted her teeth.

Patrick.

What was that old perv doing in her room? Why was he going through her and Archie's stuff?

Patrick gave her the creeps. Since he'd tried it on with her the day after she arrived, she'd steered clear of him. She didn't want a confrontation.

She slid back down the stairs and opened the front door. She slammed it shut again. Humming loudly despite her unease, she stomped up the stairs.

When she arrived at the top, Patrick was standing on the landing. He stared at her, hands on hips.

"You should tidy your room." He gestured back through the open door. "Look at it, bloody disgrace."

She met his eye, her stomach fluttering. Patrick was more than twice her age, the most experienced member of the group. He made her nervous.

"Have you been in my room?"

He blew a greasy grey hair out of his eyes. "What d'you take me for? You might want to close the door in future, though."

"Lock it, more like."

She squeezed past him and closed her and Archie's door. Patrick watched her from the open doorway of his own room. Behind him, all was tidy. So immaculate that you could imagine no one lived in there.

"That's better," he grunted.

She eyed him. "I'm going back out."

"Already?"

"It's a free country."

She barrelled down the stairs, her stomach churning.

She'd been looking forward to a quiet few hours reading her book. Maybe on her bed, maybe in the cosy sitting room downstairs. But she didn't want to be alone in the cottage with Patrick. Archie was away for his meeting and there was no sign of Crystal.

"See you later," Patrick called down the stairs. Laila shuddered and closed the front door behind her. It led directly onto a narrow strip of pavement alongside an equally narrow road that cars struggled to get down. The village of Corfe Castle hadn't been designed for modern living.

At least the sun was out. She'd wander up to the dig site, and then she might sit outside the Greyhound with a pint. They had benches out the front, filling another narrow pavement, and she liked to watch the world go by.

She hurried along West Street, glancing behind her from time to time to check Patrick hadn't followed. *Don't be paranoid.* Even he wasn't that much of a creep.

She turned the corner by the entrance to the car park then took the footpath across the fields to reach the dig site. It was quiet on a Sunday, the normal hubbub of tools and voices missing.

She could hear the trill of birdsong from the trees up ahead, cars passing beyond them.

They'd dug three trenches so far, one in the centre of the site where they believed the bailey of King Stephen's siege castle had lain. A second had been dug nearer the village, where the geophysics suggested the outer wall might have been. And a smaller test trench, near the mound where Laila stood. The two more established trenches had tents over them to protect them from the weather. It might be June in southern England, but you could always guarantee rain.

She pushed aside the flaps of the tent closest to her, the

one over the wall. She'd been working here the day before and had found coins, worn down and mud-encrusted, but hopefully from the 12th century.

She wandered out over the mounds that covered suspected fortifications, heading for the second tent. Two crows rose into the sky as she approached, disturbed by her footsteps. A short distance away, a group of wood pigeons pecked at the ground.

She grabbed the flap of the tent. This was where they were hoping to find the remains of a medieval building. Crystal and Patrick worked in here most days, along with a rotating crew of students from Bournemouth University

Startled by a bird flying out of the tent, Laila looked away. She batted at it as it brushed past her, but it was gone.

What had it found? They were careful to clear the dig site at the end of each day, cataloguing their finds and hauling them back to the cottage. They were stored in an outhouse until they could be transferred to the university. It had been drilled into them all that there was a risk not only of animal damage, but human too.

The tent was warm in the afternoon heat, muggy. There was a thick smell that made Laila's nose twitch. Someone had left a tarpaulin in the middle of the space and flies buzzed around it.

Laila bent down, puzzled. She grabbed the edge of the tarp. Had someone come in here earlier and left it behind?

She lifted the tarpaulin. A cloud of flies rose up at her. She dropped the fabric, waving her hands and spitting away the flies that tried to enter her mouth.

There was something under there. Her stomach lurched: this felt wrong. Crystal never left anything behind, and what was that smell?

Laila lifted one hand to cover her nose and grabbed the tarpaulin with the other. She pulled it up, wishing she hadn't come here.

Her mouth fell open. She was oblivious to the flies now, her body numb. She dropped the tarp.

No. She was imagining things.

Gingerly, resisting the urge to close her eyes, she lifted the fabric again.

And screamed.

CHAPTER TWO

DETECTIVE CHIEF INSPECTOR Lesley Clarke sat at the wrought iron table, sizing up the cream tea in front of her. She looked across the idyllic garden towards one of the most iconic views England had to offer.

She drew a deep breath, forced herself to sit upright, and wondered what the hell she'd done to deserve this.

She picked up her knife. Might as well make the best of it.

Jam first, or cream? She had a feeling the elderly couple who kept peering at her from the next table along would tut audibly if she got it wrong.

"We're in Dorset, mum. Jam first."

Lesley turned to see her daughter Sharon standing over her. She'd buggered off to the loo – the lavatory, as the tea room insisted on calling it – and to have an argument with the old bat who ran the place.

"I told you not to bother," Lesley said. She raised a hand to shield her eyes from the June sunshine. "You never win with women like that."

"That's not like you, Mum." Sharon sat down and surveyed her own plate of sandwiches. "What would your bosses at West Midlands Police say if they knew the woman behind the counter of a rural tea room had got the better of you?"

"She didn't *get the better* of me." Lesley put down her knife and picked up the first jam-and-cream-laden scone. She grimaced. "She probably did me a favour."

Sharon laughed through a mouthful of granary bread. "You wanted a beer, Mum. Not exactly a crime."

Lesley swallowed the first bite and leaned in. "Ah, but it is, sweetheart. Drinking a cold pint on a hot day in a National Trust tea room is clearly a crime most heinous in nature. I should turn myself in."

"Not if you've ordered a knife and fork meal," said Sharon.

Lesley scooped crumbs from her trousers. Sharon had bought them for her. Sensible ones, rain repellent. Designed to be worn on long country walks. Lesley hated them already.

"She's still sticking to that line?" she asked her daughter.

A nod. "Firm as a rock."

"I told you she'd ignore you, love. You're not even old enough to *buy* beer."

"Old enough to stand up for my invalid mum."

"Oi." Lesley reached across the table and swiped at Sharon with her knife. "Less of that."

The elderly couple at the next table muttered to each other. Lesley turned to them with a bright, sarcastic smile. They lowered their heads and turned away.

"Stop it, Mum."

Lesley spread jam on the second scone. A pot of tea stood next to her plate. *Bleurgh, tea.* She'd drunk enough of that over the last few months to fill Boston harbour. If she found a way to eat scones with a fork, would they let her have that pint?

"Stop what?" She popped more scone into her mouth and treated Sharon to a look of wide-eyed innocence.

"Winding up the locals. What if they're the victims of a crime you have to investigate?"

"They're not locals."

"Why not?" Sharon glanced at the couple. They'd shifted their twiddly wrought iron chairs so their backs were to her and Lesley.

"Guide book. Nasty his-and-hers turquoise cagoules. That *ooh look isn't everything pretty* air."

"Shush."

Lesley laughed. "I know you don't like me being rude. Your dad hates it."

"Maybe that should tell you something."

"Maybe it should." Lesley leaned back, angled herself to look at the view of Corfe Castle, and turned back again. "But when you get to my age, sweetheart, it's bloody hard to change your ways."

"You're not *that* old."

"Forty-six is old enough. You'll understand one day."

The elderly couple in the cagoules stood up from their table. The woman gave Lesley a look of disdain as they walked away. Lesley watched them leave, shaking her head.

"All that because I said *bloody*."

"And the rest of it." Sharon was gathering plates and cups onto their tray, to make it easier for the kid who was cleaning up. He didn't look old enough to be lawfully employed.

"You don't have to do that," Lesley said.

"Habit."

"You always were a considerate child."

Sharon gave her a look. Lesley knew they were both thinking the same thing: someone in the family had to be. What with Lesley's infamous abruptness, and Terry's habit of being so distracted he was incapable of noticing when someone might need his help, perhaps Sharon had spent her childhood compensating.

Lesley stood up. "Come on, then. You've got to pack. Train to Birmingham's in just over an hour."

Sharon's face clouded. "I'll miss you, Mum."

Lesley gave her a smile that hid her own emotions. "I'll be home for a visit next weekend. You'll be busy with school, you won't even notice I'm gone."

"Still. I wish they hadn't sent you down here."

Lesley put a hand on her daughter's arm. "It'll only be six months. Time for you to get settled in at your new school in September. I'll come back when I can, and you and Dad can come down here in the holidays."

"He says he's too busy with work."

What could Terry have that would keep him so busy? He was a lecturer in Anthropology at Birmingham University. Hardly high-pressure.

"He'll change his tune when he sees the house they've rented for me."

Sharon laughed. "It's tiny."

Lesley steered her towards the gate that led from the garden of the tea room to the lane leading up to the castle. "Quaint, I think they call it in these parts. Cosy." She smiled and opened the gate.

Sharon shook her head. She was sixteen, old enough to

leave home in theory. And she had a glittering future ahead of her at a specialist arts school in Birmingham.

"What was that?" Lesley turned back to the garden.

"What was what?" asked Sharon.

Lesley hurried between the tables to a fence that looked out over the fields beneath the castle. She gripped the wood. "I heard..."

From somewhere out there, a scream sounded.

"I heard it that time," Sharon said.

Lesley turned to her daughter. She knew her eyes would be sparkling. "Someone's in trouble."

"You haven't even started your new job yet. Let the local police—"

Lesley gripped Sharon by the shoulders. "I don't do this just because it's my job. And besides, local police are probably miles away. Or enjoying a cream tea somewhere."

Sharon raised an eyebrow. Lesley peered down at the fields below the castle. She could see what looked like a mound of earthworks, two tents standing on it. They reminded her of forensic tents.

A young woman ran out of one of the tents. Lesley pointed her out.

"That's her." She grabbed Sharon's hand. "Come on, your train'll have to wait."

CHAPTER THREE

LAILA STOOD in the middle of the Rings, looking frantically around. Her scream had frightened away those birds. They'd flapped off noisily, making her scream a second time.

Her mind ran over what she'd seen. The main tent covered a broad trench, in the middle of which lay a depression. Laila hadn't seen it herself, she'd been kept to the smaller trench behind which she now stood. But Crystal had described it to her: human remains. Fragments of bone, centuries old, if not a millennium. Teeth preserved by the damp soil. Sections of a gold necklace, gaps where precious stones would once have been inlaid.

But that wasn't what Laila had seen. She brought her hands up to her face and let out a long moan. She shook all over, her limbs trembling.

She sank to the ground. She was hyperventilating. Where was her inhaler? She'd barely used it since arriving in Dorset, the fresh air had been good for her. It was in her bedroom somewhere.

Her and Archie's bedroom. The bedroom that Patrick had been searching through.

She heard voices and looked up. Two women emerged from the trees between the site and the village. The taller one was in her late forties, with short blonde hair. She wore a faded denim jacket over a pair of walking trousers. The other woman was young, younger than Laila. She had long dark hair that kept catching in the breeze and she wore suede boots that were unsuited to the rough grass. Despite everything, Laila couldn't help thinking that her boots would be ruined.

The two women approached Laila. The older one stepped forward. She reached inside her jacket then tutted and shook her head. She was panting.

"Did you scream?" she asked.

Laila nodded. Her mouth was dry, her head swimming. She opened her mouth and closed it again. After a moment, wondering why she couldn't speak, she pointed at the tent.

The older one shook her companion's arm. "You stay here. Make sure she's OK." She glanced at Laila. "If she faints, call me."

Laila felt her body dip. She felt hollow, like she might float away. She wanted to stop the woman, to keep her from going in there. If no one else saw…

"My name's Lesley Clarke," the woman said. "I'm a Detective Chief Inspector with Dorset Police. Is there something in that tent?"

Laila nodded. She wanted to lie back, to let the earth hold her. Now that the birds had left, the air had gone quiet.

"Don't worry," the detective said. "You're in shock. I'm going to take a look."

"No," Laila croaked.

"What did you see?"

Laila shook her head. She couldn't find the words.

The woman exchanged a glance with her younger colleague. She made for the tent. Laila swallowed the acrid taste in her mouth.

The younger woman sat down opposite Laila. "What's your name?"

"Laila," she whispered.

The woman – not much more than a girl – gave her a thin smile.

"You're police too?" Laila whispered.

"God, no." The girl pointed towards the tent. "That's my mum."

The older woman was lifting the flap to go in. Laila moaned.

"You need me to call an ambulance?" the girl asked.

Laila shook her head. She frowned. "Not for me."

But it was too late for that. She'd known as soon as she'd seen him.

Laila and the policewoman's daughter both looked towards the tent. A group of birds had reappeared, gathered around its entrance.

"Oh, fuck," came a muffled voice from inside.

"That's Mum," the girl said with an apologetic expression. "You get used to it."

Laila stared at the tent. She waited for the detective to emerge.

"Uniform are here." The young woman stood up. Sure enough, two uniformed officers approached from the trees behind them. They must have parked in the road for Kingston. One man, one woman. The female officer had removed her hat and had it wedged under her arm.

The two constables arrived as the detective emerged from the tent. She strode towards them. Her expression had changed from concern and curiosity to professional efficiency.

"DCI Clarke," she said to them. "Major Crime Investigations Team."

"Ma'am," said the female constable. "Sorry, I didn't recognise you."

"You wouldn't."

The male constable frowned at her. "Can I see your ID, please?"

The woman's hand went towards her jacket again, but stopped before reaching inside.

"I'm due to start tomorrow. I haven't been issued with a warrant card yet."

"I'm sorry, madam," the male officer said, "but you'll have to stand back. This is a police matter."

"Simon," hissed his colleague. "Why would she be lying?"

The detective turned to Laila. "Did you go inside the tent?"

"Yes."

"You saw him?"

"Yes." Laila's voice was small.

The male constable cleared his throat. "What's in there?"

"I suggest you go and see for yourself," the woman who'd described herself as a detective said.

"I will." He strode off. The female PC bit her lip.

The blonde woman crouched down to bring her face level with Laila's. "How are you feeling?"

Laila shrugged.

"We'll need to take a statement from you. Not just yet, we'll give you some time to get your head together."

Laila told the woman her name and address. The female constable took out a notebook and wrote them down. Laila realised the older woman had a Birmingham accent. Maybe she had been lying about being a Dorset detective.

"Do you know who he is?" the woman asked her. "Did you recognise him?"

Laila closed her eyes. She thought of his body, twisted into the trench. His leather jacket, the one he never wore down here, stained with blood. The gash on the back of his head. His eyes, one obscured by blood and the other staring up at her.

God, the eyes.

She swayed, the world shifting. She felt hands on her back, steadying her. It was the younger woman, the detective's daughter.

"Yes," she muttered.

"Yes, you recognise him?" the PC asked.

"It's Archie." Laila fell back, the girl taking her weight.

"Archie who?" the older woman asked.

"Archie Weatherton. My boyfriend."

CHAPTER FOUR

LESLEY LOOKED into the young woman's eyes. She was leaning against Sharon, her lips trembling and her right eye twitching.

"He was your boyfriend?"

The woman – Laila, she'd said her name was – drew in a shaky breath. She nodded.

"She's in shock, Mum," Sharon said. "We should call an ambulance."

Lesley looked up at the female constable. "Where's the nearest hospital?"

"Dorchester's the closest A&E."

"That's bloody miles away." Lesley was used to a hospital always being in spitting distance.

"They won't have to come all that way, Ma'am. They have bases. Nearest one's a lay-by just outside Norden station."

Lesley had no idea where Norden station was, but she nodded and the PC stepped away to radio it in. Her male colleague had left the tent and was approaching them, his face pale.

Lesley stood up and brushed her godawful trousers down. "What's your name?"

"PC Mullins, Madam. This is PC Abbott. We'll take it from here, if you don't mind." He gave her a *humour the delusional person* look.

Lesley gritted her teeth. This bloody idiot was going to regret treating her like a candidate for Care in the Community.

"I suggest you call in to your station, PC Mullins. Have them identify me for you. DCI Clarke. Formerly of West Midlands Police. As of tomorrow, serving in Dorset Police."

"I'm sorry, Madam, but in the absence of ID..."

"Christ on a bike, son. I'm not a serving officer. Not till tomorrow." She resisted an urge to rap him on the top of the head.

His colleague, PC Abbott, put her radio away. "Ambulance will be here in two minutes, Ma'am. Waiting at Norden, as I expected."

"Where is Norden?"

"Station just outside Corfe," said Sharon. "It's the main stop for the steam engine."

"I know it. The Harry Potter special," said Lesley.

"Actually, no," said PC Mullins. "That's the route from Fort William you're thinking of, not the Swanage Railway."

"They filmed here though," said Sharon. "Used Corfe Station for a scene in *Fantastic Beasts*."

"I'm not sure about that," said Mullins. "But it's Corfe Castle."

"I know," replied Sharon.

"You don't," he replied. "Visitors always get it wrong. It's Corfe Castle. The village. Not Corfe."

Lesley rolled her eyes. Where was that bloody ambulance? Sharon shifted her weight. Laila, leaning against her, murmured.

"Mum, I'm worried about her." The young woman had turned very pale.

Lesley crouched next to her and put a finger on her neck. "Pulse is fine. Paramedics will give her a heat blanket, she'll be fine to give a statement tomorrow."

She stood up. "PC Abbott, let's set up a cordon. We need to protect the crime scene. You can start at the trees over there, you'll have to improvise on the other side."

"Ma'am." PC Abbott made for the trees.

A siren sounded and an ambulance pulled up beyond the trees, behind the squad car. Two burly paramedics struggled through the bushes. One of them kneeled in front of Laila.

"Hello, love. I'm Duncan. Can you hear me?"

"She discovered a body," Lesley told him. "Tells us it's her boyfriend."

The second paramedic brought a hand up to shield his eyes as he looked towards the tent. PC Abbott was stringing tape from the trees past the tent. She's left a wide margin: she knew what she was doing.

"Definitely deceased?" the paramedic asked.

"I'm a DCI," Lesley said. "I know a dead body when I see it."

"Forensics got here quick."

"The tent was already there." Lesley looked at Laila, who was being helped to sit straight by the first paramedic.

"Archaeological dig," said PC Mullins. "Tents have been there a few weeks now."

"I know the one," said the paramedic. "Bunch of hippies from Bournemouth University. Got themselves a commune in the village, I hear."

Lesley glared at him. "One of those *hippies* is dead. Another one is unlucky enough to need your care."

He shrugged. "Doesn't bother me. We'll treat anyone."

Yes, but not with respect, thought Lesley.

"I'll need to take a look," said the paramedic.

"What at?"

He nodded towards the tent. "All due respect, Ma'am, but I'd like to be sure we've got a dead body on our hands and not a living patient."

Lesley considered reminding him of her rank and her decades of police experience. She considered describing the condition of the body. But it would be quicker to show him. She didn't imagine he saw a lot of mutilated bodies, working in this backwater. Maybe it would shut him up.

She gestured towards the tent: *be my guest*.

"I'll accompany you," said PC Mullins.

"No," said Lesley. "Your colleague will."

The female PC was behind the tent, setting down stones to hold the tape in place. Lesley and the paramedic approached while PC Mullins and Sharon stayed behind, eyeing each other nervously.

"Here we are." Lesley put out a hand to stop the paramedic. They were a few paces from the tent: already too much damage had been done.

"This is a crime scene," she told him. "I don't know how many of them you've w—"

"Plenty, Ma'am."

"So you'll understand my priorities. Secure, protect,

preserve. There will be evidence inside that tent, and I don't want it walking away on your boots."

"I need access to the patient."

"Not patient, body. And you'll be able to see all you need to from the entrance."

"In which case, show me where I should stand."

"Good man." Lesley surveyed the grass at the entrance to the tent. The weather had been dry and sunny since she and Sharon had arrived in Dorset on Thursday. Which meant there was no mud for them to trample on, but also no mud for the killer to have left prints in. She wondered when the archaeological team had last been working inside.

"Right," she said. "If we stand to one side of the tent entrance, on the right, we'll be less likely to disturb the killer's route in and out. The body is on the left, so you'll get a good view."

"I'd rather we got a shift on," the paramedic said. "If he needs treatment..."

"He doesn't," Lesley replied. She suspected he already believed her, or he would have gone blustering in there already. "Come on then. PC Abbott, you stay behind. Put up another cordon by the road, keep gawkers away."

"Ma'am." PC Abbott turned towards the trees. Lesley wondered how long it would be before all this was noticed. Judging by what she'd seen at the castle, the National Trust would waste no time getting down here and selling tickets.

At the tent, she pulled the fabric aside. The paramedic leaned around her and surveyed the scene.

"Well?" she said.

"He doesn't need treatment."

"No, indeed."

The man inside was severely mutilated. His clothes were

daubed in blood and the side of his head was caved in. One eye had either been lost or congealed with blood, and the other stared at them lifelessly.

Lesley let the fabric drop. Laila was standing up now, leaning on the first paramedic and being guided towards the ambulance. Sharon sat on the grass, PC Mullins standing over her. As Laila and the paramedic reached the trees, they were passed by a man in a brown tweed jacket. He grunted at the paramedic then shuffled through the greenery, holding his arms out to keep himself from being scratched.

Lesley walked back to her daughter. "Are you OK?"

"We'll have missed my train."

"It's not the last one."

"My ticket's just for that train."

"I'll buy you another bloody ticket, love."

"I've got school tomorrow. I want to go home."

Home. Lesley kneeled next to her daughter, not caring if she got stains on her trousers. "I'm sorry, sweetheart. I didn't mean for you to get dragged into all of this."

"I know. But Laila's OK, now. She's in the ambulance. We can leave now, can't we?"

Lesley sighed. PC Mullins and PC Abbott were with the man in the tweed jacket. The pathologist?

She needed to preserve the scene. She should record who came in and out. She didn't care if this wasn't her job yet, she had to do it properly.

"I'm sorry, Sharon." She put a hand on the girl's wrist. "I'm afraid we can't leave just yet."

CHAPTER FIVE

LESLEY HURRIED towards the constables and the man in the tweed jacket. He wore heavy-framed glasses which he pushed up his nose as he approached.

"What's happened?" the man was asking Mullins. "The ambulance?"

"Ambulance has got a witness in it, Sarge. She found a body." Mullins pointed to the tent.

"Forensics got that up already?" The sergeant checked his watch. "I'm impressed."

"It's an archaeological dig, Sarge," said PC Abbott. "The King Stephen investigation at the Rings."

The sergeant looked from her to Mullins. "Show me." He strode towards the tent, Mullins following.

"Er, excuse me?" Lesley said.

The sergeant looked over his shoulder. "Madam. We'll be right with you, take a statement." He waved a hand in Abbott's direction. "See to it, would you?"

Lesley planted her feet in the grass and folded her arms. She wished she wasn't wearing these bloody trousers.

"What's your name, Sergeant?"

"Frampton. You don't need me, PC Abbott can take your statement." He turned towards the tent and stopped at the cordon.

"Mum, let's just leave them to it," Sharon said. She pulled her phone from her pocket. She jabbed at it and scowled: no signal.

"Just a minute, sweetheart." Lesley had been the first officer on the scene. As the new DCI in the MCIT only ten miles from here, she would probably be Senior Investigating Officer, or SIO.

She caught up with Sergeant Frampton. "Are you CID? It's a Sunday, maybe you're off duty." She looked him up and down: short, thinning on top with a pinched expression and weathered cheeks. "You look like CID."

"Yes, Madam. I'm CID."

"In that case, let me introduce myself." She held out her hand. "DCI Lesley Clarke. I start in the Major Crime Investigations Team tomorrow morning. You could say I jumped in early."

His jaw softened. "Ma'am."

"You don't need to ma'am me just yet."

He stiffened. "I'm a DS in that unit. I believe... I believe we'll be working together."

"Good." Lesley narrowed her eyes. "We might as well get started, then. First off, I've seen the body. IC1 male, red hair, medium height and build. The young woman who went away in the ambulance, Laila Ford, identified him as Archie Weatherton. Her boyfriend. He looks a bit old for her to me, but it takes all sorts."

"You didn't detain her?" the sergeant asked. "Ma'am."

"She was in shock, DS Frampton. No state to be making

a statement, much less an accurate one. We can send PC Abbott round to talk to her in the morning, the two of them have already built up trust."

"We don't send Uniform to take statements from potential suspects."

"She isn't a suspect. She's a witness."

Frampton squared his shoulders. "One, she claims to have found his body. Two, she was his girlfriend. Sounds pretty cut and dried to me."

Lesley took a step forward. "Cut and dried? You haven't spoken to her. You haven't even set eyes on her. You haven't examined the body, you haven't gathered forensics. You haven't identified any other witnesses. Are you people not interested in evidence down here?"

He reddened. "With all due respect, Ma'am. This is Corfe Castle, not the big city. If someone finds their husband, or wife, or partner, or best friend's dog, dead – then it's a safe bet they're the one who did it."

He spoke with a Dorset accent, a soft burr that failed to take the edge off his incompetence. Lesley held herself back. She hadn't even been introduced to her Superintendent yet. Best get the lie of the land before she started banging heads together.

"Very, well, Sergeant. If you want to adopt a working hypothesis that Laila Ford killed her boyfriend, purely for your own personal amusement, then you do so. But I intend to follow the evidence."

He twisted his lips. He was aching to tell her she wasn't on the job yet, she knew.

He turned to PC Mullins. "Come on, lad. Let's take a look."

Voices sounded behind. Frampton looked past her and his shoulders slumped. Lesley turned to see a heavily-built woman with dark curly hair and a vast holdall slung over her shoulder heading their way.

"Don't go inside," she called. "We need to check if that tent's up to the job."

The woman stopped in front of them, breathing heavily. Two men were behind her. They stopped and waited, eyes on the woman who Lesley assumed was their boss.

The woman held out her hand, her eyes bright. "Gail Hansford, Crime Scene Manager. I don't believe we've met."

She had that same soft burr, except in this case, it suited her. Lesley shook her hand. "Lesley Clarke. New DCI in the Major Crimes Team."

Gail's eyes widened. "Then it's our lucky day. I assume you're SIO?"

DS Frampton cleared his throat. Gail ignored him. Lesley decided she liked this woman.

Sharon was near the trees, pacing and waving her phone around. Lesley had no idea when the next train to Birmingham was, or if there even was another train this afternoon.

"To be honest, Gail," she said, "I don't start in the local force until tomorrow. So strictly speaking, I have no authority here." She pointed towards the tent. "We've got a dead male, IC1, late thirties or forties, severe head trauma. I assume someone has called for the pathologist to attend."

"Called him on my way here," said Frampton. "He wasn't happy being dragged out on a Sunday afternoon."

"Well that's what on-call is for," said Lesley. She turned to Gail. "The scene will need securing. Forensics gathering. You know the drill."

"I do, Ma'am."

"The paramedics came in and out the same way you did. My daughter and I came via that path over there. I assume the witness did too, but we can check that tomorrow."

Gail nodded.

"All of which means," Lesley continued, "that we've got some localised areas where the place has been trampled up. You'll need to—"

"We'll get footwear information from everyone who's been through here," Gail said. "We've already got prints and DNA for the attending police officers. Except yours, of course."

"I'll get them sent down from West Midlands." Lesley told her. "I believe I can leave the scene in your hands."

"You certainly can, Ma'am." Gail smiled.

DS Frampton grunted. Lesley turned to him. "Sergeant, you're the ranking officer on the scene. Make sure it's protected from ingress by the public. Liaise with FSM and Uniform for a search of the area."

"FSM?"

"Forensic Scene... what do you call it?"

"Crime Scene Management, Ma'am," said Frampton.

"CSI. Like the yanks. Just do the liaison, yes?"

"Of course." His voice was flat, his expression neutral.

Lesley looked up at her daughter, who was wandering across the grassy mounds, her phone above her head. A forensics nightmare.

"I'll see you both in the morning," Lesley said. "I'm assuming there won't be much of interest from the pathologist, but let me know if there is."

"Of course," Gail and Frampton said in unison. They exchanged frowns.

Lesley chuckled. "Baptism of fire." She trudged back the way she'd come, cursing the growing crowd of gawpers and hoping to hell there was another train to Birmingham today.

CHAPTER SIX

LAILA SAT on a bench outside Dorset County Hospital, her arms pulled tightly around her. She'd been taken to A&E and had waited almost an hour to be seen. The paramedics had used some kind of electric blanket to warm her up in the ambulance and one of them had given her a cereal bar.

By the time she'd arrived at the hospital she'd been fine, physically at least. Mentally, she was barely keeping herself from falling off a cliff edge.

As long as she didn't think about Archie's body, she could cling on by her fingertips. Every time the memory crept into her head, she tried to push it out by picturing Archie as he had been on Friday night, before he'd left for his meeting.

The two of them had left the confines of the cottage for the evening. He'd driven her to Swanage, where they'd eaten fish and chips on the pier. Neither of them ever had any money, despite Archie having a good job at Bristol University. Whenever she asked him about it, he clammed up.

He'd been happy, teasing her about the purple streaks

she'd dyed into her blonde hair. He'd been affectionate too, even discussing their future beyond the dig.

He lived in Bristol when he wasn't here. She lived – well, she lived nowhere, really.

A green Citroen pulled up opposite and the horn blared: Crystal. Laila dragged herself off the bench and shuffled to the car, her limbs heavy. Crystal beckoned wildly: she was on double yellows and didn't want to hang around. Laila slid into the passenger seat. Crystal drove off before she'd got her seatbelt on.

"What the hell happened to you?" Crystal asked. "Why couldn't they take you to the cottage hospital in Wareham? You'll have to pay me for the petrol."

Laila clutched the door handle. Crystal sped out of the car park, taking a corner at a sharp angle and briefly mounting the kerb.

Laila closed her eyes. It made the nausea worse. She opened them.

"Thanks for picking me up."

"Hmm. So are you going to tell me what's up?"

Laila looked out at the damp evening. Dorchester was busy, tourist traffic clogging the roads. Street lights sped past, making her dizzy.

"It's Archie," she said.

"What about him?" Crystal jerked the wheel to one side and they skidded onto the A35.

"I found him."

"What d'you mean, you found him?"

Laila swallowed. The words were too big. "Have you been to the dig site today?"

"No. It's my day off." Crystal gestured at the driver in front.

Keep your hands on the wheel. "It's been taken over by the police."

"What? Laila hen, you're making no sense. Start again. Did Archie do something? Is he in trouble?"

Laila swallowed the thick bile at the back of her mouth. "He's dead."

Crystal jabbed the brake. "Shit." She looked in the rear-view mirror. "Sorry!"

A car overtook, horn receding into the dusk.

Crystal turned to Laila. "Archie's dead? When? Did his wi—?" She bit her lip. "Explain, Laila."

"I found him." Laila tightened her grip on the door handle. "He was in one of the tents. He looked like... He looked like someone had attacked him."

"*Murdered* him?" Crystal stared at Laila. Laila pointed ahead. She should have waited till they got back to the cottage. Crystal was an erratic driver at the best of times.

Crystal blinked at the road. "You're saying someone killed Archie, and you found him. They took you to the hospital. Did this person attack you too?"

"I had shock. That's what they told me." Laila thought of the blonde detective and her daughter. The daughter had been kind. She'd looked after her. Without her, Laila would have passed out at the scene.

"So where is he now?" Crystal asked. "Archie?"

"I don't know. He was in the tent, the big one with the human remains."

Crystal grimaced. "More human remains now." She glanced at Laila. "Sorry. They'll have taken him some-where. Post-mortem. What did he look like, when you found him?"

"I... I'm not ready to..."

"Course not. Sorry, love. But the police will want to talk to you. You found him. They might think you did it."

"Why would they think I did it?"

"You were first on the scene. You were sleeping with him. And the two of you had that row."

"What row?"

"Last Wednesday, remember? You wanted to go to London with him."

Laila wiped tears from her cheek. Her skin was slick with them. "That wasn't a row."

Crystal put a hand on her knee. "It's OK. They like to jump to conclusions. But they'll know you could never do something like that."

"No." Laila was only nineteen. She was slight, although two months working on the dig had made her stronger than she'd believed she could be. "We made it up. He took me out, on Friday."

Crystal clutched her knee. "There you go. You're fine, then."

They drove on in silence until they were past the Wareham bypass. It was getting dark.

"Who would have wanted to kill Archie?" Laila asked.

"Beats me. He was a good bloke. You sure he was murdered?"

"He was... his head... He couldn't have done that to himself. I mean, I don't think so."

Had Archie been suicidal? He'd been cheerful on Friday night, the black mood after their argument had gone and been replaced by cheerfulness. On Saturday morning when she'd woken up, he'd already left. He'd never told her why he had to leave on Saturday when the meeting was on Monday.

"Shush, love." Crystal slowed the car as they drove up the

hill past Corfe Castle. She turned onto The Square and along West Street. "I'll get some of my best whisky out for you. You'll need it, help you sleep. And I'll tell Patrick what's happened. You go to bed."

Bed. The empty bed, with Archie's things in the cupboard on the other side. Laila thought of her encounter with Patrick. Had that only been this afternoon?

She couldn't face Patrick. He'd been going through Archie's things, she realised. Not hers.

Why?

She couldn't sleep, but she could investigate. She would shut herself away, and she'd work out what Patrick had been searching for.

The car pulled up in front of the cottage. Laila gave Crystal a tired smile. "Thanks. I'll take you up on that offer."

CHAPTER SEVEN

LESLEY EXTINGUISHED the headlights and leaned back in the driver's seat. A light shone through the front window; she must have left it on when she and Sharon left for the castle that morning. Either that, or there was a timer switch she didn't know about.

Her home for the next six months was a rented terraced house in Wareham, seven miles from Police HQ in Winfrith. She hadn't chosen it: somebody from the admin team had picked it out for her. It was decent enough. Clean, on a quiet if narrow street which she repeatedly got lost trying to find. Wareham was a maze, narrow back streets, one way systems and dead ends.

She wasn't hungry. The cream tea still sat heavy in her stomach and she'd eaten a pack of crisps in the snack bar at Bournemouth station. Part of a meal deal she'd bought to keep Sharon going on the train, rejected by her daughter. She was sure salt and vinegar had been the girl's favourite flavour.

She was already prepared for tomorrow. She'd hung her favourite suit up when they'd arrived on Thursday. She'd checked there were no creases in her cream blouse. And she'd placed her mid-height court shoes side by side at the bottom of the wardrobe that took up one wall of her poky bedroom. Her work handbag was ready, notebook, lanyard, and a change of tights just in case. All she needed to do was put her purse in there and she was set.

Sitting there, looking at the house, it occurred to her there wasn't much point going inside. It was quarter past eight. She had two hours to fill before she could realistically go to bed, and she didn't relish the prospect of spending them trying to make herself comfortable on the scratchy sofa in front of whatever TV Sunday night had to offer.

She started the car. She knew where she'd rather be.

Twenty minutes later she was pulling up to the car park in Corfe Castle, the same one she'd used earlier. Her ticket was still on the windscreen, good till midnight. The car park was quiet now, the tourists in pubs or tucked up inside their caravans or holiday cottages. Lesley shuddered at the thought.

She strode towards the path she'd taken with Sharon earlier and followed what she remembered of the route. The air was damp, a fine mist threatening to turn to drizzle. Maybe these trousers weren't so bad after all. She might need to rethink her polished shoes and skirt suits, if all the crime scenes turned out to be like this one.

She eased her way through a kissing gate and emerged onto the field where the archaeological dig was taking place. The low mounds were eerie in the dark and she walked slowly, aware she could easily trip. The tent where they had found the body was dimly illuminated.

She lifted the police tape and ducked beneath it. There

should be a uniformed officer out here, keeping watch. Until the forensics people had done their work.

She picked her way over the rough grass to the tent, wishing she'd thought to bring overshoes. She put a hand on the canvas.

"Hello?" She pulled the canvas to one side. "DCI Clarke here. Why is no one on watch?"

Gail Hansford was inside, alone. She crouched on the ground, examining blood spatter in the light of a torch. She turned, startled. "Ma'am."

"You're a civilian. You don't have to ma'am me."

"True." Gail stood up. "I don't know..."

"My name's Lesley. How come you're here on your own?"

"I could ask the same thing of you, Lesley."

"Touché." Lesley looked down at the ground. "They took him away already?"

"Pathologist didn't want to be kept hanging around. He was missing his granddaughter's birthday."

"I don't care if he was missing a royal bloody garden party," said Lesley. "If evidence has been compromised..."

Gail shook her head. "Don't worry. Brett and Gavin documented everything. The photographer we use was nearby, taking pics of kestrels. So we got everything we needed."

"You don't have your own photographer?"

"CSM is a team of four. Gavin and Brett were available, Sunil wasn't. Normally Gav takes the photos, but for a case like this, we use a local freelancer. He did my daughter's wedding, he's a good bloke."

Lesley hadn't thought Gail was old enough to have a

married daughter. "So what d'you do if there are multiple crime scenes for you to cover?"

Gail smiled. "Doesn't happen all that often. We've trained local CID teams to dust for prints, so that covers most break-ins and burglaries. If there's something bigger, we get involved."

"But Bournemouth is part of your patch. Surely you have serious crime there."

"Oh, we do, Ma— Lesley. It can get nasty in Bournemouth. Last month we had a stabbing in the town centre and four domestics that needed forensic analysis. Brett gets freaked by it, won't go near the place unless he has to for work."

"One stabbing and four domestics. That's all?"

"The stabbing kept us busy for a week. Closing time, crowded pub, no one making any sense. The guy lived, thanks to Poole Hospital. But his girlfriend's brother – he'll be looking at the inside of a cell for some time."

Lesley whistled. "Where I come from, a stabbing and four domestics is a quiet night."

"Don't get me wrong. We get our share of violent crime down here. But most of it doesn't need forensics. And it's dwarfed by the property crime. You'd be surprised how insecure the average holiday home can be. The grockles – that's what some people call holidaymakers – don't seem to be very good at closing windows and locking doors."

"It's not their property, so they don't pay as much attention," Lesley said.

"Exactly."

Lesley sniffed. "So what have you found here so far? And you still haven't told me why you're on your own."

"DS Frampton sent everyone home. I went home, but then it was playing on my mind."

"You live far away?"

"Swanage. With my little boy. It's five miles from here."

"I know Swanage." She and Sharon had walked along the beach on Saturday afternoon, enjoying ice creams and the feel of the sand between their toes. "Where's your son now?"

Gail looked away. "His dad has him on a Sunday night."

"Ah. So, tell me, anything useful?"

"You saw the victim's injuries?" Gail asked.

"I did. What was visible where he'd been left, anyway."

"Yeah. The pathologist said cause of death was the blow to the back of the head. Possibly multiple blows. We'll know more after the post-mortem."

Lesley resolved to attend the post-mortem in person. What she'd heard so far about the pathologist didn't fill her with confidence.

"Defensive wounds?" she asked.

"None apparent. His position would indicate that he turned after being hit, then fell to the ground. He was taken by surprise."

Lesley looked down at the ground. Gail had placed protective plates around the inside of the tent and each of the two women was standing on one. She wished the body hadn't been moved so quickly.

"I don't suppose you can show me the photos?"

"I've got them on my phone. Let's go outside."

They left the tent. Gail pulled down the top half of her forensic suit and took a phone out of her back pocket. She wore jeans and a dark fleece, with a scarf that caught the torchlight and brought out the blue of her eyes.

"Here." Gail held up a photo of the body. It had been

taken from the side, showing the twisted angle the man had been left in. She flicked through more images, including close-ups of the man's hands, which were uninjured, and the wound on the back of his head.

"Looks like a blunt instrument," Lesley commented.

"Probably. We've searched this field, as well as the under-growth along the roadside and the trees by the river. No sign of the weapon."

"So the killer took it with him."

"Or her."

Lesley raised an eyebrow. "You think it was a woman?"

"Not specifically. But I think we should keep an open mind."

"Of course," said Lesley. "So there was no sign he'd been moved?"

"No disturbance around the body. You did a good job of making sure none of the blokes trampled all around it."

"Blokes?"

"DS Frampton and PC Mullins," Gail said. "The para-medics. Lots of blokes round here."

"PC Abbott was here too."

"Tina's a good girl. I hope she gets the recognition she deserves." Gail eyed Lesley. "I bet she was the only one who listened to you earlier. Did as you said."

"You could say that."

"See? Blokes, the lot of them. You'll be the most senior woman your department has had since... well, since forever."

Lesley was used to working with men and women. She didn't like to dwell on it too much.

"I'm sure it'll be fine," she said. It was almost dark now; she could barely make out the route back to her car. "We're not going to get much more done here tonight. Where's your car?"

Gail pointed. "Back there, in a field. Why don't we go for a drink? I can fill you in on what to expect of Dorset Police."

Lesley smiled. "That's kind of you. But I'd rather keep an open mind. And I need to get an early night."

Gail gave a mock salute. "No problem, Lesley. It was nice meeting you. I'm sure our paths will cross again very soon."

"I'm sure they will." Lesley looked towards the village. There was no way she was finding her way back to the car. "I will ask you a favour though."

"Name it."

"A lift to my car? I'm on West Street car park."

Gail laughed. "No problem. Come with me."

CHAPTER EIGHT

"Morning." Lesley walked into the MCIT office and placed her bag on an empty desk. DS Frampton, sitting at the next desk along, looked up and half-rose from his chair.

"Ma'am. Good to see you again." He tugged at his tie. It was the same colour as the tweed jacket he'd been wearing yesterday, but today it was teamed with a dark blue suit that even Lesley could tell clashed with it. "I was expecting to meet you in the reception area."

Lesley smiled. "Thought I'd save you a job." She held up the lanyard she'd brought with her, along with the ID attached to it. A Dorset Police badge would follow. "I'm official now. No one can accuse me of intruding on a crime scene."

She surveyed the group of desks. They were to one side of an open plan office, large windows behind them overlooking the patch of grass in front of the modern police building and the road beyond. Two other men sat at two of the group of four desks. One was in his mid-thirties, with scruffy blonde hair and a too-tight suit. The other was ten years younger, with light brown skin and closely cropped hair. His suit looked cheap but at least it fitted him.

"So?" she said. "You going to introduce me?"

The two younger men stood up, each looking awkwardly at the sergeant. Frampton ran the flat of his hand across his hair, which had been smoothed down with far too much of some kind of cream.

Frampton gestured towards the man in the tight suit. "This is DC Johnny Chiles, Ma'am. Been on the team for eight years."

DC Chiles leaned towards Lesley and extended his hand. He smelled of cheap aftershave. Lesley shook his hand.

"DCI Clarke, but you already know that. Eight years on Major Crimes, and still a DC?"

His face tightened. He looked sidelong at Frampton, who ignored him. So there was tension there.

Lesley turned to the remaining man. "And you are?"

"DC Michael Legg, Ma'am." He had a Dorset accent, stronger than Frampton's or Gail's. He didn't put his hand out, and neither did Lesley.

"So this is the team," she said. She nodded at the empty desk. "I'm assuming that's not mine?"

"Vacancy, Ma'am," said Frampton. "DC Graves retired."

"Good for him. We'll need to find someone new then, won't we?" Lesley looked around the office. Another group of four desks was further along by the same set of windows, occupied by four uniformed officers.

"Our neighbours?" she asked.

"Temporary," said DC Chiles. He sucked his teeth. "We were hoping that now we had a new DCI, the team might grow."

"And what's wrong with that lot?" Lesley surveyed the

four uniformed officers. She recognised one of them: PC Abbott from the crime scene.

"They're Uniform, Ma'am," Chiles said. "Support officers. We need detectives."

"Uniformed officers can be an invaluable resource as part of a major crimes team," she said. "Don't underestimate them."

Frampton and Chiles shared a look. DC Legg watched, saying nothing.

"So where am I?" Lesley asked. "Over there?" she pointed towards an empty office.

"Yes, Ma'am." Frampton shuffled towards it and opened the door. She picked up her bag and followed. He stood at the door as she entered and smoothed her hand across the desk.

The office was bigger than the one she'd had in Birmingham, with tall windows at the front of the building. In her last office, she'd had a high window that opened onto a light well in the middle of the building. She'd never turned the lights off.

Here, the light, even today's thin sunshine, was blinding.

She crossed to the window. "I'll need blinds."

"Ma'am?" said Frampton.

She balled a fist and pushed it against the wall. "Bloody main road's right out there. Can't have any Tom, Dick or Harry looking in at what we're doing."

"Err..." said Frampton.

"What?" She placed her bag on the desk. It wouldn't take long to settle in.

Frampton gestured to Chiles, who was in the doorway. Legg was still at his desk, typing into his computer. Either he was the industrious, antisocial type, or this team didn't get along.

Chiles returned with a glass jar. A pile of pound coins and fifty pence pieces sat in the bottom.

"Your charity drive isn't going very well." Lesley reached inside her bag for her purse. "What you fundraising for?"

"It isn't a charity drive," said Frampton. "It's a swear jar."

Lesley stared at the jar. She stared at Frampton, blinking back at her. She stared at Chiles, holding the jar out, his lips pursed. She put her purse back in her bag.

"I've never heard anything so damn ridiculous," she laughed. "You're kidding me, right?"

Frampton shook his head. "50p for a..." He cleaned his throat. "For a 'damn'. A pound for your previous infraction."

"Infraction? You mean me saying *bloody main road*?" She leaned against the desk. "I've never heard such crap in my life, Sergeant. Get that thing out of my face and don't try to tell me how I should talk. I'm a copper, not a fucking nun."

A muscle below Frampton's left eye twitched. He muttered under his breath. Was he counting? Tallying up her *infractions*?

She'd show him bloody infractions.

DS Frampton nodded at his colleague who left the office, taking the offending jar with him. He placed it in a filing cabinet. DC Legg watched, still saying nothing.

A man's face appeared around the door: mid-fifties, skinny, wearing uniform and a Chief Superintendent's badge.

"DCI Clarke, I assume?" He strode in and grabbed her hand, pumping it ferociously.

"You must be Detective Superintendent Carpenter, Sir," she replied.

He winked. "I don't normally dress like this, on my way to some godawful thing with the Chief Constable. We'll talk properly later." He finally let go of her hand. "You been getting into trouble with the language police?"

Lesley eyed DS Frampton. He'd been rude to her at the crime scene and he'd pissed her off by telling her how to talk. But he was a member of her team.

"Just getting to know my new team, Sir. I expect we'll be hitting the ground running."

"The Corfe Castle incident, yes. They've already brought you up to speed?"

"I've been to the crime scene, Sir. I was in the village when the body was discovered."

"Lucky you." Carpenter's face brightened.

"I wouldn't put it like that, Sir."

He waved a hand. "You know what I mean. Tragic event, life cut brutally short and all that. But bloody fortunate that our new DCI is on the scene when it happened."

"Not when it happened, exactly. Now *that* would have been lucky." She smiled. "I could have prevented it."

"Ha! Of course you could." He patted her shoulder. "Anyway, must be off. You're SIO, of course. I'll expect a briefing, my office, 6pm. One of your lads will tell you where to go."

"Of course, Sir."

He left her office and waved at the officers sitting outside as if he was minor royalty. They straightened at their desks. Lesley rolled her eyes.

She clicked her fingers to pull her team members' attention away from the senior officer.

"Right, folks," she said. "In my office. Let's work out our plan of attack."

CHAPTER NINE

"Right," said Lesley as the three detectives gathered in front of her. "Drag a couple more chairs in, will you?"

DS Frampton nodded to DC Chiles, who left the room and came back dragging a chair. DC Legg followed and did the same. The three men stood awkwardly for a moment, then shuffled onto the chairs.

"Someone shut the door?" Lesley suggested. Chiles did the honours.

Lesley placed her elbows on the desk, her fingers entwined. "OK, we've got a murder inquiry to get cracking with but first, let's set some ground rules."

Frampton tugged at his collar. Legg brought out a pad.

Lesley smiled at her team. "We didn't get off to the best start. You pissed me off at the crime scene, Sergeant, and then there was all this crap with the swear jar."

The DS opened his mouth to speak. Lesley raised a hand to stop him.

"But," she said, her gaze flicking towards the door and the half-glazed partition wall it sat in. "And this is an important 'but'. We're a team. I've got your back, so long as you do your jobs. I run a tight ship, no cutting corners, no excuses for lack of attention to detail, no running around after wild hunches."

Lesley thought of DI Zoe Finch, her favourite team member back in West Midlands Police. Zoe had done her share of running around after hunches. But her instincts had been good, and she'd spent years proving that to Lesley. And when Lesley had needed to rein her in, to remind her of procedure, she'd listened. Mostly.

"When we're facing the public, or for that matter, senior management, we present a united front. No going behind your colleagues' backs. No contradicting other members of the team, except when you're in this room. That make sense?"

"Yes, Ma'am," said DS Frampton. He glanced at the other two in turn, Chiles first. Always Chiles first, Lesley noted. The DCs murmured agreement.

"And while we're on that," Lesley said. "You don't need to ma'am me all the time. We'll be spending a lot of time together. It makes me feel like the bloody Queen. Call me boss, or guv."

"No problem, boss," said Frampton.

"Good." Lesley smiled at him. "And I don't want to keep using your titles. Remind me of your full names."

Frampton cleared his throat. He gave Chiles a look.

"Johnny Chiles, Ma'am. I mean boss," said the constable.

"Johnny. That what you prefer to be called?"

He nodded.

"You sure?"

Another nod.

"Fair enough. Johnny it is. I'll try not to laugh." She turned her gaze on the other constable.

"Michael Legg. Mike. Boss." He scratched behind his ear.

"Mike. That's more like it. What do you two tend to call DS Frampton here?"

"Sarge," said Johnny.

"Even though the two of you have clearly been friends for yonks?"

The constable frowned at her.

"That means for a very long time," she told him. "I'm going to have to learn to speak Dorset."

"DC Chiles and I have worked together, on and off, for twelve years," said the sergeant.

Again Lesley thought of Zoe. Her relationship with DS Mo Uddin, who she'd met in training back in 2001.

"So I bet when you're in the pub you call him by his first name. Which is?"

"Er, Dennis," said Johnny.

"Don't worry, son. You can carry on calling him Sarge when you're in the office. I'll stick with Dennis."

All these blokes' names, she thought. Maybe Gail had a point.

"OK, so that's the introductions out of the way," Lesley said. "I've told you how I work, I'll come to learn how you work. How about we get on with finding Archie Weatherton's killer, yes?"

The tension in the room fell. Lesley looked through the glass partition to see PC Abbott watching them. She gave the younger woman a nod and Abbott looked away. Lesley wondered how soundproof these walls were.

"Someone fetch a bloody board, will you?" she said to her team. "We've got evidence to collate."

CHAPTER TEN

GAIL WAS POURING resin into a faint footprint she'd found at the back of the tent. It probably belonged to the paramedic or the heavy-hoofed PC Mullins, but she could always hope. She was disturbed by Gav's voice outside the tent.

"Hey! This is a crime scene. You can't just walk in."

Gail opened the tent flaps. Gavin Larcomb was a bear of a man, six-foot-five and built like a brick shithouse. He'd had to get forensic suits specially made to avoid wandering round crime scenes looking like a kid in last year's school uniform.

In front of him stood a skinny woman with dark spiky hair. She had her hand on the cordon tape and had placed one foot inside.

"This is our place of work, pal," she said in an accent Gail recognised as Glasgow. "You can't keep us out."

"It's a crime scene." Gav grabbed the tape. He clearly itched to grab the woman too, but they all knew how it would look if the biggest bloke on the team was photographed with his hands on this scrawny sparrow of a woman.

"Can I help?" Gail stepped out of the tent, peeling off

her gloves.

"Who are you?" The woman slapped a hand to her forehead. "Jeez, there are delicate 12th century artefacts in there. You'll...." She stared at Gail, her chest rising and falling. She looked like she might cry.

"There's also evidence relating to a suspected murder," Gail told her. "And if you're who I think you are, it's the murder of one of your own."

"Archie." The woman's expression slackened. "Poor bastard."

Gail was in front of the woman now. She'd dropped the tape, thank God.

"Look," she said. "I don't know if you're aware of forensic methodology, but we're being incredibly careful in there. We have plates on the ground to protect it from our boots and we're cataloguing everything as we go."

"You have no idea how precious that stuff is," the woman said, her voice hoarse. "Coins, bones, jewellery."

"We're not interested in any of that. All I want to know is what was left behind when your colleague was attacked."

"What's your name, love?" Gav asked.

The woman gave him a look of disdain. "Don't *love* me, you Neanderthal."

Gail suppressed a laugh. The insult was appropriate, she supposed, for an archaeologist.

Gail looked at the woman. "What's your name?"

"Crystal Spiers. I'm in charge of this dig."

"Has anyone been to see you? I imagine CID will want to talk to all Mr Weatherton's associates."

"Associates? You are full of it, you lot, aren't you? No, no plod have come knocking on our door just yet. We still have that pleasure to come."

Gail nodded. Gav had left them and gone to join Brett, cataloguing evidence bags and placing them in containers ready to go in the back of her car. They'd taken mud samples and some seeds and pollen from nearby plants. Anything they could use to place a suspect at the scene. Unfortunately there was still no sign of a weapon.

"We'll be done in a few hours," Gail told the woman. "And then you can have your site back."

"Have you found anything?"

"I'm afraid I can't—"

"Come on. It's my bloody tent you're using. Archie was a colleague, a pal. If someone did away with him, I want to know who."

"We haven't got as far as identifying a suspect yet. But you'll need to take this up with the Major Crime Investigations Team."

"Hmm."

The woman lowered herself to the ground. The grass was still damp with the morning's dew, her sturdy brown trousers would get wet. "I'm not going anywhere till you do," she said. "And I'm watching everything that comes out of that tent. You find anything of archaeological significance, you damn well tell me, yes?"

"We'll do our best," Gail replied. Truth was, she had no idea what archaeological significance would look like if it hit her in the face with an early medieval brickbat.

"Good." The woman shuffled on the grass, her lip twitching. She was cold and uncomfortable by the looks of it, but she wasn't about to admit it.

Gail sighed and turned back to the tent. Gav was back. "You want me to keep an eye on her?"

She nodded. This was going to be a long morning.

CHAPTER ELEVEN

MIKE LEGG HAD WHEELED in a movable whiteboard which
Lesley had placed against one of the windows.

"It's difficult to see it with the sun in our eyes, boss," said
Dennis.

"I don't want people wandering up to our windows being
able to see what we're up to."

"Can't we move it just for now," suggested Mike, "and
then put it back after?"

Lesley waved her pen at him. "Fair enough." She moved
the board against a wall.

"I'll want photos printed off, helps get the cogs whirring,"
she said. "But for now, you'll have to put up with my scrawl."

She smiled at her team. The two constables smiled back
nervously and Dennis rearranged his tie.

She wrote Archie Weatherton's name on the board,
followed by Laila Ford's. She drew an arrow from Archie to
Laila and wrote *girlfriend*.

She jabbed her pen into Laila's name. "She found him.
We don't know much more yet, she was in a right state."

"Maybe cos she killed her fella," Johnny Chiles suggested.

"Maybe indeed," Lesley replied. "We don't have any concrete evidence pointing to her as a suspect just yet. But we have to assume she could have done it."

"The injury to his head, Ma'am," said Mike. "I mean boss, sorry. D'you think she was strong enough?"

"The FSM reckons – sorry, CSM, I'll have to get used to your local jargon. Anyway, she reckons he was taken by surprise, given the position he was in and the fact that it looks like only one blow. Someone could have entered the tent, he turned, they walloped him and he went down. With the right instrument, no reason it couldn't have been a woman."

"You've spoken to the forensics team?" Dennis asked. "That's something I normally—"

"I went back to the scene last night. Didn't get much of a look earlier on, what with Laila looking like she might faint and me having my daughter in tow."

Dennis frowned. "You met Gail Hansford at the crime scene?"

Lesley turned to him. "She told me you'd sent everyone home. Not sure who gave you authority to do that."

"With respect, Ma' am..."

She raised an eyebrow. He took a breath. "Boss. We already covered this yesterday. You weren't in post yet, and you needed to get your daughter home. You left me in charge."

"And you left a murder scene unprotected."

He eyed the constables. Johnny was sitting back in his chair, legs out in front of him, arms folded. His gaze was on the DS. Mike, by contrast, sat with his feet tucked beneath his chair and his eyes down.

"I'd appreciate it if we could have this conversation later, boss," Dennis said.

Lesley met his gaze. The man had a point. Leaving a crime scene unattended was a bloody inept thing to do. But she didn't need to tell him that in front of the rest of the team.

"Fair point." She turned to the board. "So we've got Archie and Laila, and an archaeological dig. We need background on Archie, whether he'd pissed anyone off recently. Who else was involved in this dig, and what are relations like. Any tensions. We have an address..."

"Boss." Legg attached a card to the board. It held an address in West Street, Corfe Castle.

"This is Laila and Archie's address?" Lesley asked. She'd been there when PC Abbott had noted it down the day before. But she wasn't yet familiar enough with the local towns and villages for it to lodge in her head.

"The whole dig team, from what I've heard," said Johnny. "Bunch of hippies got themselves a commune. Probably all hopping in and out of each other's beds."

Mike smirked. Dennis suppressed a smile.

"Wow, you lot really are from the dark ages, aren't you?" Lesley said, ignoring Dennis's pinched expression. "A group of colleagues shares a house and you're all imagining soft porn."

"Sorry, boss," muttered Mike.

"I want open minds about these people. I don't care that you lot don't take to folks from the outside world. Yes, one of them could be our killer. But they might not. Archie might just have pissed off a local farmer and—"

"Come on, boss," said Dennis. "It's wise to have an open mind about rural communities too, I think. Including the farming community."

Lesley licked her lips. The sergeant had a point. She'd never met a farmer in her life, and she was sure they had exactly the same propensity for violence as anybody else. Maybe.

"OK," she said. "So we need to know who else Archie had dealings with. We still don't have a murder weapon, but I'm hopeful the post-mortem can narrow that down."

She remembered what Gail had told her about the pathologist. *Hopeful* was the right word. She would prefer *confident*.

"We'll regroup later today to look at other leads we can be following." She jabbed her pen into Laila's name. "But first I want to talk to the dig crew. Johnny, you find out who we're dealing with here. I want names, professional backgrounds, relationships if possible. Do any of them have a record, you know the drill."

"Err...." Johnny looked at Dennis.

"Mike normally does that kind of thing, boss," said the sergeant. "Johnny comes out with me to do the interviews."

"Well we can give each of you lads an opportunity to stretch a different set of muscles, can't we? "Lesley replied. She spotted Mike's small smile.

"Come on, you two. I want to get statements off these people before they've had too long to agree on a story. I'll drive. Johnny, phone the sarge with information as soon as you have it."

"Will do, boss." Johnny looked from her to Dennis. He was waiting for the DS's permission, she realised.

Lesley clapped her hands. "Let's move, fellas! We may be in rural Dorset, but the clock ticks at the same pace it does everywhere else."

CHAPTER TWELVE

As THEY LEFT HER OFFICE, Lesley spotted PC Abbott at her desk. She called over.

"PC Abbott, are you busy right now?"

The constable turned in her chair, her gaze going from Lesley to Dennis and back again. "Well, I'm... but I can be available, if you need me."

"Good. You have access to a squad car?"

"Yes."

"You go with Mike here. I'll drive the sergeant."

"Mike?" PC Abbott asked.

Mike Legg gave the PC a pointed look and pointed at himself, drilling his finger into his chest.

"DC Legg, Constable," Dennis told her.

"Of course. Sorry. Yes, give me five minutes."

Twenty minutes later they'd left the Wareham bypass behind and were on the A351 heading towards Corfe Castle. The road was flanked by wide fields filled with gorse. Clouds sat low on the horizon ahead but right here, the sun was out.

Lesley wasn't used to being able to see the weather approaching. It made her uneasy.

"Why did you want PC Abbott to bring her panda car?" Dennis asked. "Surely we don't want to draw attention to ourselves."

"It'll bring the neighbours out. Can you imagine, a narrow street like that? We need all the eyewitness reports we can get."

"Surely we can achieve that by knocking on doors."

"I want them to know we're taking this seriously."

They were approaching the castle. The sun was behind them and the ruins were illuminated, details of the battered walls picked out by the bright light. The road ran around its northern side, so close that it felt like the castle was on top of them. As they climbed the hill into the village, the sergeant's phone rang.

"Frampton... yes... good... OK... that should make things simple... Thanks."

"That was Johnny," he told Lesley. "There are – were – just four permanent staff on the dig, supplemented by a revolving crew of students."

"Names?"

"Archie and Laila we already know about. The head honcho is a woman called Crystal Spiers. And there's a fella called Patrick Donnelly. All living at the same address." He gave her a pointed look but didn't mention communes. "Johnny wanted to know what else he should be getting on with."

Lesley turned to him. They were entering what looked like a former market square, stuck behind a car that was attempting to reverse into a parking space. The old guy at the wheel looked harassed.

"Surely Johnny can work that out for himself?" she said.

"He can. But you've been giving the orders so far. I wanted to be sure we were doing what you wanted."

The car finally made it into the space and Lesley pressed down on the accelerator. She wasn't sure which was more frustrating: the leisurely Dorset traffic, or her even more leisurely colleagues.

"What do you suggest, Sergeant?"

"We know about the dig team. We still don't know if the deceased had family, or if there were any personal or professional issues back home."

"Bingo." She turned once again into West Street car park. She had a feeling she was going to become familiar with this place. "Give him a quick call and make sure he's not twiddling his thumbs, will you Dennis? While you go and get us a parking ticket."

"You'll need to join the National Trust," he said as he opened the car door.

"What's that got to do with the price of eggs?"

"They own most the car parks on Purbeck. Beaches, too. It was bequeathed to them along with the castle."

"Someone owned all this?"

He gestured back towards the castle. "Bankes family. Local legends, or at least one of their ancestors is."

She screwed up her nose. "They just gave it away?"

"Would you want the bill for upkeep of that place?"

"I thought that was the whole point. Ruined castle."

"I'll educate you one day." He left the car.

"Please don't," she muttered. She got out of the car and walked to the squad car. It was parked on a verge: PC Abbott had no need for parking tickets or National Trust membership.

"I'm afraid there was nowhere to park outside the house, Ma' am," the constable said. "Double yellows all the way along West Street. So we'll have to leave it here."

Lesley surveyed the tourists leaving the car park for the castle. It was a Monday morning in term time and not one of them was under the age of sixty. Brightly coloured waterproofs, grey hair, tasteful jewellery. A few of them looked sidelong at the squad car but no one approached.

"It'll be fine," she said. "This isn't Chelmsley Wood."

"What's Chelmsley Wood?" PC Abbott asked.

"Don't ask."

DC Legg emerged from the squad car. Dennis returned with the parking permit. Lesley looked between them, wondering if she could pinch herself and go back home.

"Come on then you lot," she said. "We've got witnesses to interview."

CHAPTER THIRTEEN

Susan Weatherton ended the call, her heart racing.

Tony wasn't supposed to call her at home. He wasn't supposed to call her when she was with her daughter. And mostly, he stuck to that rule.

Today had been different.

She clutched the phone to her chest and stepped inside through the patio doors, unaware of the rain that plastered her fringe to her forehead.

"Mum! where's my reading book?"

Millie.

Susan pushed down the guilt at allowing herself five minutes to step outside not only the house, but her role as a mum. She cleared her throat and shoved the phone into a drawer.

"It's right here, sweetie."

"Where?"

"In the kitchen." The book was on the table, right next to her.

Millie barrelled onto the room, the pigtails Susan had pulled her hair into already messy.

"I'll get into trouble."

"No, you won't." Susan grabbed the book and waved it at her daughter. "Where's your bag?"

Millie frowned. "I thought you'd know."

Susan pushed down her irritation. She pointed to the bag, which had been slung into a corner last night.

"Thanks, Mum."

Susan smiled. Millie was eleven years old and in her final months at primary school. Sometimes she was like a teenager already, worldly and dismissive. But other times, like today, it was Reception class all over again.

"Don't forget your lunch," Susan said. She nodded towards the lunch box on the counter.

"Yeah." Millie stuffed it into her rucksack, not caring that she'd be squashing the library book that had just been thrown in underneath it.

"Ready?" Susan grabbed her keys. The school was a mile away, a pleasant walk through Clifton, one of Bristol's most desirable suburbs. This house had belonged to Susan's parents. Her husband Archie was always broke, he'd never have been able to put a roof over their heads. Despite having a good job at the university.

At the thought of Archie, her gaze went to the drawer where she'd hidden her phone. Her thoughts switched to Tony, and her insides softened.

She opened the drawer and plunged the phone into her skirt pocket. "Let's go."

Millie paused at the mirror in the hall, trying in vain to straighten her hair.

"Maybe I should do it the minute before we leave the

house," Susan said. But even that wouldn't be enough. In reality, she should leave it till they were at the school gates, if she wanted her daughter to start the school day looking presentable.

She opened the front door. Two men were walking up her path, wearing dark uniforms.

Susan's hand flew to her throat.

"Hello?" she croaked. "Can I help you?"

The older of the two policemen gave her a concerned look.

She knew that look. She felt her stomach slide.

Millie banged the front door shut. "Mum?"

Susan grabbed the sleeve of her daughter's cardigan, her eyes on the two police officers.

"Is your name Susan Weatherton?"

She nodded.

"Is there any chance we can come in?"

She looked up and down the street. Old Mr Gill next door would have spotted the police car parked a few doors along. He'd be at his front window, peering through those dusty lace curtains.

"I have to get my daughter to school. We're running late."

The constable's eyes crinkled. His expression shifted from concern, to pity.

Oh God.

Susan's grip on Millie's cardigan tightened.

"It's about your husband, Mrs Weatherton. I'm afraid this can't wait."

Susan could barely breathe. There was only one reason the police would come knocking at this time of day.

She swallowed. "You'd better come in."

CHAPTER FOURTEEN

THE ARCHAEOLOGICAL DIG team occupied a flat-fronted terraced cottage on West Street. The front wall of the building abutted the narrow pavement, where Lesley and Dennis now stood, occasionally having to move aside for passers-by, as they waited for someone to open the door.

"Maybe there's no one in," suggested Dennis.

Lesley pointed upwards. "I saw that curtain move when we got here."

"Right." He hammered on the door.

Lesley winced. The young woman they were here to see was a witness, for now. She'd been through an ordeal. And from what Lesley had seen of her yesterday, she was emotionally fragile.

At last the door opened. Lesley gestured to Dennis, who held up his ID.

"I'm DCI Clarke, this is DS Frampton," she said. "You and I met yesterday."

Laila stared back at her. Her skin was less pale than it had been at the crime scene, but she still had an ethereal quality, with her flowing white-blonde hair and stick-thin limbs. If this woman had murdered her boyfriend, Lesley thought, then she'd never have been able to move him. It fitted with Gail's theory.

"How are you, Laila?" she asked.

"Better. They discharged me quickly."

"Good. Can we come in?"

Laila looked back inside the cottage, then back at the detectives. She shrugged. "Course."

"Thank you," Dennis said. He raised his eyebrows, waiting for Laila to move aside, then walked past her into the house. Lesley followed, her eyes on Laila's face.

Laila closed the front door and stood next to it, tugging at the sleeve of her floral blouse. "Sorry. It's a bit..."

The room looked tidy, to Lesley. A newspaper lay on the floor next to a threadbare green armchair and there was a half-finished plate of toast on the sofa. Apart from that, the room held just a narrow dresser and a low stool with books piled on it. There was no coffee table: no space. And no TV either.

Lesley shunted around the sofa and took a seat on it. She shifted the plate of toast onto the stool of books. Dennis took the armchair. A door behind him led into a small kitchen and another doorway to the side had a steep flight of wooden stairs beyond it.

"Cosy," Dennis commented as he shuffled in his chair.

Lesley patted the sofa next to her. Laila was still by the door, chewing her wispy hair.

"We won't bite," Lesley said. "You can sit down."

Laila gave her a tight smile and perched at the other end of the sofa, next to Dennis's chair. He picked up the newspaper, folded it and placed it on the arm of his chair. Lesley frowned at him.

"They're all out," Laila said. "Crystal went down to the Rings. That's the dig site. Patrick... I don't know where Patrick is."

"That's OK," Lesley told her. "It's you we wanted to talk to."

Laila gripped her sleeve tighter.

"I know this is hard, Laila. But I need you to describe what happened yesterday."

"Yes."

"Can you start by telling us why you were at the dig site?" Lesley nodded to Dennis who pulled out his notepad and started to write.

"I wouldn't normally be, on a Sunday." Laila's voice was shaky. "But I'd... I'd had an argument with Patrick."

"Patrick Donnelly?" Dennis asked.

"Yes. I came home from the shops. He was in my room. Mine and Archie's room. Going through things." She sniffed. "He had a go at me about the mess."

"He had a go at you?" Lesley asked. "Not the other way round?"

"You found him snooping in your room," Dennis pointed out.

Red spots had appeared on Laila's cheeks. "I came back downstairs before he saw me. I made lots of noise so he'd know I was here, then I went back up. I didn't want a confrontation."

"Had you seen Mr Donnelly going through your belongings before?" Lesley asked.

"That's just it. He wasn't going through my stuff."

Dennis looked up. "You've just said..."

"He was going through Archie's things," Lesley suggested. "Wasn't he, Laila?"

The red spots intensified. "Archie and me, we kept our stuff separate. Patrick was in his bedside table."

"Did he find anything?" Dennis asked. Lesley gave him another frown.

Laila shrugged. "I don't know. I didn't..."

Lesley leaned forward. "Have you had a chance to check Archie's belongings since his death?"

"I was going to. But when I came home last night, I couldn't..."

"I understand," Lesley said. She looked at the DS. "We're going to need a forensics team in here."

"Gail Hansford's already at the crime scene."

"Surely we have more than one team of CSIs?"

"There's one in Weymouth. But..."

Lesley sighed. They could continue this conversation later. She turned to Laila.

"So you came upstairs for a second time, and where was Patrick?"

Laila glanced towards the door leading to the stairs. "On the landing. He knew I was coming."

"Was he holding anything? Did you see him move anything?"

"No."

"OK. So you argued with him about the state of your room. What did you do then?"

Laila's eyes were bright with tears. "I didn't kill him, you know. I loved Archie. Love."

"I didn't say you did."

"I know what you're doing. You're putting together a timeline. Working out my movements."

"We just want to know when and how you found him," Lesley told her.

"It's in your interests to cooperate, "Dennis added.

Lesley gritted her teeth. "Go on," she said. "Tell us what happened next."

"I left the house. I wanted to get away from Patrick. I was angry that Archie had gone off to London early. I just wanted some—"

"Hang on," said Lesley. "You said Archie had gone to London early."

"He had a meeting on Monday." Laila's face clouded over. "Today. Something about funding for the dig."

"And he left the cottage to go to London when?"

"Saturday morning."

"Did he normally do this?"

A shrug. "He sometimes went away at the weekend. But he hates London. He's got – he had – nowhere to stay there. So I couldn't see why he'd have left early."

"Laila, do you think Archie might have gone to London and then come back here?" Lesley asked.

"The meeting wasn't till Monday."

"But he went somewhere."

The young woman slumped. "Yeah."

"Do you know of anywhere he might have gone?"

"He's employed by Bristol University. I guess he might have had a flat there, or something. He never mentioned it."

Lesley and Dennis exchanged glances. Lesley thought back to the phone conversation she'd had with Johnny Chiles on the way here from the dig site. Johnny had tracked down Archie's next of kin. Bristol Police would probably be knocking on her door right now.

"Did Archie tell you he had a family in Bristol?" she asked.

Laila's hand stilled on her sleeve. "His parents? I thought they'd died."

"Not his parents."

Laila shook her head.

"Archie had a wife in Bristol." Lesley watched the young woman carefully. "Her name's Susan."

Laila's head shot up. "He didn't. That's a... you've got it wrong."

"Little girl, too," said Dennis. His tone was harsh. "Eleven years old."

"But..." Laila looked between the two detectives.

"I'm sorry, Laila," Lesley said. "But it looks like Archie was lying to you."

CHAPTER FIFTEEN

"You didn't know?" Lesley asked the young woman.

"He told me he was divorced. Never mentioned a daughter."

Lesley narrowed her eyes. They would have to speak to the others in the house, find out if Laila was telling the truth.

If Laila had known Archie was married and they'd argued about it, then maybe...

"You mentioned that you and Archie had an argument," she said.

"I wanted him to wait until Monday morning to go to London. He had plenty of time, and I'd have given him a lift to the station." She looked up. "He lets me drive his car. It wasn't the first time he's gone away at the weekend. There were meetings with his Dean in Bristol. A visit to a site at Avebury." She paused. "He was going home to his wife, wasn't he?"

The young woman looked like she might cry. Lesley shuffled her feet. In Birmingham, she'd had a bigger team to shield her from the need to do witness interviews. Emotional suspects irritated her.

"Bristol Police will have visited Mrs Weatherton by now," Dennis said. "I imagine she'll be distraught."

Laila nodded. "If I'd known..." She rubbed her face with her increasingly damp sleeve. "Eleven years old, you say?"

Dennis eyed her. "How old did you say you were, Miss Ford?"

She blinked. "Twenty. Archie thought I was..."

"You told him you were older?" Lesley asked.

"I didn't... they all just assumed."

Convenient, thought Lesley. She wondered if Crystal Spiers, as the manager of the team, had known Laila's real age.

Lesley tugged at her fingers, making the knuckles crack. She was hungry, and she wanted to track down the other two residents of this cottage before they went AWOL.

"Let's get back to yesterday's events. Did you go straight from the cottage to the dig site?"

"Yes. It was the only place I could think of to go. I thought maybe if I did some work, distract myself."

"Was it normal for members of the team to work alone?"

"Normally there's a bunch of us. The four of us, plus some students from Bournemouth Uni. A couple of National Trust volunteers. Maybe if we need a specialist on hand, one of them too." She rubbed her face. "It changes every day. But yesterday was the first time I'd been alone down there."

Except you weren't alone, thought Lesley. "Describe what happened when you arrived at the site."

"It was empty. There was a man further along the field. A dog walker. You're not supposed to let dogs off their leads on those fields, but I noticed him because his dog was chasing rabbits. Tourist, probably."

Lesley glanced at Dennis, who was still writing. Tracking down the dog walker would be a priority.

"What next?" she asked.

"I went inside the other tent first, the smaller one. That's where I've been working. with Patrick." She shivered. "I realised I didn't have any equipment with me, any tools. We keep it all locked up here. There's an outhouse." She gestured towards the back of the cottage.

"What time was this?"

Laila's brow furrowed. She'd lost the colour in her cheeks and her skin was once again almost translucent. "About three, I think?"

"What did you do next?"

"I had pins and needles in my feet, I went outside and shook them out. I decided to take a quick look in the big tent and then go to the pub. Lie low for a bit."

"So you went to the big tent..."

A nod. "And he... Archie was in there." Laila's voice caught.

"Describe what you saw." Dennis pushed his specs up his nose and resumed his note-taking.

Laila looked from him to Lesley, her eyes welling. "There were flies." She shuddered. "A tarpaulin. I picked it up. I wish I hadn't..." She wiped her cheek. "He was facing away from me. His head... "

She put her hand on the sofa and clawed at the fabric. "I... I knelt down. I grabbed his arm and gave him a shake. But his head... the wound..." She closed her eyes, her hands trembling. "I can't get it out of my head."

"Then what?" snapped Dennis. Lesley eyed him; they really would have to discuss interview technique.

Laila looked up at him. Her eyes were dull, like she was struggling to focus.

"I realised there was nothing I could do. I ran out of the tent. I must have called out, or screamed." She looked at Lesley. "And that's when you came."

CHAPTER SIXTEEN

SUSAN HUNG up from her second phone call of the morning, trying not to think about the first one.

Mrs Hancock, the administrator at Millie's school, had been kind but intrusive. Nobody at the school had ever met Archie. His work took him all over the country and sometimes the world. They'd chosen a house near his university base, but Susan often wondered why they'd bothered. In fact, she often wondered if the staff at the school assumed that Archie was just a figment of her and Millie's imaginations.

Not any more.

She hauled herself upstairs, her limbs heavy. The two police constables had been kind, too. They'd broken the news as gently as possible in the circumstances: lowered voices, respectful tones. Hats on their laps. A Family Liaison Officer would be around later on. Possibly members of the Dorset Major Crimes Team, too.

Major Crimes Team.

Susan lowered herself to the top step and plunged her fist

into her mouth. She wanted to slide into bed, to bury herself under the duvet and pretend today had never happened.

"Mummy? What did the policemen want?" Millie stood over her, her face full of worry. Two police officers turning up when you were on your way to school, that was a scary experience for a child.

"Are we going to school now?"

"You've got a day off." Susan couldn't look her daughter in the eye.

"Really? Brilliant!"

Millie ran into her room, all thoughts of the policemen gone. She threw herself onto her bed and grabbed her phone.

Susan wanted to protect her. To give her the joy of a day off school without the heartache of knowing why. She could take her into town, buy ice cream at Oliver's. Maybe even head out to Weston, go on the rides. One final day together before she brought Millie's world crashing down.

Millie stood in the doorway. "I WhatsApped Hayley. She's not picking up. You sure it's a day off, Mum?"

Susan pulled herself upright. *Be strong.* She gave her daughter a weak smile and looked past her into the bedroom.

Where to do this? This would be one of those moments Millie would always remember. The room where it happened would forever be associated with it.

She reached for the girl's hand. "Come downstairs, sweetie. I've got something I need to tell you."

CHAPTER SEVENTEEN

"WHAT WAS ALL THAT ABOUT?" Lesley asked DS Frampton as he closed the front door of the cottage behind them.

He gave her a pointed look and started walking back towards the car park. She kept pace with him.

"You treated that woman harshly," Lesley said. "She's a witness, not a suspect."

He stopped and turned to her. "I do know that."

"Then why the tone? We needed to gain her trust. To get her to open up."

"She's a liar, Ma'am." He resumed walking.

"I've already told you not to ma'am me. You don't believe her evidence?"

"It's not that. She isn't much more than a child, and she's pretending to be in her mid-twenties. Carrying on with a man old enough to be her father."

"Archie was thirty-seven."

"His daughter is only eight years younger than her."

"That's hardly relevant. And I think you'll agree that it

was Archie doing the lying."

They arrived at the car park. Mike Legg was sitting in the squad car along with PC Abbott.

Dennis put a hand on Lesley's arm. She flinched. "Boss. She was sleeping with a married man. Lying about her age. And probably giving some wild story about herself to the rest of her colleagues. Laila Ford has questionable morals."

Lesley spluttered out a laugh. "Christ on a bike, Dennis! If you suspect everyone who shags someone they shouldn't of killing them, we'll have more people in jail than we have walking around on the outside."

"Please don't use that kind of language."

She suppressed another laugh. "What? Shagging?"

He frowned and reached into his jacket pocket, pulling out a notepad. Not the black police-issue one but a pale blue one. He wrote in it.

"What's that? What are you writing?"

He turned it to her. She read: *Swearing +2. Blasphemy.*

"Oh my God, Dennis. You've not only got a swear jar, but you've got a fucking swear notepad, too?"

His eyes widened. He licked his lips and wrote again. Lesley resisted the urge to snatch the pad off him.

"I regret the fact that you don't share my – our – moral values, Inspector. I know that where you come from—"

"No you don't, Dennis. I come from Birmingham, not from bloody Baltimore."

His nostrils flared.

"I'm not going to change the way I talk, Sergeant, and we need to get that straight if we're going to work together. Now I know you operate at a different pace down here, and you have a... how shall I say it? A different worldview. I know I'll have to get used to that. I've already learned to say CSI instead of FSI, haven't I?"

"Boss, that isn't—"

Lesley raised a hand. Over Dennis's shoulder, she could see Mike getting out of the car. He and PC Abbott would be wondering what the hell was going on.

"Now," she said. "You're going to pop that notepad back in your pocket for me. You'll notice that I refrained from swearing in that last sentence, which believe me I was sorely tempted to do. We're going to forget this conversation ever happened. I'm going to pretend that jar of yours doesn't exist."

"It's for a good cause, boss. The money goes to my chur—"

"Are you listening, or not? Because I'm about to make a far more important point than any petty nonsense about my use of Anglo-Saxon."

Mike was a few paces away. He looked between Lesley and Dennis, shifting on his heels.

"Yes, Mike?" Lesley snapped. "What is it, that it can't wait?"

"I wanted to give you an update, boss." Mike looked like he wished he'd never got out of the car. "PC Abbott and I went to the dig site. We spoke to Crystal Spiers. And she told us where Patrick Donnelly is."

"Which is?"

"The Greyhound. They open early for breakfast."

"I know it." The Greyhound pub was close to the tea room from where she'd heard Laila yesterday. "Come closer. I want you to hear this too."

Mike glanced back at PC Abbott in the car. "Er... OK." He stepped forward.

"Good," said Lesley. "Some information has come to light about Laila Ford that DS Frampton here believes casts a shadow on her morals. If you ask me, it tells us more about the kind of man the victim was, but he's not here to defend himself."

Mike looked at Dennis, whose gaze went just over Lesley's shoulder, towards the castle.

"I want to make something very clear to you gents," said Lesley, "and that is that we don't make assumptions about witnesses, or about suspects. If we draw conclusions about the motives, behaviour, or mental state of the people we have cause to question, we do so on the basis of *evidence*." She eyed Dennis. "*Not* on our view of what kind of person they might be."

"Of course, boss," said Mike. "We build a case."

Lesley smiled. At last, one of these bumpkins spoke her language.

"Glad you understand, DC Legg. Dennis?"

DS Frampton cleared his throat. "Yes, boss. Loud and clear."

Lesley squinted at him. Had that *loud and clear* been laced with sarcasm? Was Dennis even capable of sarcasm?

She would give him the benefit of the doubt.

"Good," she said. "Now let's get on with finding a killer."

CHAPTER EIGHTEEN

"OK," said Lesley. "Did you question Ms Spiers?"

"Question?" asked Mike.

"Did you ask her where she was yesterday? Establish an alibi?"

"She was having an argy with the crime scene investigators. It wasn't..."

Lesley looked away from Mike, towards the castle. *Don't lose your rag with him.* It was her first day, she needed to make some friends.

"OK, DC Legg, where is Crystal now?"

"Still at the crime scene. Observing."

"In that case, you and I are going down there to talk to her."

"Boss." He looked like he was about to salute her. Lesley turned to Dennis.

"You and PC Abbott can go and interview Patrick Donnelly. I want to know if he had a motive to kill Archie, what he was doing in the man's room. Whether he had an alibi."

"We don't have a time of death yet," replied Dennis.

"True. Where are we with the post-mortem?"

Dennis and Mike exchanged glances.

"What?" asked Lesley.

"Doctor Whittaker. He was called out yesterday. He'll probably start late today, make up for it." Dennis looked sheepish.

"He's got a murder victim on his hands and he... never mind. Tell me when you know his plans. I want to sit in."

"Boss."

"Good. Come on then, Mike. I'll see you and PC Abbott back here shortly, Dennis."

"About that..."

Lesley raised a finger. "PC Abbott was here yesterday. She's bright, and she's good with the public. I'm not having her sit idle in the car because you don't like involving Uniform in investigations."

He eyed her. "Ma'am." Lesley gestured for PC Abbott to leave the car.

The constable hurried towards them, then walked towards the village with Dennis, neither of them looking comfortable. Passers-by turned to look at her uniform, intrigued.

"Most excitement this village has had in years," Lesley said.

"Since the Civil War, probably," Mike added.

"Huh?"

"There was a siege. I won't bore you with it."

"Thank Christ for that. Let's get to the crime scene."

· · ·

Crystal Spiers was sitting next to the police cordon when they arrived, her face hard.

"Ms Spiers?" Lesley approached her, cursing the tussocky grass. Her shoes already had mud stains.

"That's me." Crystal eyed Mike. "But you already know that. Where's your mate?"

"My name's DCI Clarke," Lesley said. "DC Legg and I have some questions we'd like to ask you."

Crystal leaned back. Her hands were splayed on the grass behind her and she might have been sunbathing, enjoying the midday sunshine. Apart from the look of thunder on her face.

"I'll talk to you if you get these bastards off my dig site."

"It's a crime scene," Lesley said. "And I'm sure they've already told you that you don't get anyone more careful with a search than a CSI."

"It's not a *search*, it's an excavation. Anything they move will threaten the integrity of our findings."

"We haven't disturbed the soil inside the tent." Gail stood outside the tent where Archie's body had been found. "You don't need to worry."

Crystal pushed herself up to standing.

Gail put her hands on her hips. "Look, lady. Most of the evidence in there is blood spatter. Your mate got a... you don't need to know that. But we don't want to disturb the evidence any more than you do. We're measuring, photographing. Triangulating."

"You're stomping around on land where there could be important artefacts just below ground level."

Gail peeled off her gloves and rubbed her hands. "This field is a public right of way. People have been stomping around on it for centuries. And we're using protective plates. That's the only place we stand."

"Thanks, Gail," Lesley said. This argument could go on forever. She looked down at the grass: no way was she sitting on that in her peach skirt.

"Gail," she called, disturbing the other woman before she re-entered the tent. "Can we borrow your car?"

Gail frowned. "Going somewhere?"

"Just want a place to sit."

"Fine." Gail threw her keys to Lesley. "Don't leave a mess."

Lesley had been in Gail's car last night. She knew that any rubbish she or Mike added would be unnoticeable in the litter-strewn interior.

"We won't keep you long," she said to Crystal, and led her to the car.

Lesley got in the driver's seat, with Crystal beside her and Mike in the back. He was surrounded by crisp packets, sweet wrappers and empty juice cartons.

"Thank you for giving us your time," she said to Crystal, who folded her arms. "Had you known Archie Weatherton long?"

Crystal gazed out at the trees that separated them from the crime scene. She twitched all over, like she was crawling with ants. "I first met him in 2003, at a conference. But this was the first time we'd worked together. I specialise in early Medieval history, he's more of a technical guy. Was."

"How long have you been working with him on this project?"

"Two months, ten days."

"That's very precise."

"I have a good memory."

"Have the rest of the team been here for the same length of time?"

"Patrick, yes. Laila came along afterwards. Five weeks ago."

"And in that time, she established a relationship with Archie?"

Crystal shrugged. "It's a close-knit environment. Things tend to intensify pretty quickly."

"Did you and Archie ever have a relationship?"

"God, no. I don't go for younger men."

"How *was* your relationship with Archie?"

Crystal glanced at Lesley, then looked back at the trees. "Fine, I guess. I mean, he could be an irritating bugger, but we got on OK."

"Irritating? How?"

"He thought he should be in charge. He was doing more to bring in funding, I admit. But it was my project. I've been lobbying the National Trust for access to that site for over sixteen years."

"We've been told that Archie was supposed to have been away from the village this weekend. A funding meeting, in London."

Crystal shook her head. "The funding meeting was real enough. Scheduled for Monday afternoon." She pinched the skin above her nose. "I'll have to rearrange it. But he hadn't gone to London for the weekend."

"Where did you think he was going?"

Crystal turned to Lesley. "He's got a wife, in Bristol. The others didn't know. Especially not Laila."

"But he told you?"

"Like I said, I've known Archie on and off for years. I met

Susan a couple of times. She's nice, if dull. He told Laila he was divorced."

"But he didn't tell you that?"

"Academic circles are gossipy. I'd have known."

"And you didn't tell Laila?"

"None of my business."

"Do you think there's a chance Laila might have found out about Archie's wife?"

Crystal shoved her fingers between her knees. It was chilly in the shade of the trees. "They had an argument on Wednesday night. It could have been about that, I suppose."

"You didn't listen in?"

"I don't know what you think we're doing in that cottage, Detective. But we respect each other's privacy. Patrick and I went to the pub. Save having to listen to them going at it hammer and tongs."

"They argued a lot?"

"It was a volatile relationship. She's immature. He was jittery. They'd row, and then they'd make up. And you can believe me, Patrick and I did *not* want to listen to the making up."

Mike leaned forward, putting his weight against the back of Lesley's seat. She'd forgotten he was there.

"So if Archie didn't go to London and he didn't go to Bristol, where did he go?" he asked.

Crystal shrugged. "Beats me. He left the cottage early on Saturday morning. I was the only one up."

"What time was this?" asked Lesley.

"About six thirty."

"Did he normally leave that early, when he went to visit his wife?" Mike asked.

"Sometimes. Wasn't anything out of the ordinary." Lesley made a mental note to have Susan Weatherton questioned. She wondered how long it would take to drive to Bristol.

"Where were you between Saturday morning and three o'clock yesterday afternoon?" she asked Crystal.

"Saturday I was in the cottage, mainly. Laila and Patrick were both there in the morning, then Patrick went out for his breakfast. Laila can vouch for me till half six in the evening, then I went out for a walk."

Lesley wondered how long Laila had stayed in her room. She wouldn't have known if Crystal had stepped out.

But then, what was Crystal's motive? She had no reason to kill her colleague, certainly not compared to his wife and mistress.

"What about Sunday?" Lesley asked.

"In the cottage till early afternoon. Then I went for a walk."

"Where?"

"To Swanage. Over the downs."

"Alone?"

"I didn't kill him, Detective. Why would I have wanted to?"

Lesley nodded. "Thanks for your time. We'll be in touch if we have more questions."

"I'd rather you gave me my bloody dig site back."

Lesley said nothing, but got out of the car and gestured for Crystal to do the same. She beckoned to Mike, and the two of them walked back to the village, Lesley wondering how closely Patrick's story would match Crystal's and Laila's.

CHAPTER NINETEEN

Dennis hurried along West Street, PC Abbott at his heels. When they arrived at the Greyhound Inn, he turned to face her.

"I'll do the talking. I'm CID."

"Sarge."

He nodded: *Good*. He turned away from her and entered the pub.

It was dim inside, the glare of the morning only emphasising the contrast. An elderly couple in matching cagoules sat by a window enjoying a fry-up. Two old blokes sat at the bar, nursing cups of tea. Dennis wrinkled his nose. He couldn't understand the need to come to a pub before lunchtime, even if no alcohol was involved.

The female half of the elderly couple tapped her husband's arm. He looked up with a clatter of his knife and the two of them peered at PC Abbott. She gave them a friendly smile in return.

Not for the first time, Dennis wondered why the DCI had lumbered him with this uniformed woman instead of his most trusted detective constable, who she'd left languishing at the office.

"Talk to the barman," he told PC Abbott. "Find out if Donnelly's here. I need to make a call."

He stepped out into the beer garden. It sat in the shadow of the castle, with a view straight up the slope to its walls.

His call was picked up on the second ring. "Sarge."

"Johnny, how's it going? Not losing your mind stuck between four walls, I hope."

"I'd be lying if I said this was what I signed up for."

"Sorry, mate. I'll make sure she doesn't do it again. How are you getting on tracking down Weatherton's associates?"

"His wife has had a visit from local police. You know about that. I've tracked down his boss at Bristol University. Dr Alman. Not sure if we need to set up an interview with her."

"We do."

All these women in charge, Dennis thought. He wished more of them were like his wife Pam.

"Anything else?"

"Nothing yet, Sarge. I thought I'd see if I could get Archie's financial records. Maybe if he was having money troubles..."

"This wasn't suicide, Johnny, if that's where your thinking's going."

"I thought it best not to rule—"

"You've seen the photos. An injury to the back of the head that severe, that's never self-inflicted. We're looking for a murderer."

"Who does the boss think did it?"

Dennis frowned. "DCI Clarke doesn't think anything

yet. She says we have to keep an *open mind*. For my money, the girlfriend is suspicious."

"Laila."

"She slept with a married man, Johnny. She lied about her age. Goodness knows what else she's hiding."

"OK, Sarge. If that's what you think..."

"Have you got a time for the PM yet?"

"Pathologist says this afternoon."

"I'll let the DCI know."

"Anything else you need me to be working on, Sarge?"

Dennis checked his watch. "You're fine. Take an early lunch break. We'll be back by the time you're done."

"No problem."

Dennis hung up to find PC Abbott hovering behind him, in the doorway to the pub.

"What?" he snapped.

"Patrick Donnelly's waiting for you, Sarge. Says he hasn't got all day."

"Well seeing as we've closed down his place of work, he has, hasn't he?"

He pushed past the constable. He was irritated with her, irritated with his arrogant new boss, irritated with himself. If only DCI Mackie hadn't...

"Sergeant!" A short man with dark floppy hair waved to him from the other side of the pub. Dennis sighed and approached him, ignoring Mr and Mrs Cagoule whose eyes followed his every step.

"Patrick Donnelly."

"You must be Sergeant Frampton." Donnelly gestured towards PC Abbott. He had a broad Irish accent. "Your charming colleague here told me all about you."

"I need to ask you some questions, about Archie Weatherton. And your other colleagues."

"Of course you do. I'm happy to help."

Dennis pulled out a chair. This man was open, affable. He couldn't imagine him sneaking around people's bedrooms.

"Thank you for taking the time to speak to me." Dennis didn't acknowledge PC Abbott, who had sat down next to him. What was the point in bringing a uniformed constable to a witness interview? The girl would be better off on traffic duty.

"My pleasure," said Donnelly. "Such a tragedy about poor Archie. Can you tell me how he died, exactly?"

"I'm afraid I can't right now. Sorry."

Donnelly gave him a knowing nod. "Of course. Completely understand, fella."

"Did you know Mr Weatherton well?"

Donnelly screwed up his mouth in thought. He took a deep breath. "Well, I shared a house with him for more than two months. I know what brand of toothpaste the man used. And I know more than I'd like to about his sexual preferences, from hearing what he got up to with that Laila. Those cottages aren't as solidly built as you'd like to think."

Dennis didn't want to know about Archie Weatherton's sexual proclivities. The man should have saved that sort of thing for his marital bed.

"How was his relationship with Laila? Smooth? Rocky?"

Donnelly laughed. "Tempestuous, I'd say. But then, she's a tempestuous kind of girl. Poor Archie didn't stand a chance."

Dennis raised an eyebrow. "What do you mean, didn't stand a chance?"

Donnelly's eyes widened. "Oh I don't mean that, fella.

She didn't kill him. At least, I don't think she did. But that's your job to work out, isn't it? No, I just mean that when she turned her sights on him, he was dead meat. Not real dead meat. There I go, shooting my mouth off. You know what I mean."

Dennis was unsure what Donnelly did mean. But he wasn't saying Laila killed Archie. These were just turns of phrase, weren't they?

No. Dennis shook his head. Donnelly didn't have a subtle bone in his body, from what he'd seen.

"How long had Laila been Mr Weatherton's mistress?" he asked.

"Mistress. Now there's a grand word. Now, she started in the second week of May, I remember because that's when we got started with the second trench. Then after she... after a week or so, the two of them were an item. Not sure how it started up, though."

"Did something significant happen in her first week?" PC Abbott asked. Dennis gave her a disapproving look.

Donnelly turned his smile on her. "Why would you think that?"

She looked down at her notepad. "You said 'after she,' and then you changed tack and said 'at the end of her first week.' Did she do something, in that first week? Something to do with Mr Weatherton?"

Donnelly leaned towards her. "It's just my way of talking, sweetheart. You have to ignore me." He turned back to Dennis. "Fat lot of good I am as a witness, eh?"

Dennis returned his smile. He remembered what Laila had said. "Laila told us she saw you in her room, the room she shared with Archie."

Donnelly looked taken aback. "No. When?"

"Yesterday afternoon. Before she found his body. She seemed to think you were looking through his things."

Donnelly reached inside his t-shirt and fingered a chain around his neck. It caught the low sun through the window: a crucifix. Dennis instinctively patted his own, under his buttoned-up shirt.

"She came back to the cottage at about half past two, maybe a bit later. I was in my room, reading a book. *God's Library*, you won't have heard of it. I heard her slamming around, then she came upstairs."

"Did you speak to each other?"

"I made a complaint about the mess in her room. She'd left the door open and I could see dirty plates inside. It never got like that when Archie was around, but we had a rodent problem. If she kept on leaving food in her room..." He shivered, then broke into a smile. "I'm sure you can imagine, Sergeant."

"I can."

Dennis had no idea what it would be like to have a rodent problem. His own modern house was immaculate; Pam took good care of it. He'd never taken food upstairs in all the years they had lived there.

"So you weren't in Laila and Archie's room?" PC Abbott asked. "You weren't searching through Archie's things?"

Dennis wished he could kick her under the table without getting into trouble for sexual harassment. He gritted his teeth.

Donnelly held his arms out wide in a gesture of innocence. "The girl's lying to you, Constable."

"Something she does a lot?" Dennis asked.

Donnelly laughed. "You have no idea, Detective. You have no idea."

CHAPTER TWENTY

"So where will I find the post-mortem?" Lesley asked Dennis as they drove back to HQ.

"Poole Hospital," he told her. "Take the A351 and the A35 for Poole then follow the signs. You want me to accompany you?"

"You go back into the office. I want to know all about Archie Weatherton's personal and professional circumstances."

"Boss, we're doing all this digging into Weatherton and his colleagues. You haven't considered it might have been nothing like that?"

"How so?"

"Maybe he got into a fight. Annoyed somebody in the pub. Could be random."

"How many random murders do you get each year, in Corfe Castle?"

"None, but..."

"The Isle of Purbeck as a whole?"

"Occasionally, in Swanage..."

"How many?"

"One. Two years ago."

"Exactly." She indicated to leave the A352 and approach the office. She was beginning to become familiar with the roads, at least the roads between Winfrith and Corfe Castle. "There's nothing random about what happened to Archie Weatherton. Forensics show no sign of a struggle, no blood spatter outside that tent. Whoever killed him, they knew he'd be in there. We just have to work out *why* he was in there, and not in London or Bristol."

She pulled to a halt outside the front doors. "Send Johnny Chiles out, will you? His turn to get out from behind a desk."

Dennis unfastened his seatbelt. "You're finding excuses to work with each of us, one by one. You're sizing us up."

"Well done, Poirot. I'll find a space as close as possible."

He grunted and got out. There had been no talk of the swear jar on the way home, no arguments about Laila's loose morals. But Lesley knew it was all still there, under the surface.

Johnny darted out of the front doors and dived into the car. "Boss."

"Someone was keen to get out of the office."

"Boring, boss. Bloody boring."

Lesley suppressed a chuckle. Either Johnny was showing his true colours, or he was trying to get on her good side. She'd soon find out which.

Forty minutes later, they were being led into the morgue by a young female technician wearing Doc Martens with her lab coat. Johnny kept grinning at her but she wasn't biting.

"He's already begun," she said as she opened a set of double doors. "Put these on, please."

Lab coats hung from a row of hooks, wellies beneath them on the floor. Lesley removed her muddy shoes and slipped her feet into the chilly boots. In a few moments, she and Johnny were ready.

"Through here." The woman led them through another set of doors to the mortuary. A man with grey-white, thinning hair stood over a man's body which lay on the wide metal bench. He'd already been cut open.

"Doctor Whittaker," Lesley said. "My name's DCI Clarke. This is—"

"Yes, I've heard all about the new DCI from up north. You're late."

"We were interviewing witnesses."

He grunted. "Stand back and don't get in the way." He eyed Johnny. "And if you feel queasy, well for God's sake, bugger off to another room."

Lesley smiled. At least this wasn't another man with a swear jar. Johnny gave her an exasperated look which she didn't return.

The pathologist worked over the body for a few minutes in silence. He extracted the internal organs and handed them to his colleague. After a while he stood back, hands on the small of his back.

That was a bloody quick post-mortem, Lesley thought.

"So you'll want to know the cause of death," Dr Whittaker said.

"Of course," replied Lesley.

"No big surprises, I'm afraid. The blow to his head caused significant inter-cranial bleeding and damage to his cerebral cortex. He would have lost all control over his bodily and mental functions, then lost consciousness. And then, of course, he died."

"How long would each of those stages have taken?"

"How long would they have taken, or how long *did* they take, on this particular chap?" He leaned back, surveying the body. "Loss of control was virtually instantaneous, or that's my best guess. He'd have dropped to the ground like a grouse in hunting season. Loss of consciousness... well, that could have taken anything between a couple of minutes and ten."

"So he could have been lying on the ground staring at his killer for ten minutes?" Johnny asked.

The pathologist gave him a *don't interrupt* look. "Death would have been slower. Maybe an hour, maybe two."

Johnny whistled. Dr Whittaker's cheek twitched. Lesley nudged the DC: *shut up*.

"Time of death?" she asked.

The pathologist wiped his glasses and scratched the bridge of his nose. "When I attended the scene yesterday, rigor mortis was still apparent, although it was beginning to fade. Now, it's almost completely gone."

"Which puts death around twenty-four hours before we found him," Lesley said.

He shook his head. "It isn't as simple as that, Detective Chief Inspector. One must take into account the temperature and climatic conditions after death. The weather has been warm recently, and there was cloud cover on Saturday night, so the temperature wouldn't have dropped overnight."

"It was twelve degrees," said Johnny.

"You're a meteorologist, are you son?"

Johnny held up his phone. "Weather app. Twelve degrees on Saturday night in Corfe Castle."

The doctor sniffed. "Well I must bow to your superior judgement, in that case."

Johnny's lips twitched. Lesley peered at his phone: he was right.

Hating herself for feeding the man's already sizeable ego, she looked at the pathologist. "So taking into account the temperature, what's your estimated time of death?"

"A warm environment means that rigor is slowed. Rigor mortis is the process of heat passing from a warm body, no longer able to regulate its own temperature via the circulation of blood, to a cool external environment. If it's a warm day, this slows."

I know all this, Lesley thought. "An estimated time?"

He sniffed. "Between 9am on Saturday morning and 3pm the same day."

"Thank you."

That meant Archie wouldn't have had time to leave for London: he'd stayed in the village, gone to the dig site for some reason, and been killed there.

"But that's not the interesting part," the pathologist said.

"No?" replied Lesley.

He smiled, his small eyes crinkling. She wondered what kind of man he was at home. If he had been this pompous at his granddaughter's birthday party.

"No, indeed," he said. "Before you so tardily arrived here today, we ran blood tests. Our victim had an abnormal concentration of a sedative in his system."

"Which sedative?"

"Zoplicone. It's used in prescription sleeping tablets. Normal dose is seven and a half milligrams; his blood levels indicated he'd taken four times that."

"He was on sleeping pills?" Lesley said.

"He took an overdose?" Johnny asked.

"If he did, it wasn't enough to kill him. Of course, and I'm

sure you won't need me to point this out to you, Detective
Chief Inspector, but there is the possibility that the pills were
administered by another party."

"By the killer," Johnny said.

Lesley frowned at him. It made no sense. There was no
sign of Archie being forced, or dragged, into the tent. It
looked like he had been taken by surprise.

But the sedatives....

Keep an open mind, Lesley had told her team. She had to
follow her own advice when it came to the forensic evidence,
too.

"Come on Johnny," she said. "We need to talk to the rest
of the team."

CHAPTER TWENTY-ONE

LESLEY PERCHED on her desk as Dennis and Mike filed into her office. Johnny was already with her, not having left her side since the post-mortem.

"Let's bring PC Abbott in as well, if she's around. Mike?"

Mike hurried out and went to PC Abbott's desk. The PC looked surprised but pleased.

Lesley gave her a nod as she entered. "Hope we're not keeping you from anything."

"Paperwork, Ma'am. Traffic violations, and a—"

"Thanks. I don't need chapter and verse."

"Ma'am." PC Abbott looked down.

Lesley pulled the board out from its position in the window. The team had added to it during the day: photos of the archaeological team plus Susan Weatherton, more crime scene shots, and a printout of the toxicology report. There was also a map of Corfe Castle showing the cottage and the crime scene.

"Let's recap on what we have so far," Lesley said. "Johnny, tell us about the post-mortem."

"But you were there, boss."

"I know I was, but the rest of the team wasn't. And someone needs to report back. Might as well be you."

Johnny cleared his throat and shared a look with Dennis. He approached the board and pointed at a photo of the victim.

"Cause of death was this blow to the head. We still don't know what the weapon was. Haven't found it yet."

There was a knock at the door. Gail was outside, a nervous smile on her face. Lesley beckoned her in.

"Sorry if I'm interrupting. I wanted to bring you up to speed on what we've been up to today."

"You've found the weapon?" Lesley asked.

Gail's previously animated face fell. "Sorry."

"OK. It's good that you're here. Johnny's just running us through the PM."

"Ah." Gail leaned against the door to listen.

"Can I carry on?" Johnny looked from Lesley to Dennis.

"Of course," said Lesley.

"Yeah, so... Like I say, cause of death is the wound to the head. Pathologist reckons he's been dead since Saturday morning."

"More specifically, he put time of death in a window from 9am to 3pm," added Lesley.

"So he was killed just a few hours after he left the cottage?" Mike asked.

"Seems that way," Lesley replied. "What do all the dig crew say they were doing at that time?"

PC Abbott had her notepad out. "Patrick Donnelly was in the Greyhound. It was deserted this morning, but it might have been busier on Saturday."

"It wasn't Donnelly," Dennis snapped. "He's not a

killer."

Lesley leaned against the desk. "So I assume his moral values were more to your taste than Laila's?"

"If you must ask, yes. The man was open and honest with us. He was happy to answer our questions. And he clearly doesn't belong in that house, seeing as he's a practising Catholic."

Mike snorted. Dennis glared at him. Lesley grabbed a biro and pressed the top repeatedly.

"He was at church when the murder took place?" she asked.

Dennis frowned. "Of course not. He was in the Greyhound. All day breakfast."

"In that case, I fail to see what his religion has to do with the probability of his guilt or otherwise."

"It speaks to his character, boss."

Lesley noticed Gail smirking at the door. She turned to PC Abbott. "What was *your* judgement of his... character?"

The constable blushed. "He was friendly, Ma'am. Bit creepy, though."

"Creepy?"

"He kept looking at my... at my chest, Ma'am. He touched my knee when I stood up to leave."

"Does that sound like a fine upstanding citizen, Dennis?"

"There's no law against looking at a woman. And he could easily have brushed PC Abbott's knee by accident." His eyes went to the constable's legs then quickly to the floor.

"OK," sighed Lesley. She didn't want yet another public disagreement with her DS. "Laila was claiming he was going through Archie's things. That he was in her room. What did he say to that?"

"He denied it, boss." Dennis's stare was hard. "Said she

was lying."

"Why would she make something like that up?" asked PC Abbott.

"Deflect suspicion away from herself," replied Dennis, "onto Donnelly. "I'd have thought that was obvious."

"So it's her word against his," said Lesley.

"Not necessarily," said Gail. "We can dust for his prints."

"The cottage isn't a crime scene," said Dennis.

Gail met his gaze. "If Laila consents to us searching her room, then we can. If she thinks it would reveal evidence of Patrick Donnelly searching through the victim's things, she'll be only too happy."

"And if she's lying," added Dennis. "She won't consent. I'm happy with that."

I bet you are, thought Lesley.

"So that's Patrick Donnelly." She jabbed a thumb into his photo. "Inappropriate behaviour towards women, doing his best to make us think he's co-operating, claims to have been in the Greyhound on Saturday. We'll need to check that alibi out with whoever was working in the pub."

"I can do that," said Mike.

"Thanks. Why don't you fill us in on Crystal Spiers?"

"I don't think there was any love lost between her and Laila," he said.

"Why not?"

"She was very keen to let us know Laila and Archie argued. Described their relationship as volatile."

"And you think that means she didn't like Laila?"

"I got the feeling she was jealous, boss."

Lesley hadn't got this impression. "Why?"

Mike shrugged. "Donnelly's ten years older than Crystal, thirty years older than Laila. Which meant Archie was the only eligible man in the house. Not surprising the two women had a rivalry going over him."

Lesley sighed. And Mike had been showing so much promise.

"Did Crystal say she fancied Archie?" she asked. "Did she give any indication in that direction?"

"She was unhappy about Archie and Laila's relationship. She knew how young Laila was. Maybe she resented—"

"Dear God." Lesley dug a hand into her hair. She ignored Dennis clearing his throat at her use of what he would consider blasphemy. "What did I say to you all, when we were in the car park at Corfe Castle?"

Johnny raised his hand. "Er. I wasn't there."

"No. But this applies to you as much as to anyone else. What did I say?"

"Don't make assumptions," said Dennis.

"Gold star to that man. What else?"

"Evidence, Ma'am," said PC Abbott. "Build a case."

"Exactly." Lesley raised a hand and started to count off on her fingers. "One, Patrick Donnelly being a practising Roman Catholic does not necessarily make him a fine upstanding citizen. I believe quite a few members of the IRA share that trait."

Dennis opened his mouth to speak.

"No." Lesley stopped him. "I come from Birmingham, remember. The first sergeant I worked for was on the scene at the pub bombings."

Dennis closed his mouth, his face still red.

Lesley continued. "Two, on the flip side. Donnelly looking at your" – she stopped herself from looking that way – "chest, PC Abbott, might make him a creep. But it does not make him a murderer."

PC Abbott nodded, her shoulders hunched.

"Three, just because Crystal Spiers and Laila Ford were two women sharing a house with a man who everyone here seems to think was eligible but to my mind looked too much like an ageing Ed Sheeran, doesn't mean they both fancied him. And it doesn't mean one of them would have killed him because of that."

Johnny cleared his throat. "Sorry, boss."

"Accepted. And going back to Laila, and indeed to Archie's wife in Bristol." She turned to the woman's photo on the board. "Susan Weatherton. Archie was stringing both of these women along. We still don't know if Susan knew about it, but Laila certainly didn't, or claims not to have known, at least. This gives both of the women a potential motive. But it doesn't say anything about their character or their moral values."

"You've already made that clear." Dennis had shifted to the back of the room, his face dark.

"So I have." Lesley took a breath. Right now, she longed for Harborne Police station and the familiar faces of her old team. Zoe, Mo, Frank. Even bloody David Randle.

"Right." She turned to Gail. A smile played on the CSM's lips. "Let's turn to the evidence, shall we? Gail, what have you got for us?"

"I thought you'd never ask." Gail stepped towards Lesley and put out her hand. Lesley looked down at her own hand, then passed her the whiteboard marker she was gripping.

"Thanks." Gail continued to the board. She circled a photo of the inside of the tent.

"Blood spatter," she said. "There's bloody loads of it, which when you're a forensics tech, is like Christmas and Easter Sunday rolled into one." She pointed to the photo.

"Direction of spatter indicates multiple wounds, but the first blow was the fatal one. See the dotted lines on the canvas? This one, with the larger spatters and the clear sideways direction, was inflicted on the victim when his pulse was strong. Arterial spray is possibly the most impressive I've ever seen. Then we have other trails, with different points of origin. All arterial spray, indicating violent blows. Three of them, according to the maths."

"Maths?" asked Johnny.

"Trigonometry," replied Gail. "We use it to calculate the angle and intensity of blood loss, and so to determine where the victim was when he was hit." She pointed to a photo of the victim. "The final blow was when he'd reached the ground. Much weaker spray, he'd already lost a lot of blood."

"Can you tell what the weapon might have been?"

"We've found some hair matted with blood on the ground. Tiny metal fragments mixed in with it. They've gone to the lab. But it was blunt, and heavy. Possibly a hammer, but the fragments don't tally with any hammer I've seen."

"An archaeological tool?" Johnny suggested.

"Something they dug up?" Mike added.

"Let's not jump to conclusions," Lesley replied.

"It has to be worth considering," Dennis said.

Lesley nodded at him. "Let me know as soon as the analysis comes back," she told Gail.

"Of course."

"Do you think the weapon was heavy? Could it have been lifted by a woman weighing around nine stone?" asked Dennis.

"Laila," muttered PC Abbott. Lesley grimaced.

Gail shrugged. "Difficult to say. Even a child can lift your average hammer, although they wouldn't be very precise with whatever they hit with it."

"Thanks," said Lesley. "Anything else? Footprints?"

"Sorry. Grass is too dry, this time of year."

"Fine. We've also got the sleeping pills that were in his system. Johnny, you forgot that."

"I meant to…"

"It's OK." She'd interrupted him when Gail had arrived. She turned to the team. "Archie had four times the usual dose of Zoplicone in his system. Yeah, I've never heard of it either. We need to know if he had a prescription for the stuff or anyone else in the house did." She watched their faces: who was thinking, and who was just waiting to be given instructions?

"And we need to follow up alibis. We've got a time window now, so we go door to door asking if anyone saw anything. Prioritise the cottage's neighbours and the houses near the path down to the dig site. And someone find the bloke who Laila claims was walking his dog when she found Archie."

"What about Susan Weatherton?" asked Dennis.

"I'll go and visit her tomorrow, you can come with me. You allocate roles to the constables, will you? I've got a meeting now."

She checked her watch: quarter to six.

"Ma'am," said PC Abbott. "Do you still need me? Only I've got a mountain of paperwork."

Lesley remembered that, and knew that it had only got worse in the twenty years since she'd been a PC. "You're fine, PC Abbott. Thanks for your help."

She clapped her hands. "Come on, then! Everybody bugger off out of my office."

CHAPTER TWENTY-TWO

"LESLEY. COME IN." Detective Superintendent Carpenter closed his laptop and sat back on his chair. "How was your first day?"

"Fine, Sir."

"You don't have to be so formal, you know. Sit down." He gestured at the chair she stood behind.

Lesley sat and smoothed her hands on her skirt. Truth was, she was tired and her head pounded. But she wasn't about to tell her new boss that.

"So how's it going with the Weatherton case?"

"We're making good progress. Forensics have been helpful, we've interviewed the three people who shared a house with the victim. Tomorrow I'll be visiting his wife."

"She's a suspect?"

"She lives in Bristol with her eleven-year-old daughter, so it's unlikely. I'm looking for background, on her husband."

"I'd heard you were all about the evidence. Building a case."

"I am, Sir." She didn't tell him she'd had to remind her team of this twice today.

"But you're looking for background?"

"We need to identify who might have had a motive to kill him, Sir. But that's only one angle. We—"

He drummed his fingers on the desk. "It sounds like you've got it all under control. Question is, can you handle a murder inquiry so soon into your posting?"

"I have years of experience of this kind of case. Many far more complex and dangerous. In the West Midlands force—"

"Yes, yes. I'm sure we're small beer compared to what you're used to. But you were sent here for a slower pace, if I'm not mistaken."

"I appreciate the sentiment, Sir. But like I say. I'm more than up to leading a murder inquiry. We've got potential suspects coming out of our ears, I'm sure we'll pin it to one of them soon."

He frowned. "Make sure you choose the right one."

"We'll go where the evidence takes us."

"Glad to hear it."

She shifted in her chair. Carpenter's office was bright and modern, large windows to one side and three almost identical pieces of anodyne modern art on the wall behind him. The sun filtered through Venetian blinds and hit her face, making her squint.

"Is that all, Sir?"

He opened a file on his desk. "You've been summoned."

"Sorry?"

"Back to the West Midlands. They want you to—"

"But I've only been here one day."

"Let me finish. They want you to attend a meeting with a Superintendent Rogers. Wednesday morning."

"That'll be a case I was working on."

"They need you to go all the way back to Birmingham? Can't you do it over the phone?"

She swallowed.

Carpenter would learn about this eventually: best coming from her.

"Superintendent Rogers is from Professional Standards. He'll need me to give a statement clearing up a case I was involved with."

"You were investigating police corruption?"

"I can't talk about it I'm afraid, Sir. But I'll make sure my team have work to do before I go. I'll be on the first train back."

"I'm sure you will." He closed the file. "I've heard good things about you, Lesley. I hope you live up to them."

"As do I."

"Indeed." He surveyed her. The informality he'd insisted on when she'd walked in was gone. Was it the mention of Professional Standards?

"Dismissed." He opened his laptop.

Lesley left his office, her muscles tight.

CHAPTER TWENTY-THREE

LAILA SLID down the stairs from her bedroom, her limbs aching. She'd spent most of the afternoon lying face-up on her bed, memories of what she'd seen in that tent flashing through her mind.

Crystal was in the kitchen, cooking dinner. They'd all had a day off, with the police taking over the site, but Crystal had gone down there anyway. She was determined to make sure they didn't damage anything.

Laila eased onto the bench behind the kitchen table, saying nothing. Crystal hummed to herself as she cooked. Laila watched, wondering about Crystal and Archie's relationship. They'd known each other before this dig, but Archie hadn't told her how well.

"Crystal?"

Crystal dropped the wooden spoon she was holding and turned.

"Bloody hell, Laila. How long you been sitting there?"

"Five minutes, maybe?"

"It was a rhetorical question. Give me a hand, will you. I need someone to cut the bread, lay the table."

"Does the table really need to be laid?" Back home, Laila's mum had just plonked food onto a plate and left Laila to decide what to do with it.

"*Yes*, the table needs laying." Crystal snapped a tea towel at her. "Come on, it'll do you good to do something useful."

Laila pushed herself up and opened the pine dresser where they kept plates and cutlery. She placed three settings on the table, her chest tight.

She stood back and gazed at the empty space where Archie's plate should be.

Crystal put a hand on her shoulder. "Don't dwell on it, eh? I've made bolognese, that'll cheer you up."

"I'm vegetarian."

"No you're not. You ate Archie's chicken wings last week, didn't you?"

Laila shrugged. She'd been thinking about going veggie for a while, but Archie had discouraged her.

Maybe now was the time.

She sat down. "Did the police talk to you?"

Crystal tensed, her back to Laila. "They did. After they'd trampled all over the dig site."

"We trample all over it, all the time."

Crystal turned. "We know what we're doing. If they damage something important..." She frowned. "No wine?"

Laila looked at the table she'd laid: glasses, but nothing to drink. "It didn't feel appropriate."

"Don't be daft." Crystal reached into the fridge and brought out a bottle of Pinot Grigio. She slammed it on the table. "Drink some. Pour some for me, while you're at it."

The front door clattered open and a gust of air rushed

through to the kitchen. Crystal rolled her eyes. "Back from the pub."

Patrick stood in the doorway. "Smells good."

Crystal gave him a dark look. "It was supposed to be your turn."

"Ah hell, I'm sorry." He stepped towards the stove. "Here, I'll finish off."

Crystal slapped his hand away from the pan. "I'm almost done. You can cook tomorrow."

"Of course." Patrick turned to Laila. "How's our waif and stray doing?"

"I'm fine." Laila huddled over the table.

"Those detectives talk to you?" he asked as he took the seat opposite. She shuffled along the bench, not wanting to meet his eye. He leaned back. "They were pleasant enough, though. The fella in charge didn't seem to think *I* could have done it."

Laila winced. How could he be so casual?

"It wasn't a *fella* in charge," Crystal corrected him. "It was a woman. A DCI, no less."

"Only woman I saw was a uniformed lassie. Pretty young thing." He rearranged the cutlery in front of him.

"Paddy, I'll thank you not to talk about women like—" Crystal began.

"Yeah, yeah. I'm a dinosaur. So shoot me." He winked at Laila, who knew he was a lot worse than a dinosaur. She pulled her feet under the bench, shrinking away from him.

"Grub's up." Crystal placed two pans on the pine table: the spaghetti and the sauce. "Where's the bread, Laila?"

"Sorry." Laila shuffled out from behind the table and fetched the bread she'd already sliced.

Crystal sat on the bench, spooning spaghetti onto her plate. "I bloody need this, after the day I've had."

"Sitting on yer arse watching the coppers," Patrick commented.

"Preserving the dig site. It took me sixteen years to get—"

"Yeah, yeah. We all know the sob story. Poor Crystal, spending half her life fighting the bleedin' National Trust. Save it."

Crystal eyed him across the table. Laila shuffled a little further away. She was going to fall off the bench if she wasn't careful.

"What's got into you?" Crystal asked Patrick. "You normally hide your obnoxiousness behind a veneer of Irish charm."

Laila held her breath. She knew Crystal and Patrick had worked together before. Years ago, Crystal had been Patrick's junior on other digs. Now, she was in charge.

Patrick laughed. "And I do a damn fine job of it." He shovelled spaghetti into his mouth, giving Crystal a wide-eyed look. He swallowed then turned to Laila.

"So who d'you reckon did it? Was it you?"

Laila clutched her knee under the table. "What?"

"Leave her alone, Paddy," Crystal said. "If she's guilty, that's for the police to get to the bottom of."

Laila stared at her. "I didn't kill him."

"Course you didn't, love. Neither did I. And neither did Paddy here, if you ask him."

"Weren't me, officer." Patrick raised his hands.

"There you go," Crystal said. She leaned forward. "But somebody did, didn't they? I know I'll be locking my bedroom door tonight."

The air in the room shifted with the implications of what

Crystal had said. Laila looked between the other two, who were staring back at her.

"I'm not hungry." She pushed her plate away and squeezed out from behind the table, wishing she hadn't sat this side. "I'll be in my room."

"Archie's room, too!" Patrick called after her as she climbed the stairs. "Police'll want to search it, I bet."

She closed the bedroom door behind her. When she'd caught Patrick snooping in here, he'd shown none of his usual bravado. He never did, on the rare occasions they were alone.

She shuddered. *Don't think about it.* Archie's things were still here. They wouldn't be for long. Even if the police didn't want access, his wife would turn up to take everything away.

What had Patrick been looking for? Had he found it? His hands had been empty when he'd confronted her at the top of the stairs.

Laila took a deep breath and opened the top drawer of Archie's bedside cabinet. She had to know.

CHAPTER TWENTY-FOUR

LESLEY SLID her grubby shoes onto the floor and sank back into the sofa.

She wasn't used to days like this. In Birmingham she'd spent much of her time behind a desk since becoming a DCI. But here, with less staff and no DI reporting to her, she was back to working in the field. She reckoned she'd enjoy it, as long as she could persuade her team to behave themselves. Especially Dennis.

She peeled the lid off the takeaway curry she'd grabbed on the way home and picked up her phone to call home. It rang out four times.

"Yeah?"

"Sharon, love. I was expecting your dad to pick up."

"He's gone out. Some work thing."

Lesley paused, her fork in mid-air. "You on your own?"

"I'm fine, Mum. You let me get a train all the way home from Bournemouth, didn't you?"

The girl had a point. "Thanks for your text."

"You wanted to know when I got back. I'm more reliable

than you give me credit for. Dad's pissed off about it, though."

"Why?"

"I dunno. He thinks you should have set me up as an unaccompanied minor, or something. So they'd keep an eye on me."

"I didn't even know they did that."

"Me neither. Dad was at New Street when my train got in, though. Messaging me every two minutes after the train left Rugby. He's worked out WhatsApp, you know."

Lesley chuckled. She couldn't imagine her tech-averse husband on social media. He didn't even have a Facebook account.

"What you doing?" she asked her daughter.

"French exam in the morning. Revising. Je suis, tu es, vous êtes."

"I hope your vocabulary goes beyond that."

"It does Mum, don't worry. Don't expect too much of me with French though, will you?"

Lesley swallowed a mouthful of her Chicken Jalfrezi. "You have too little confidence in yourself, sweetheart."

"It's called realism. I've always been crap at French, always will be."

Lesley was about to comment on Sharon's language, but the thought of Dennis stopped her in her tracks.

"You want to know how my first day went?" She'd been hoping to share this with Terry. She needed familiarity right now.

"Sorry Mum, but I really have got a mountain of revision to do. Tell me quickly."

Lesley sighed. She eyed the takeaway carton; she should fetch a plate.

"It's OK, love. You get back to your work. Give your dad a hug from me, yeah?"

"Do I have to?"

Lesley laughed. "Tell him hello, then. Get him to call me."

"Will do." The line went dead.

Lesley gazed at her curry. It was bland and watery, unappetising. What did she expect, from a rural town like Wareham?

She took it to the kitchen and put it in the fridge, which was all but empty. Just a carton of milk and a multipack of Mars Bars. She'd take a couple of those into work tomorrow, keep her going if she had to spend another day out of the office.

She'd noticed a pub a few doors down from the takeaway: the Duke of Wellington. It was only a two minute walk.

Five minutes later she was huddled at a corner table, a glass of red wine in front of her. She'd wanted to order a pint but the way the barman frowned when she pointed to the taps had put her off. So it was this glass of bitter Merlot instead. She wondered how long the bottle had been open.

She sipped her drink and watched the pub's clientele. It was quiet, the fact it was Monday trumping the fact this was Dorset in June. Two men sat at a table in the far corner, talking quietly over pints of cider. They had weather-worn faces and their hair looked wind-dried. Beyond them, a young couple sat at the bar. The man was skinny, with blotchy red skin and short blond hair. His hand kept darting out to touch his girlfriend: her knee, her elbow, her shoulder. The girl, for her part, was plump with long brown hair and bright green eyes that danced every time he touched her.

Lesley guessed that this pair hadn't slept together yet, but that they soon would.

She finished her wine and went to the bar for a second. Maybe a bag of crisps too: the hunger had returned. Terry liked to make hints about her eating more healthily, maybe even going on a diet. She ignored him: none of his damn business what she ate.

The barman had been replaced by a woman. She held a glass up to the optics, her back to Lesley. Her hair was thick and wavy, almost black and hanging just past her shoulders. Lesley ran a hand through her own hair, short, blonde and thin.

The barmaid turned and placed a glass of vodka in front of the young couple. She glanced at Lesley, her eyes crinkling. She was older than Lesley had expected, with laughter lines and faint crows' feet.

"What can I get you?" she asked as the couple left the bar and found a table.

"Large red wine and a packet of cheese and onion crisps, please."

"You sure about that? Lethal combination."

Lesley laughed. "I'm made of stern stuff." She patted her belly. This woman was probably a couple of years older than Lesley, but there was something about her that made Lesley feel ancient.

"You on holiday?" The woman placed a glass and the bag of crisps in front of Lesley. "You don't look like a tourist."

Lesley was still wearing her peach skirt and cream blouse, plus the muddy shoes. She should have changed.

"Here for work. Just moved in round the corner."

The woman smiled. "Maybe we'll see you again." She

walked away to serve a group of three women who'd just entered.

Lesley watched her for a moment. Was it worth trying to make friends here?

No. And if it was, befriending a barmaid was a bit of a cliché.

She took her glass and crisps and returned to her table. She'd make this her last: she needed to be alert tomorrow.

CHAPTER TWENTY-FIVE

LESLEY OPENED HER OFFICE DOOR. "DENNIS?"

The DS and the two DCs looked up. It was 8:30am and she'd been impressed by the fact that Dennis and Mike had been here when she'd arrived ten minutes earlier, with Johnny not far behind.

She took her chair behind her desk. Dennis entered and sat opposite her.

"What's the plan of action for today, then?" she asked.

"Witness interviews. Susan Weatherton is available this morning. We need to find out more about Laila's movements on Saturday, and establish alibis for the other two, if they have them."

"I want to talk to Archie's boss at Bristol University, too."

"No problem. Johnny's got her details."

"We might as well hit the road then. How far to Bristol from here?"

"Two hours, with decent traffic. But if it's all the same to you, boss, I think it's best if I stay behind. I should be co-ordinating the interviews in Corfe Castle, we can't leave the DCs to it on their own."

"Fair enough. I'll take Johnny, you have Mike."

"I was thinking—"

"Johnny has the information on the Bristol interviewees."

"Well, I don't think—"

"Dennis. If you rein in your urge to argue with me every time there's a decision to be made, you and I will get on a hell of a lot better."

His hand went to his pocket but he didn't pull out his notebook. That goddamn swear book. Could Lesley curb her language, if he could put a lid on his contrariness?

"Right." She stood up and grabbed her bag. "We'll reconvene here, late afternoon. Let me know if there's anything interesting in the meantime."

"Boss."

Two hours later, Lesley was skirting the south of Bristol on the A370. She'd let Johnny drive, glad of some rest. The bed in her rented house was bloody uncomfortable.

"Which part of Bristol does she live in?" she asked.

"Clifton. I've got it on the satnav."

"Already?"

"I programmed it in when we left the office, boss."

She peered at the satnav screen. "You'll have to show me how to work that thing, when we're done here. It seems to always want to send me to Dundee."

He grinned. "It's just tech, boss. If you're confident with it, it'll do as it's told."

She grunted. They turned a bend and followed a river. The bridge appeared ahead, way over their heads.

"Clifton Suspension Bridge," Johnny said.

"I know it well," Lesley replied. "Studied Isambard Kingdom Brunel at school."

She waited for him to make a quip about how long ago that would have been. Forty-six wasn't all that old. Young enough to have taken GCSEs and not O levels.

He turned right then left then right again and brought them to a street of grand if slightly unkempt Victorian houses.

"Nice," she said.

"Bristol's got one of the priciest housing markets in the country," Johnny said. "Outside London. I guess our victim was worth a penny or two."

"Or his wife is."

They found a parking space and walked to the Weathertons' house. A curtain shifted in the bay window next door and an elderly man looked out.

The door opened to reveal a red-faced woman with mid-length brown hair and an air of solidity. She was about as far removed from Laila Ford as it was possible to get. She looked a few years younger than Lesley, which made her a few years older than her husband.

"Mrs Weatherton?"

"Susan, please. Come in." She stared at the bay window next door and the curtain flicked closed.

Lesley showed her ID. "DCI Clarke, this is DC Chiles."

"I was expecting you. Please, come in."

They followed the woman through a dark hallway into a large kitchen towards the back of the house. Dirty dishes littered the worktops and there were clothes draped over chairs.

"I'm sorry, it's not normally like this." Susan picked up a child's t-shirt from the back of a chair and folded it.

"You don't need to tidy up on our account," said Johnny. Susan put the folded t-shirt on the table.

A slender woman with a blonde bob and the same angular nose as Susan appeared in the doorway. She looked at the two detectives and then at Susan. "Everything OK?"

"Thanks, Fi," Susan said. She looked at Lesley. "This is Fiona, my sister. I know you sent a liaison officer, but I'd rather have someone I know..."

"The Family Liaison Officer can help keep you informed of progress on the investigation," Lesley said. "It's a good idea not to send them away."

What she didn't say was that the FLO was also the investigating team's eyes and ears in the family home. They could report back on suspicious behaviour.

"If I have to..."

"It's not an obligation," Lesley said. "But it is advisable."

"OK." Susan grabbed another t-shirt from a second chair.

"I'll do that," said Fiona. "You need to talk to these officers. I'll put the kettle on." She guided her sister into the now-empty chair.

Susan lowered herself into the chair. The redness in her cheeks had gone, replaced by a blanched pallor. Lesley and Johnny took the chairs opposite her, ignoring the washing.

"Thank you for agreeing to see us today," Lesley said. "I understand this can't be easy for you."

"I don't imagine I have much choice," said Susan.

Lesley exchanged a glance with Johnny. Hostile witness?

"You do, Susan. You're not under caution and we have no

reason to compel you to talk to us. But as I'm sure you can imagine, it's very helpful for the investigation into your husband's death."

"His murder," Susan muttered.

Lesley nodded. "His murder."

Fiona put a tray holding a teapot and mugs on the table. She took a seat next to her sister. "Help yourselves."

Lesley indicated to Johnny, who poured a cup for her. He then poured for Susan and Fiona and finally himself. Lesley spooned sugar into her tea, watching the two sisters.

"Can you tell us when you last saw Archie?"

Susan cupped her hands around her mug. "Just over two weeks ago. He came home for the weekend."

"Did he do that most weekends?"

A shrug. "Depended."

"On what?"

Susan sighed. She looked Lesley in the eye. "On whether he had a woman on the go in the dig team."

Johnny coughed, his tea going down the wrong way. Fiona frowned at him. She hadn't blinked when her sister had mentioned Archie's affairs.

"Did he make a habit of sleeping with the women he worked with?" Lesley asked.

"Thank you for that." Susan nodded. "Not mincing words. Archie liked to shag younger women, and his job gave him ample opportunity." She grabbed a tissue from a box on the table and blew her nose.

"Always younger women?" Lesley asked.

"Yes."

Fiona put a hand over her sister's. Susan chewed her bottom lip.

"Students?" Lesley asked.

"Not to my knowledge. He knew that would get him fired. But there were often women in their twenties in his teams. Archaeology has only properly opened up to female excavators in the last fifteen years or so."

"As far as you knew, was there a woman at the Corfe Castle dig?"

"Crystal Spiers was in charge. I met her a couple of times, didn't like her."

"Any other women?"

"You're talking about Laila. I don't know her surname."

"Laila Ford," Johnny said.

"I don't care what her surname was. Archie said she was too young for him – as if that ever stopped him. He denied being involved with her."

Susan gulped her tea. Lesley waited for her to continue.

"But I know he was lying," Susan said.

Fiona's grip tightened on her arm. "You don't need to worry about that any more."

Susan's hand jolted but her sister kept hold of it. Lesley leaned back.

"How did you know he was lying?"

"Because she told me." Susan looked up and into Lesley's face.

"Who told you?"

"Laila."

Johnny's pen stopped moving across his pad. Lesley leaned forwards. "Laila told you about her relationship with your husband?"

"I thought you weren't going to do that. She didn't have a *relationship* with him. She'd only been on site for five weeks. She was fucking him, the little bitch."

Fiona's hand left her sister's. Susan picked up her own hand and shook it out.

"When did Laila tell you?" Lesley asked.

Susan's hand came to rest on the table. "She called me. On my mobile. Said I could forget about him, he was hers now."

"When did this happen?"

Susan shifted position. Fiona let out a long sigh and turned to face her sister. She leaned in and muttered in Susan's ear.

Susan raised a hand to bat her away. "Fiona says I should retain a solicitor."

Fiona pulled a business card out of her pocket and placed it on the table. "I'm a corporate lawyer. I can't represent Susan in this. But I believe this interview should stop now."

"Why?" Johnny asked. Lesley put out a hand to silence him.

"Susan?" she asked. The woman had let them in. She'd given them tea. She'd volunteered information. "Do you want to tell me when Laila told you about her and Archie?"

Susan blinked back at her, her body very still.

"Suze..." Fiona said, her voice low.

Susan nodded at Lesley. "It was last Thursday. She rang me and told me all about her *relationship* with my husband on Thursday." She emphasised "relationship," enunciating every syllable clearly.

Fiona stood up. "Susan, shut up. Officers, I'd like you to leave."

CHAPTER TWENTY-SIX

DENNIS KNOCKED on the door of the archaeological team's cottage. Mike was in the Greyhound, tracking down punters who'd been there on Saturday morning. PC Abbott, thank God, was out somewhere doing whatever uniformed officers were supposed to be doing these days.

Laila answered the door. "Oh. Hello again."

He gave her a dry smile. "Just a couple more questions. Won't keep you long."

"Of course. I'm the only one in. Crystal and Patrick are down at the dig site. I should be there but..."

Dennis surveyed the room. A pot of tea sat on the side table and another plate of toast was on the sofa. Laila wore pyjamas and a dressing gown. At half past nine in the morning.

He didn't bother sitting down. "I just need to ask you where you were on Saturday, between nine am and two pm."

Her open expression dropped. "You've done the post-mortem."

"We have." Not that he was about to tell her anything

about it. That kind of information was reserved for the victim's wife. "Can you answer the question please?"

"Yes." She looked away towards the kitchen. "Well, I was here until about ten. So were the others, well Crystal at least. She was down here when I went out."

"What time was that?"

"A bit before ten, I think."

"And you were with her before that?"

"I was upstairs, in my room."

He took out his notepad. "So where did you go after that?"

"I went to the Pink Goat café for breakfast. It's on the way to the castle."

"Anyone see you there?"

"My friend Caz works there."

"Caz?"

"Karen Dawes. She was there the whole time. She had her break, we chatted, then I had another pot of tea and read a book."

"What time did you leave the cafe'?"

"About half twelve. It was getting busy, I thought I'd better give them the table back."

He raised an eyebrow.

"I came back here. I was... I was tired. I wrote a few emails, watched a film."

"What film?"

"I don't remember. It was on Netflix."

"Was anybody else here?"

"Patrick got in at around two. Crystal was later than that. Five, I think."

"So you were alone from twelve thirty till two."

"I was here. I wasn't out killing Archie. Look at me, d'you think I could have overpowered him?"

"Miss Ford, did Archie take sleeping tablets?"

She shook her head. "Not that I know of."

"Do you?"

"God, no."

"Anyone else in the house?"

"I wouldn't know. I don't think so."

"We can check GP records, you know."

"I'm telling the truth." She looked like she might cry. Dennis had come across plenty of women who could do that. Turn on the tears, for effect.

"Would you consent to a forensic search of your room?"

She tensed. "Why? You don't think he was killed here?"

"You said that Patrick Donnelly was searching through Archie's things. We want to know if Mr Weatherton was taking sleeping pills. Or hiding anything."

"Like I said, he was—"

He eyed her. "Do you consent, or not?"

His phone buzzed in his pocket. He ignored it.

Laila glanced at it. "Maybe you need to get that."

"It can wait. Do you consent to a search?"

"Yes. I consent." She sat on the sofa, tipping the toast to the floor. "When?"

"I'm going to ask you not to go into your room again until we've searched it. The CSIs are waiting nearby."

She was holding herself very still, as if she didn't want to reveal her true feelings. "I'll go out."

"It's alright. You stay down here, with me. Put the kettle on, maybe."

"Of course." She went to the kitchen. He grabbed his

phone to call Gail Hansford. There was a voicemail from the DCI.

"Dennis, where are you? Call me, we've got new information about Laila."

He fired off a quick text to Gail – *Consent given. Ready for you* – and dialled the boss.

"Dennis, where are you?"

Laila clattered around the kitchen. She was pretending to make enough noise so she wouldn't hear him. He knew better than to trust that.

"I'm at the cottage in Corfe Castle. Laila Ford is in the next room."

"Good. I need you to ask her about Susan Weatherton."

"What about her?"

"According to her, Laila knew Archie was married. She called Susan on Thursday last week."

"What did she say to her?"

"Susan's sister's a lawyer. She shut the conversation down before we were able to get anything else. But Laila did apparently tell Susan she was having an affair with Archie."

Dennis shifted position to get a better view of Laila, who was pouring hot water into a teapot. He thought of the girl's reaction when they'd told her Archie was married. The apparent shock.

"I know what you're thinking, Dennis."

He cupped his hand around the phone and edged towards the door. "She's a liar. A very convincing one."

"Assuming Susan Weatherton isn't the one who's lying."

"You think a grieving widow would lie about something like that?"

"I don't *think* anything, Dennis. Talk to Laila, though.

See if you can find out what the truth is. And if she did know, why did she call his wife?"

"Shouldn't we do that under caution?"

"I don't think we're quite there yet. How's her alibi?"

"Patchy."

"OK. Check out the alibi, then call me back. We'll decide whether she needs to be cautioned once we know what else we've got."

"Boss." He hung up as Laila returned with the teapot. There was a knock on the door behind him.

He threw it open. "Gail."

"Sarge." Gail was with her ridiculously tall colleague. "Where d'you want us?"

"Front bedroom, upstairs. Make sure she doesn't leave."

"Isn't that your job?"

"I need to speak to a witness." He squeezed between the two CSIs and hurried towards the café.

CHAPTER TWENTY-SEVEN

"What was all that about?" Susan asked as Fiona reappeared in the kitchen. Her sister had shown the detectives out, anxious for Susan not to answer any more questions.

"I'm sorry, Suze. Why don't you sit down?"

Susan slammed the cutlery drawer shut. Her sister was four years younger, married without children. She always made Susan feel dowdy and slow. Today had been no different.

"I don't need to sit down. Just tell me."

Fiona sat at the battered pine table. The detectives' half-finished mugs of tea were still cooling.

"You found out Archie was having an affair on Thursday, and he died on Saturday. They'll have you pegged as a suspect."

"That's ridiculous. He died in a field in Dorset."

"You'll need to prove where you were on Saturday. Provide an alibi."

"That's easy enough." Susan leaned against the worktop,

her mind fuzzy. "I went shopping with Millie."

"Did anyone see you? Do you have receipts?"

Susan joined her sister at the table. "Fi, I know when I called you on Friday morning I said I'd bloody kill him. But you do know I didn't mean it, don't you?"

"Of course I do. But you sent me a text, too. Thursday night, remember?"

Susan's chest hollowed out. "But I didn't..."

"I know that, and you know that. But the police don't know you. They—"

"They'll find out that I put up with Archie's philandering for ten years and never did anything about it. Why would that change now?"

"You know why."

Susan stared at her sister across the table. "What do you take me for?"

Fiona leaned in. "I don't *take you* for anything. I'm not saying I think you did it, and you know I'm not." She cleared her throat. "But they'll be asking you for a solid alibi. And I imagine they'll ask Tony, too."

Susan's heart picked up pace. "They don't know about Tony."

"They'll find out. Don't hide it from them, Suze. Be honest with them. You start lying, and they won't believe anything you say." She pulled out her phone. "I've got a colleague, a criminal law specialist. I'll call her."

Susan's mouth was dry. "I don't need a lawyer."

"*Only guilty people need lawyers*, that's what you're thinking, isn't it? But the truth is, you need one more if you're innocent."

"If?"

"Don't put words in my mouth." Fiona raised a finger to

silence her. "Fiona Reynolds here, for Jacinta Burke. Thanks."

Fiona put her hand over the phone. "And call Tony. Tell him Archie's dead, and that you can't see him for a while. Nothing more."

CHAPTER TWENTY-EIGHT

THE PINK GOAT was a homely double-fronted cafe almost exactly halfway between the archaeologists' cottage and the castle. A bell over the door clattered as Dennis entered.

All eight tables were taken, mainly by middle-aged to elderly holidaymakers. One table held a young family with a toddler who slammed into Dennis's legs as he approached the counter.

"Charlie! I'm so sorry. He's a bit exuberant today." The child's father grabbed his son by the hand and gave Dennis an apologetic grin.

Dennis looked from the man to the boy, to whom he reluctantly gave a stern smile. "You need to be careful." The dad's grin morphed into a frown and he pulled the child away.

A woman in her sixties with the look of someone about to impart bad news was waiting for Dennis behind the counter. "Takeaway only right now, my dear. Unless you don't mind waiting."

He showed her his ID and she stood almost to attention. "Oh I'm sorry, officer. Wait, I'll..." her gaze darted around the café, no doubt assessing which table she could remove the occupants from for him.

"Don't worry, madam," he said. "I don't need to sit down."

"Is this about that" – she lowered her voice and brought her hand to her mouth as if sharing a secret – "murder at the Rings?" She blinked, her eyes damp. "So sad. That poor man."

"I need to speak to one of your employees. Karen Dawes."

"I don't see what Karen's got to do with it."

"Please. I won't keep her long."

The woman wiped her hands on her apron and disappeared through a door behind her.

The café had gone quiet, all the customers listening in. Dennis turned, careful not to make eye contact, but knowing they'd all be averting their eyes anyway. The toddler squawked and his mum shushed him. Conversation resumed at a couple of the other tables.

Dennis turned at the sound of the door opening behind him. A young woman with brown hair tied back in a ponytail and an acne-scarred complexion looked at him nervously.

"Sheila says you need to talk to me."

He gave her what he hoped was a reassuring smile. "I won't keep you long. It's about Laila Ford."

A nod. "How is she? She must be..." Karen shook her head.

"She told me she was in here on Saturday morning, that she spent some time with you."

"She was."

He brought out his notepad. "Can you tell me what time?"

"Err... she got here at about quarter past, half past ten. I went on my break and sat with her for a bit. Then she hung around." She glanced towards the door, behind which Sheila would no doubt be listening to the conversation. "She made a pot of tea last until a bit after midday, then Sheila kicked her out. Needed the table."

"Were you here the whole time?"

"Yeah. I work eight till three on a Saturday. She sat at that table there." She pointed to the table where the toddler was now standing on a chair, dancing – at least, Dennis thought it was supposed to be dancing. "She had to pop out at one point, go to the cash point. But other than that, she was here."

"She went out to get money?"

"She needed to pay for her tea. I said I'd lend it to her, but she insisted. She was a bit..." The young woman frowned and stopped talking.

"She was a bit...?"

"She was upset." She squared her shoulders. "He was a bastard, you know. Treated her like shit. Maybe she'll be better off wi—" She caught his frown. "Sorry. But that's just the way it was."

"How long did she go out to the cash point for?"

"It wasn't working so she had to go into the National Trust shop, get cashback. They made her buy jam."

"How long?"

A shrug. "About half an hour, I guess? It was early on, before eleven. Or I'd never have been able to save the table."

"Thank you, Karen. You've been very helpful."

"I haven't got her into trouble, have I?"

"Don't worry. I appreciate your help." He noted her look of dismay as he left the cafe.

CHAPTER TWENTY-NINE

THE DEPARTMENT OF ARCHAEOLOGY and Anthropology was housed in a grand Victorian building in the centre of the university. The reception was staffed by a young man in a rainbow tie and black shirt.

"Doctor Alman is with students right now, but she'll be available in fifteen minutes."

"We'll wait," said Lesley. "Tell her not to go anywhere."

"I don't see why she would."

Lesley wandered to a row of low chairs next to a vending machine. Johnny took the seat next to her.

"I'll call Dennis while we're waiting," she said. He nodded and she headed outside.

"Boss." Dennis sounded out of breath.

"Have you been running?"

"I'm walking back to the house from the café where Laila spent Saturday morning."

"And?"

"She left for about half an hour. She was on edge, apparently. And her friend said she'd be better off without Archie."

"That doesn't mean she killed him."

"With respect, Ma'am. The girl has been lying to us. She pretended not to know the victim was married, she's been throwing accusations at Patrick Donnelly, and she didn't tell us that she wasn't at the café the whole morning."

"And she was alone during the afternoon," Lesley added.

"You're coming round to my way of thinking."

"No, Dennis. Not yet. A flimsy alibi and an argument or two with the victim isn't enough evidence."

"But the lies..."

"We need concrete evidence. Forensics. And where's the bloody murder weapon?" She ignored his tut. "Has she consented to a search of her room?"

"Gail Hansford is in there right now."

"Good. Let me know if you get anything useful."

"I'm back now. If you wait a moment."

She heard him banging on the cottage door, then silence. More banging.

"What's going on, Dennis?"

"There's no one here. I told Gail to make sure the girl didn't go anywhere."

"That's not her job, Dennis."

"I gave her clear instructions."

Lesley sighed. She heard a woman's voice on the other end of the line: Gail. So she hadn't deserted her post. Dennis was talking to her, his words muffled. It sounded like they were arguing.

"Boss?" Johnny was behind her. "Doctor Alman is ready for us."

"Dennis, I've got to go." Lesley wasn't sure if he could hear her.

She pocketed her phone and followed Johnny back

inside. A tall woman with salt-and-pepper hair pulled back into a bun was waiting for them.

"Doctor Alman?"

"I thought you'd buggered off."

Lesley smiled. She pulled out her ID. "I'm DCI Clarke, this is DC Chiles. We need to ask you a few questions about Archie Weatherton."

"Of course. We're all devastated." The woman ushered them into her office. It was long and narrow, lined with books. A window filled one of the narrow ends and the contrast in light levels between each end of the room made Lesley's eyes hurt.

"Take a seat. I'll get someone to bring us coffee."

"We're fine."

"I insist." Doctor Alman picked up the phone on her desk and barked an order for three coffees and a jug of milk. Smiling, she joined them in a low seating area. Three well-worn sofas squeezed around a coffee table.

"Sorry it's a bit cramped. My tutorial groups have eight students in them, hence all the sofas. Makes things cosy." She sat back. "So, what can I do for you?"

Lesley attempted to sit back in her own sofa, but it had dreadful back support. She sat up straight, her knees at an awkward angle to avoid being squashed by the coffee table.

"You've been informed that Archie was murdered on Saturday?"

"Local police came round yesterday afternoon. His wife must be in pieces."

Lesley wasn't sure whether *in pieces* was the phrase she'd use, but then everyone experienced grief in a different way.

"We need to get as much background information on Mr Weatherton as we can," she said.

"Dr Weatherton."

"Yes. Anything we can find that might give someone a motive for killing him, would be useful."

"So it wasn't a random attack?"

"It took place in Corfe Castle, a village with fifteen hundred inhabitants. Random attacks don't happen in a place like that."

"You'd be surprised."

"Doctor Alman, you'll understand that I can't give you all the details of what happened to your colleague. But the evidence doesn't indicate a random attack."

"But who would want to kill an archaeologist, for God's sake?" The doctor shivered. "We're not exactly attention seekers."

"How much did you know about Archie's personal life?"

Doctor Alman nodded. "Now I get you."

Johnny leaned in. "Now you get us how?"

"He had... he had a reputation. Young women, colleagues on digs. Never went near any students as far as I'm aware, thank the Lord, but I imagine he thought about it."

"You knew he had multiple affairs?" Lesley asked.

"Archaeological digs can get claustrophobic, Detective. Especially when people are living on site. And gossip travels. I imagine half the bloody university knew about Archie's exploits."

"Including his wife?"

"Now that, I wouldn't know. Most faculty social events are partner-free. Those that aren't, well, let's just say the conversation is more circumspect."

"Might there have been a woman who wanted revenge? Or a husband?"

The doctor laughed. "Quite a few, I'd imagine. But I

don't see them travelling to Dorset to finish him off. I suspect you'd need to look closer to home."

Lesley and Johnny exchanged a look.

"Can you explain what you mean by that?" Lesley asked.

"Well, seeing as he was killed in Corfe Castle, shouldn't you be interviewing his colleagues on that dig? Especially any young women."

Another glance: *Laila*.

"We already are," said Johnny.

"Good." The professor made to stand up. "Now if you'll excuse me, I have a seminar to prepare for."

"How was Archie's relationship with the other members of the dig team?" Lesley asked. "Any tensions?"

"I don't even know who half of them were. The project was run by Bournemouth University. Archie was drafted in for his experience excavating jewellery and other delicate items."

"Did you know the woman in charge?"

The doctor nodded. "Crystal Spiers. Yes, I know her. Plenty of history between her and Archie."

Lesley raised an eyebrow.

"Crystal and Archie go way back, Detective. I've no doubt they slept together, when she was young enough for him to be interested. But I do know he wasn't happy with her management of this project."

"Why not?"

"He reckoned she was too close to it. It was her baby, her life's work. She couldn't see past that. And she was bloody awful at managing the finances."

"In what way?"

"He told me she'd lost a major backer. She had no control over the budget. He had to keep bailing her out, finding alternative sources of income. He talked to me about some of it, probably kept quiet about the rest."

"Why would he do that?"

The doctor stood up. "I'm not sure it's my business to speculate. And I really do need to bid you farewell now." She nodded towards the door: a group of students was visible through the glass. "Sorry I can't be more help."

Can't, or won't? Lesley gritted her teeth as the professor half-ushered, half-shoved them out onto the corridor.

"Not much use, eh boss?" Johnny said as the students shuffled past them.

"You don't think so, Constable? I think that was very useful indeed."

CHAPTER THIRTY

GAIL OPENED the door to find Dennis Frampton outside, looking like he'd swallowed half a beehive.

"Where is she?"

"Come in, why don't you? We're nearly done."

He stormed past her. Gavin was coming down the stairs, stooping to avoid hitting his head.

"What did you do?" Dennis snapped at him.

"Sorry, mate." Gav looked past Dennis at Gail, who shrugged.

"We had no legal right to detain her," she said.

"Where did she go? I told you to keep her here."

"And I told you that's your job. Are you planning on arresting her?"

He looked like he wanted to hiss at her. "Not yet. But I have my suspicions about that young woman."

"Has the DCI authorised an arrest?"

"I already told you, not yet, "he snapped. "But I wanted to see her reaction to whatever you found."

"Oh, we can help you with that." Gav sounded amused.

Gail bit back a smirk. "She stayed down here the whole time we was up there. Hovering around the door, I reckon. She wanted to know what we were doin'."

"And?" Dennis balled his fists on his hips.

"And what, *mate*?"

Dennis rolled his eyes and crossed himself. "Sometimes I wonder why we bother with you lot. What did you find? How did she react?"

Gail stepped in. "In answer to your first question, we found three distinct sets of prints."

"Whose?"

"We still need to establish that. Archie's we can get from the pathologist. The others in the house, we'll have to take elimination prints. One set will be Laila's, of course."

"So you took her prints?"

Gail shook her head. "Didn't get a chance."

"Why not? What were you playing at?"

"Sarge." Gav put a hand out.

Dennis brushed it away. "Where did she go?"

"I can't tell you that, Sarge," Gail said. "But I can tell you she grabbed something out of that drawer," she pointed to a chest of drawers crammed in next to an easy chair, "and took it with her."

Dennis crossed to the chest of drawers.

"I looked," said Gail. "There's nothing in there except a stack of board games."

"She can't have taken a board game with her."

"Unlikely."

Gail looked at Dennis. His colour had dropped, the tension in his face loosened. Dennis had been like this when she'd first joined the team; she'd avoided him as far as possible. DCI Mackie had calmed him, had managed to rein his temper in. But then DCI Mackie had committed suicide. Gail couldn't imagine Dennis was too pleased about his old boss and mentor being replaced by a woman from the big city.

"We'll dust that chest," she told him. "Technically we don't have permission, but..."

"Do it," Dennis said. "If we don't know what she got out of there, I at least want to know who else might have had it."

Gail gave Gav a nod and he took out his fingerprinting kit.

"You going to go looking for her?" she asked Dennis.

His cheek twitched. "Of course."

Gail turned at the sound of the front door opening. Laila stumbled in, looking shocked to see them all. Quickly, Gail stepped in front of Gav, who was already shoving his equipment back into a bag.

"What's happened?" Laila's gaze flew from Dennis, to Gavin, to the chest of drawers and back to Dennis.

"Nothing." Gail gave her a smile. "We're just finishing up."

Laila nodded. She didn't ask what they'd found in the bedroom.

Dennis flexed his fingers at his sides. He was itching to arrest Laila, Gail could tell. He didn't approve of women like Laila, and the threshold of evidence became lower for him when he was dealing with them. Or at least it had done, until DCI Mackie had worked his magic.

"Come on, Sarge," she said. "The DCI is expecting us all back at base."

He stared at Laila for a moment. The young woman blinked back at him. He pursed his lips then followed Gail and Gav out of the house.

CHAPTER THIRTY-ONE

"WELCOME BACK, EVERYBODY," Lesley said. "I hope we all had productive days."

The team murmured assent as they shuffled into her office. Johnny yawned. The drive back from Bristol had been grim: the beginning of the rush hour as they left the city, and then half an hour stuck in a long line behind a tractor as they'd approached the office.

She pointed to the board. "Let's start with Crystal and Patrick. How are their alibis looking?"

"Not brilliant for either of them," said Mike. "The barman at the Greyhound said he spoke to Patrick a couple of times, but can't vouch for him being in the pub the whole time. And Crystal has already said she was out walking alone. I asked around to see if anyone in the village had seen her heading out. Nothing."

"What about motive? Either of them got a reason to want Archie dead?"

"There were those financial problems Archie's boss told us about," said Johnny.

"Fill everyone else in, will you?"

"Yeah. Course." He turned to the room, his eyes on Dennis. "Archie and Crystal had known each other for years. His boss reckons they were an item, when they were younger. But they didn't see eye to eye on the way this project was being run. There were financial problems, and Archie reckoned they were Crystal's fault. Then there was what Doctor Alman told us about Archie's sex life..."

Lesley stopped him. "We'll come to that when we look at Susan. We're going to need financial forensics. Accounts for the dig, budgets, however it is these things work. Johnny, you get onto Bournemouth University about that tomorrow."

"Boss." Johnny eyed Dennis, who frowned.

"OK," said Lesley. "What about Laila?"

"She said she was at a café in the morning," replied Dennis. "But the girl working there said she had to go and get cash around eleven. Apparently she took a while."

"Long enough to get to the dig site and back?"

"Half an hour."

Lesley took one of her Mars bars out of her pocket and unwrapped it. "So none of them had alibis. We're missing something."

"The blood," said Gail.

Lesley took a bite and gave Gail a thumbs-up, her mouth full.

"It was a series of head wounds," Gail said. "One of which was fatal. If Archie had been facing away from his killer then it wouldn't have completely covered them. But they couldn't have avoided having at least some blood on their clothes."

Lesley swallowed her second bite of the Mars bar,

enjoying the rush of the sugar perking her up. "Does the blood spatter show a gap where the killer was standing?"

"Not really. There's less of it in the entrance, but that's largely because the wound was on the other side of the victim's head."

Lesley picked up a pen from her desk and mimed hitting out with it, imagining someone doing the same to Archie Weatherton.

Gail gave her a look. "D'you want me to demonstrate?"

A ripple of laughter passed through the room. Lesley pushed the last of the Mars bar into her mouth and tossed the pen to Gail.

Gail approached Lesley's desk, dropped the pen and picked up a few sheets of paper.

"Is this important?" she asked Lesley. Lesley hadn't checked any of the paperwork that had landed on her desk yet. She shook her head.

"Thanks." Gail rolled the paper lengthways to make an imitation weapon.

"Whatever hit him, it was hammerlike. The intensity and trajectory of the spatter and the angle of the wound indicate that it was brought round in a wide arc, hitting him on the rear of his skull, left hand side. The killer was right-handed."

She took a swing with her right hand. She brought the rolled up, slightly crumpled, paper down and pointed to the far end. "The head of the weapon was protruding here. We found traces of iron in his hair, it's mentioned in the pathology report too. No modern hammer is made of iron."

"An ancient hammer?" Mike asked.

Gail shrugged. "Not necessarily ancient, but pretty old. Possibly a find from the dig site."

Johnny whistled.

"Under normal circumstances," Gail continued, "I'd make contact with the dig manager and ask about missing items and about the composition of weapons from the period they're studying."

"But she's a potential suspect," Lesley said.

"Exactly. With your permission, Ma'am, I'd like to seek advice from an expert. Not Bournemouth University, though."

"For obvious reasons," muttered Dennis.

"Do it," Lesley said to Gail. "And for God's sake, please stop ma'aming me. You're a civilian."

Dennis cleared his throat. Johnny's gaze went to the filing cabinet next to the DS's desk outside, the swear jar sitting reproachfully on top.

"The nature of this weapon will help us determine the strength of the killer," Lesley said. "And of course it'll be covered in forensic evidence. Finding that is a priority."

"We've combed the field," Gail said.

"Maybe we should ask if anything's gone missing," Johnny suggested.

Lesley didn't like the idea of asking the archaeologists such a direct question. "We ask about inventory," she told him. "They'll document what they find. We need a copy of whatever records they keep."

"Boss."

Dennis was watching her, his hand raised ever so slightly.

"This isn't school, Dennis. Jump in whenever you have something to say."

He nodded. "Surely the forensics are enough for us to seize those records. We don't have to ask."

"You're right. Dennis, you work with Johnny on the Bournemouth University angle. Find whoever looks after the records. Get a copy and start working through, looking for anything that tallies with Gail's description. Find out where things are stored and check for discrepancies."

"Boss."

"Thank you." At last he was cooperating. "So moving on from Laila to Susan..."

Dennis raised his hand then dropped it again when he saw his boss's expression. "There's still her claim that Patrick was searching through Archie's things."

"So there is. She consent to a search?"

Lesley dipped her hand into her bag, mindful of the second Mars bar. Once again, she'd failed to eat lunch.

"She did," Dennis replied.

"We found three sets of prints," Gail said.

"Do we have fingerprint samples from the house's inhabitants?" Lesley asked.

"Not yet," said Dennis. "Another job for tomorrow."

"Good. Mike, take a mobile sampling kit with you to the cottage, or the dig site. Get prints from all three of them."

"I was about to suggest that," said Dennis.

Lesley sighed. "Let's move on to Susan. She knew her husband was having an affair with Laila."

"Yeah, it was Laila who told her," Johnny said. Dennis tutted and shook his head.

Lesley continued. "Laila made out that she had no idea Archie was married when we first interviewed her."

"And she ran off while the search of her room was taking place this afternoon," Dennis added. He gave Gail a pointed look.

"If she's lied to us about this," Lesley said, "she could be lying about other—"

"Including Patrick searching her room," Dennis interrupted.

Lesley scratched her cheek. "The prints will either back up her claim, or they won't."

"Most likely won't."

"Let's not assume, eh?"

He shrugged.

"Anything else from the search?" she asked.

"Nothing of interest," Gail said. "His bedside table and chest of drawers just had clothes in them."

"Did you check Laila's clothes?" Dennis asked. "She might have dumped whatever she was wearing when," – he glanced at Lesley – "*if* she killed him."

"We did," Gail replied. "Nothing."

"Anything more on Susan Weatherton?" Mike asked.

"She shut us down," Johnny replied. "Didn't she, boss?"

"Her sister's a lawyer. After she told us about her phone call from Laila, the sister kicked us out."

"Which is suspicious, if you ask me," said Johnny.

"It's just what lawyers do," Lesley told him. "But I do want to know more about Susan. Her... relationship with Archie, her whereabouts over the weekend."

"Another thing for tomorrow," Dennis said.

"Good thinking." Lesley checked her watch. "I need to catch a train. I won't be in till the afternoon tomorrow, I have a meeting I can't get out of." No matter how hard she tried.

"Leave it with us," Dennis said. Lesley looked from him to Gail, who nodded.

"Excellent," she said. "Good work today, everyone. Let me know if you get anything important while I'm gone."

CHAPTER THIRTY-TWO

GAIL PLACED her empty glass on the table. "I'd better be off. Babysitter to relieve."

Dennis watched the CSM as she left the pub. Gail was good at her job. But he didn't approve of her leaving her son with a babysitter so she could come out drinking after work. Even if she'd only had a shandy.

"Go easy on her, Sarge," Johnny said. "I know that look."

"What look?"

"You think she should be at home with her kiddy."

"I don't think anything."

Johnny laughed and necked the last of his pint. "Fair enough. I hope you're still good for that lift."

"I promised you a lift, mate. I wouldn't go back on a promise."

"Course not." Johnny turned to Mike, who was nearly at the bottom of his own glass. "You getting the next one in?"

"Uh..." Mike looked at Dennis, who held up his empty glass: Diet Pepsi. Pam's idea, stave off the middle-aged spread.

"Good lad," Johnny said as Mike gathered up the glasses and left for the bar. He turned to Dennis. "I don't like the way he's brown-nosing her."

Dennis screwed up his face. "That's a horrible turn of phrase."

"You know what I mean. He's even started swearing around her. When he thinks you're not listening."

Dennis sucked in a dry breath. Mike was at the bar, flirting with the barmaid. She leaned towards him, her low-cut top gaping.

"Sarge?"

Dennis turned back to Johnny. "Sorry. He's ambitious. I'm not surprised he wants to impress her."

"He's only been in MCIT for eighteen months."

That was the issue, Dennis knew. Johnny had been on the team for eight years, and was still a DC. He resented anyone who might leapfrog him. But Johnny was a good copper. Loyal, reliable. Dennis depended on him.

"So what do you make of her?" Dennis asked, not wanting to talk about Mike.

A shrug. "She's efficient. Never worked so hard as I have the last two days. She seems thorough, though."

"Why a woman who demands meticulousness in the gathering of evidence can't be more like that in her behaviour is beyond me," Dennis replied.

Johnny cocked his head. "You'll have to say that in words of one syllable, Sarge."

Dennis patted the constable's hand. Johnny wasn't the brightest tool in the shed. It made him a good DC as far as Dennis was concerned. No surprises.

He leaned in, checking the bar. Mike was still chatting to

the barmaid. She kept touching her hair. A man didn't have to be a detective to know what that meant.

"I did some background research," he told Johnny. "Into the new DCI."

Johnny rubbed his hands together. "Go on then."

"I did it for a good reason, you understand. After what happened with DCI Mackie I, well, I wanted to be prepared."

"Wanted to know the new one had control of all her marbles."

"I wouldn't put it like that." Dennis paused, staring down at the table. It had only been three months, but it felt like yesterday the old DCI had passed away.

"So does she?"

Dennis felt his shoulders slump. He'd found it hard to square what he'd heard about Lesley Clarke with the intelligent, forceful woman who'd become his new boss.

"This is confidential," he said.

Johnny gave a mock salute. "Scout's honour." He hiccupped.

Dennis rolled his eyes. "She was injured, four months ago. The bomb attack in central Birmingham."

"The one at the station, or the airport?"

"Central Birmingham. The one at the station."

"She looks OK to me."

"It was a head injury. Maybe neck, I couldn't get consistent accounts."

"Who d'you get this stuff from, Sarge?"

A young woman pushed behind Dennis to get to the next table. He shuffled his stool in and lowered his voice.

"Never you mind. But word is, it affected her mentally."

"She's lost it?"

"PTSD."

Johnny sat back. At the bar, Mike had given the barmaid his card and was gathering up the drinks.

"Don't tell anyone, Johnny," Dennis said. "Especially not her. But our new gaffer may have a screw loose."

CHAPTER THIRTY-THREE

Tony picked up on the second ring. "Hey, gorgeous."

For the first time all day, Susan felt her muscles relax. "Hey."

She pushed the phone closer to her ear and sat down at the kitchen table. Millie was in her room, getting into her pyjamas. She wouldn't be long. Susan was planning a quiet evening in with her, maybe watching a film. Anything to provide distraction for them both.

The doorbell rang.

"Shit. I'm sorry Tony, I can't talk for long."

"What's up? You've spoken to him?"

She screwed her eyes shut. "He's dead."

"What? Who is?"

"Archie. He... he died on Saturday."

Silence. The doorbell rang again.

"Tony?"

"How?"

"I can't talk to you about it. My sister has told me not to be in contact with you for a while."

"Why not?"

There was hammering on the front door. Susan heard Millie's voice from the stairs. "Mum?"

"You don't think I killed him, do you Susie?"

"Of course I don't. But I imagine the police will want to talk to you."

"You told me nobody knew about us."

"The detective who came here was pretty sharp."

She suppressed a sob. She still couldn't believe Archie was dead. She couldn't imagine he wouldn't be back at the weekend, breezing in as if everything was fine and their marriage wasn't falling apart.

"Mummy? Grandma's at the door."

Susan tensed. *Grandma* meant Archie's mother. "I have to go, Tony. I'm sorry. I'll call you when... when things have settled down."

"You're free. We can get married, like we said."

"I don't want to talk about it."

Archie had cheated on her God knew how many times. She loved Tony. She wanted to be with Tony.

Didn't she?

"Susan!" Her mother-in-law had opened the letterbox and was calling through. She would be able to see Millie.

"I have to go. I love you."

"Me too. Take care, Susie. Call me if you need me."

She nodded and blinked back the tears.

Phone safely in her pocket, she stepped out of the room and took her daughter's hand. *Deep breath.* She opened the door to her mother-in law, her teeth gritted.

CHAPTER THIRTY-FOUR

As the Selfridges building came into sight, Lesley felt the warm glow of home blanket her. She hadn't wanted to come back so soon. She'd been even more reluctant about the meeting with Superintendent Rogers tomorrow. But after the stresses of the last few days, it felt bloody good to be arriving at New Street Station.

She fought her way through the evening crowds and walked to the taxi rank. She had only a small overnight bag with her, a fresh blouse for the morning and the files she'd been sent in preparation for the meeting. She hadn't brought anything from the Weatherton case: that was all in her head. Reluctant as she was to admit it, Dennis was probably right. It would prove to be a straightforward case, with Laila the likely killer. The girl had a motive, she would have had access to the weapon if it was an archaeological find, and she had next to no alibi. Add to that the fact that she'd found the body and was now behaving strangely. Lesley had to concede that she was looking likely.

But they needed more evidence. Forensics. Witnesses.

She'd check if someone had tracked down the man Laila claimed to have seen walking his dog, when she'd found the body.

At last Lesley reached the front of the queue and slid into the back of a cab. She gave the driver her address and leaned back in her seat. It felt good to be driven past the familiar lights of the city. Hell, there were probably more people in her line of sight right now than she'd clapped eyes on in almost a week in Dorset.

The taxi pulled up outside her house and she rooted around in her purse for the fare. The driver scowled at the meanness of the tip. He'd only driven her a mile and a half, what did he expect?

Standing on the pavement, she looked up at the house. A dim light shone in the hallway and her bedroom light was on. It was quarter to nine, Terry would be doing some work or maybe enjoying a glass of wine in front of the TV. She'd spoken to Sharon on the train; her daughter was at a friend's for a revision session and sleepover. Lesley wasn't sure how she felt about this on a Tuesday night with GCSEs in full flow.

Terry's phone had gone to voicemail, and she hadn't left a message. Her flying visit home would be a surprise.

She unlocked the front door and removed her shoes, placing them in their usual spot under the radiator. Terry and Sharon's shoes were lined up next to them, neater than usual.

The kitchen light was on at the back of the house. Lesley passed the closed doors to the living and dining rooms and stood in the kitchen doorway. She yawned.

The fridge door was open. Terry's hand gripped its edge but his body was hidden behind it. Lesley cleared her throat.

The fridge door closed with a bang. The person standing in front of it wasn't Terry.

For an excruciating moment, Lesley thought she had the wrong house. Had the driver brought her to the wrong address? Was the brain damage after the bomb attack worse than she'd thought?

No. Those had been her family's shoes next to hers in the hall. This was her kitchen: grey units, scratched wooden work top, family photos on the wall over the sink.

And that was her silk dressing gown, being worn by the dark-haired woman standing in front of the fridge.

"Who the fuck are you?"

The woman's gaze rested on Lesley then went past her. "Terry!"

Lesley heard footsteps on the stairs. She turned to see Terry stumble off the bottom step, tying the cord on his own dressing gown.

She stared at him. "What are you doing? Who is this?"

It didn't make sense. Her husband was an idiot. He bored her half out of her mind and he'd long since ceased being attractive.

The woman in the kitchen had a narrow waist, and sleek, wavy black hair that tumbled down her back. Lesley had to accept that she looked bloody gorgeous in her own dressing gown.

Terry, have an affair? With this beauty? Never.

"Where's Sharon?"

Terry approached her, arms raised. "At a friend. Lesley, I can explain."

"I'm sure you can." Lesley turned to the woman. "Who are you?"

"Julieta. I'm Terry's colleague. Who are you?" She had an accent, but her English was flawless.

"Who am I?" Lesley didn't know whether to laugh, or spit. "I'm only his bloody wife."

The woman paled. "Oh."

"*Oh*," Lesley barked. The woman's accent was Spanish, she realised.

Holy fuck. Drop-dead gorgeous, ten years Terry's junior, and Spanish?

She turned to her husband. "How the hell did you manage that?"

He frowned. "I'm sorry?"

"I mean, look at her." She looked her husband up and down. "Look at *you*. What did you do, tell her you were a millionaire?"

"Don't."

"I think I can do what I fucking like, seeing that I've just caught you shagging a hot Spanish woman in the marital bed." She glanced back at the woman. "You're welcome to him."

She shoved her way past Terry, grabbed her shoes, and slammed the door on her way out.

CHAPTER THIRTY-FIVE

ANOTHER MEAL, another argument. This time it had been between Crystal and Patrick. Crystal was tense about damage she claimed the CSIs had done inside the tent. Patrick just wanted things to get back to normal. He'd made a mess cooking dinner, and Crystal's griping at him had escalated into a full-scale row.

Laila dried the dishes while Crystal washed. Crystal kept asking questions, but Laila shut them all down. Crystal knew the police had been back. She knew they'd searched Crystal and Archie's room. She didn't know why.

When everything had been put away, Laila left the kitchen. Patrick was in the cramped living room, cricket blaring from a tinny radio he kept for that purpose. Laila grimaced and went upstairs.

She paused at the top, hand on her door handle. Coming in here was getting harder each time. The room still smelt of him, every time she opened a drawer she was faced with his belongings, and she'd taken to sleeping as far over on her own side of the small double bed as she could.

They'd laughed about the lack of space, the fact they had no choice but to be intimate. For her first three weeks in the house she'd shared with Crystal, who had two single beds in her downstairs bedroom. Moving up here had been a relief, even if she had been forced to endure some disapproving looks from Crystal. It had got Patrick off her case, at least.

She pulled her duffel bag out from under the bed. She couldn't stand it here anymore. She'd sent a text to her sister, Jade. *I sent you a parcel. Keep it safe.*

But Jade hated her.

She'd open it, and then what? What if the police decided to go to the house, interview her family?

She heard movement outside, followed by a knock on her door. She opened it, her foot behind it for security.

"We need to talk." It was Patrick.

"I don't have anything to talk to you about."

"Ah, don't be daft, girl."

He pushed at the door. She held it firm.

"Please. Leave me alone."

"They searched your room."

"How did you know?"

"Don't be daft, Laila. Let me in." He gave the door a shove and was inside.

"I'll call Crystal," she said.

He leaned against the door. She backed away from him.

"And what'll she think, knowing what a little slag you are? Archie's dead, move onto the next fella."

A shiver ran across her skin. Patrick was old enough to be her dad. And he was gross.

"Go away."

"Tell me why they searched your room."

"I don't know, do I? They wanted to go through Archie's things, I suppose. Look for clues."

"*Look for clues.* Don't be so naive. They were looking for something specific."

She met his gaze. *Don't blink.* "I don't know what you're talking about."

He shoved his forefinger into his mouth and poked between his teeth, then withdrew his finger and surveyed it. She watched, disgusted.

"Well, they'll have it now, I suppose." He took a step towards her. "Unless you found it?"

She shrank back, her legs hitting the bed. "Like I say, I've got no idea what you're talking about."

He nodded, twisting his lips. Another step forward. She leaned back.

"Did you tell them about us?" he murmured.

"Us?" She put a hand out behind her but it fell through space, nearly taking her with it.

"You and me, stupid."

"There never was a you and me."

He smiled and raised his hand. He left it hovering, centimetres from her face.

Don't fall. Don't close your eyes. Don't let him win.

He stroked her cheek. She screwed up her eyes.

"You're a cute little thing, for a trollop." He blew into her face, very gently. She wanted to scream.

After a long moment, he pulled back. "You'll be out of here soon."

"What?" She opened her eyes and regained her balance. Did he know she'd been about to pack her bags?

"Crystal only kept yer on cos Archie insisted. He had power over her. Now he's gone..."

There was no answer to that. She was the most junior member of the team, and she didn't have the qualifications she pretended to. Only Crystal knew about that.

But they were too far into the project for Crystal to start recruiting. And Laila was cheap.

"Leave my room, now."

"Only too happy to." He pulled the door open and clattered down the stairs.

Laila sank back onto the bed, her body quivering. Archie had been her protection. From Crystal and her mistrust. From Patrick and his wandering hands. Without him, she had nothing left. She didn't want to be an archaeologist. The six months she'd spent at university before dropping out, and the five weeks on this dig, had taught her that. She'd only got up in the mornings because she loved Archie. And he'd loved her, too.

Hadn't he?

She pulled out the duffel bag. She didn't have many belongings. What little cash she had saved would buy her a train ticket home.

She stopped.

Home. She hadn't even told her dad she'd dropped out of uni. Jade knew, and she held the knowledge over Laila like a weapon. Dad had been an empty shell for the last two and a half years, since Mum had died. He barely knew what his daughters' names were, let alone what they were studying. But her getting a place at Durham University had made him smile for the first time in months.

She dropped the bag. She couldn't go home.

Where, then?

She heard footsteps in the room next door. Patrick. She

wished her room had a lock. Could she ask Crystal if the older woman would share again, now Archie was gone?

Crystal would ask questions. It would be an excuse to throw Laila off the team.

Laila yanked her door open and hurried down the stairs. It was dark out. She didn't want to go to the pub: they'd all be talking about her.

But she had to get out of the house. "I'm going for a walk," she told Crystal. There was a route up to the hills above the village, she often went up there for some time to herself.

Crystal glanced up from her book. "Put a coat on."

Who are you, my mum? Laila felt tears prickle. She flung open the front door and half-fell into the street, ignoring the chill.

CHAPTER THIRTY-SIX

LESLEY STOOD OUTSIDE HER HOUSE, her heart racing. It had started to rain. *Bloody typical.*

She turned back to the house. The curtains had been drawn in the bedroom. *Her* bedroom. Where her toad of a husband was shagging a woman who was way out of his league.

She shouldn't have stormed out like that. It was her house. She should have kicked the Spanish woman out. *Julieta.* Terry, too.

She sighed, imagining the legal wranglings over the house. Then there was Sharon to think of. With Lesley stuck in Dorset for the next six months, Terry would want custody.

She shook her head. The rain was making her face wet. Not tears. She was too angry for tears.

She'd been too busy with her career over the years to cultivate the kind of friends whose doorstep you could arrive at unannounced at ten o'clock on a Tuesday night, dripping wet and steaming with anger.

It would have to be a colleague. She should phone ahead,

but her new Dorset Police-issued phone didn't have the numbers of her old colleagues.

She flicked her phone on and brought up the Uber app.

Twenty minutes later she was standing outside a narrow terraced house in Selly Oak. She pushed her hair back, knowing she looked a state.

A curtain flickered in the bay window next door: a young man looking out at her. She gave him a sarcastic wave and he pulled the curtain shut. She took a breath and rang the doorbell.

A light came on, visible through the glass over the front door. She was home, at least. After a few moments, the door opened.

A woman in her early forties with long red-brown hair stood in the doorway. She had a grey tabby cat in her arms. When she recognised Lesley, her jaw dropped.

"Ma'am?"

Lesley shook her head. "I'm not your boss any more."

Zoe looked past Lesley as if she was expecting to see a fleet of police cars behind her. "Everything OK?"

"I'm getting pretty wet."

"Sorry. Come in."

Lesley shuffled past DI Finch into a narrow hall. The cat yawned at her as she passed. Zoe remembered she was holding it and let the creature drop to the floor before closing the front door.

Lesley walked through to a chaotic living room. Empty Chinese takeaway cartons littered the coffee table and a pair of black Doc Martens had been slung on the floor next to the sofa. Zoe had never been known for her tidiness.

Lesley turned back to the woman who'd worked for her

until a few short months ago. Zoe Finch had been her best DI, the only person she could trust with all this crap.

"Did Dorset not work out, Ma'am?"

"Call me Lesley, please. Dorset's fine. I had to come back for an interview with Superintendent Rogers. First thing tomorrow morning."

"Ah." Zoe would know all about that. The interview was about the Jackdaw case, investigating Lesley's corrupt former boss, Detective Superintendent David Randle. Without Zoe's input, Rogers and his team wouldn't have collared the man.

"Do you need something from me, Lesley?" Zoe looked awkward saying her name.

"This is bloody embarrassing. And it's confidential, you understand?"

"Of course."

Lesley eyed the takeaway cartons. All she'd eaten since the two Mars bars in the briefing had been a packet of custard creams on the train.

"Don't suppose you've got any leftovers, have you?"

Zoe laughed. "Shedloads. Nicholas is out with his boyfriend. I over-ordered, and the cat was having none of it."

Lesley sank to the sofa. She wanted to curl into a ball and sleep for a week. Images of Julieta kept flashing through her head. Of Terry with her.

She shuddered.

"Here. I'll get you a plate. We might need to stick it in the microwave."

"That would be fantastic. Thanks."

"No problem. Is that what you need from me? Food?"

Lesley rubbed her temple. "I also need a bed for the night."

Zoe paused as she was picking up the takeaway cartons. Lesley could sense the questions. But Zoe would never pry.

"Of course." She took the cartons into the kitchen. "You can have the spare room," she called out as she opened the microwave.

Lesley nodded. The grey cat, not much more than a kitten, jumped onto her lap. After a moment's hesitation, she stroked it.

Bloody Terry. Why the hell had she decided to surprise him?

CHAPTER THIRTY-SEVEN

Rollington Hill was partway along the Purbeck Way, a line of windswept hills with panoramic views across the Isle of Purbeck. To the north, Poole Harbour stretched out below. Behind, Corfe Castle rose up on its hilltop perch. On a fine day you could see as far as the Isle of Wight in the east and almost to the New Forest beyond Bournemouth to the north east.

Today was not a fine day.

Dennis tugged at his grey tweed jacket, wishing he'd thought to pick up his coat on the way out of the office. Pam had bought it for him. It was sensible: green, waterproof, designed for long country walks.

He didn't imagine the manufacturers had envisaged it being worn at a crime scene.

Behind him, Johnny stamped his feet and blew on his hands. Mike had been the lucky one: back in the office, trying to get hold of the boss and tracking down the next of kin.

Ahead of him, Gail Hansford and her team of two burly CSIs struggled with a forensic tent. The wind whipped at the canvas, tugging it back and forth and as often as not taking one of the techs with it.

"Shouldn't we give them a hand, Sarge?"

Dennis sighed. Truth was, he'd been enjoying watching them struggle. Gail Hansford could be irritating, with her unladylike brusqueness and those dreadful heavy boots she wore. There were rumours about Gail, rumours Dennis liked to hold himself aloft from. But she'd never given anyone a satisfactory explanation as to why her husband had left her three years ago. Her ex, Bob Hansford, was a good guy, worked as a traffic warden in Poole. He lived alone up there, no girlfriend or new wife. It didn't make sense.

"Sarge?"

Dennis snapped out of his thoughts. "Of course."

Johnny hurried towards the CSIs. Unlike Dennis, he was suitably attired, a black fleece over his creased blue suit. Dennis hated fleeces.

Johnny grabbed the fourth corner of the tent and helped bring it under control. Dennis joined him.

"Thanks guys," Gail panted. "Be careful not to disturb her. This is bloody delicate work."

Dennis raised an eyebrow, wishing he'd managed to persuade the Crime Scene Manager to include her team in the swear box. The Church Roof Fund would be significantly the richer for it.

"Got it." Gail slammed a peg into the ground, narrowly missing Dennis's foot. She scooted round to the other corners of the tent, securing pegs while the four men held the structure steady.

She stood back, the wind whipping her hair across her face. "Let go."

The four men each loosened their grip on their respective corners and stepped back. Dennis held an arm in front of his face. He wouldn't have been surprised if the whole thing came tumbling down on him. But it held.

He heard a shout behind him and turned to see the ageing pathologist heaving his way up the hill. He stopped next to Dennis, panting.

"Damn steep, up that hill," he breathed.

"Thank you for coming."

"Only doing my job. Good job you got me on a weekday this time, eh?"

Dr Whittaker struggled forward and into the tent. Gail and one of her CSIs were already in there, while another one was crouched on the ground outside, examining something.

"Watch where you step," the CSI said as the pathologist passed him.

The doctor waved an arm in dismissal. "I've been doing this since you were in nappies, young man." He yanked the tent opening aside, making Johnny wince, and disappeared inside.

"Stay here," Dennis told the constable. "Call Mike, find out what's going on."

"Sarge."

Dennis passed the CSI, mindful of where he put his feet. Forensic plates had already been placed on the ground: they didn't want any more footprints. Dennis pulled the tent fabric aside and slid inside, glad of the relative quiet and stillness.

Gail and Dr Whittaker were huddled together over the body. Dennis could only see the young woman's hair and legs; the rest of her was obscured. The pathologist muttered to Gail who nodded.

Dennis stared at the white-blonde hair, his mind numb.

Less than twenty-four hours ago he'd been talking to this woman. He'd made judgements about her character. He'd believed her to be a murderer.

And now...

Getting herself killed didn't mean she couldn't have already killed too, he reminded himself. She might have been attacked by someone who wanted revenge for what she'd done. She might have been unable to live with her crime and come up here, to the roof of the county, to end her own life.

When the pathologist and CSM drew back, he knew she hadn't killed herself. Laila Ford's face had been caved in by a blunt instrument. Her cheek had been smashed and her jaw broken. It wasn't a pretty sight.

The pathologist stood up. He winced and wriggled his shoulders. "I'm too old for this."

Doctor Whittaker had been threatening retirement for six years. He never would.

"I don't imagine you need me to tell you the cause of death."

"I'd rather you confirmed it," Dennis replied.

"From what I can see here, her cheek and jaw bones fractured after impact from a blunt object. A piece of bone" – he bent down and pointed – "has come loose and ruptured her carotid artery." He indicated bleeding inside her skull, behind the shattered jawbone. "It might have lodged in her trachea as well. From her skin colour, I don't suspect asphyxiation so I imagine she died of cardiac arrest."

"Her heart stopped, because of a blow to her face?"

The pathologist turned to look at him. "The head is a complicated thing, Sergeant. You'd be surprised."

"I am." Dennis grimaced. Whatever this girl's morals had

been, she didn't deserve this. She was only two years older than his niece.

"Any sign of a weapon? Fibres? Footprints?" he asked Gail.

"No weapon as yet. It could be the same one that was used on Archie Weatherton, but I don't want to jump to conclusions until I've got more data. Footprints, we're still checking out. There'll be some from Uniform, and from the elderly couple who found her."

The couple were still nearby, huddling on a rock with foil blankets around them. A uniformed PC had found a flask of tea in their rucksack and was all but force-feeding it to them.

"Fibres? Defensive wounds?"

"Too early to say on fibres, Sarge, but there are defensive wounds." Gail pointed to Laila's right hand. "Her fingernails are broken."

He nodded. Hopefully her killer would still be bearing the scratches.

He shivered. The effect of insulation inside the tent had worn off and his toes were blocks of ice.

He could leave this to the techs.

"We're trying to get hold of the DCI," he said. "She's in a meeting, but hopefully Mike's spoken to her by now."

"She'll be SIO?"

"It'll be part of the same investigation as Mr Weatherton, so yes. But come to me until she gets back, yes?"

"Will do." Gail returned to her work.

Dennis emerged from the tent only to have the wind slam into his face. He suppressed a yell. Johnny was talking to one of the CSIs.

"Has Mike managed to speak to her yet?" Dennis called

as he started walking towards the path down into Corfe Castle.

Johnny jogged to catch up. "His mobile's engaged, Sarge. Hopefully that's good news."

"Good." Dennis picked up pace, anxious to be out of this dreadful wind.

CHAPTER THIRTY-EIGHT

SUSAN WAS WOKEN by banging on her door. She groaned and checked her alarm clock: nine o'clock. She had a brief moment of panic before she remembered why she hadn't set it last night. Archie was dead. Millie had the week off school, and her boss had told her to 'take as much time as you need.'

She slumped back onto the pillows, gazing at the ceiling. She wanted to sleep for a week. Until the funeral, at least. *God.* She had an appointment at the undertaker's today, with her mother-in-law. They hadn't released Archie's body yet. But in her usual efficient way, Rowena Weatherton had insisted they should start getting things organised.

The door banged again. Susan dragged herself out of bed and picked up her dressing gown – pink towelling, faded and grubby at the cuffs – from the floor. She tied the belt as she opened the front door.

"Are you OK? You didn't take sleeping tablets, did you?" Her sister Fiona stood at the door. At the far end of the path, beyond Fiona, a police car was pulling up.

"What's going on?" Susan asked.

Fiona bundled her inside and closed the door. "They've assigned you a Family Liaison Officer. They'll tell you she's here to look after you, to keep you updated on the investigation. But her real job is to spy on you."

"There's nothing to spy on. Fi, please stop being so paranoid."

"What about Tony?"

"I'm going to tell them about Tony."

"You should consult with Jacinta, before you do that."

"Jacinta?"

"Your solicitor." Fiona went into the kitchen. Millie was at the top of the stairs.

"Mum?"

Susan hurried up the stairs and folded her daughter in a hug. She wished to God the girl didn't have to go through this. Bloody Archie, what had he done to get himself killed in a place like Corfe Castle?

"Come on, sweetie. I'll get you some breakfast."

"I'm not hungry." Millie's voice cracked. Susan thought her heart would crack with it.

The door banged again.

"Oh, just go away," Susan muttered. She and Millie needed to be left alone.

She bent down and smoothed Millie's hair away from her cheeks. "You're always hungry."

A sniff. "Not today."

Susan pulled Millie to her and guided her down the stairs. Fiona was at the door, a uniformed policewoman on the doorstep.

"Let her in," Susan told her sister. "I've got nothing to hide."

The policewoman gave Susan a sad smile as she entered

the house. Susan would have to get used to people looking at her like that.

"Come in the kitchen," Fiona said.

"I'll put the kettle on," the policewoman suggested. Fiona rolled her eyes.

Susan steered Millie into the living room at the front of the house. The curtains were still closed. She would leave them that way, what with old Mr Gill sticking his nose in day and night.

She flicked the TV on and navigated to CBBC. She gave her daughter a kiss on the forehead. "I'm going to get you some breakfast." *And find out what the FLO has to say for herself*, she thought. She would get a quick update, then return. She planned to spend the day in here, cocooned in the dark with her daughter. The undertaker could wait.

She closed the living room door gently and hurried to the kitchen. More knocking at the front door. Impatient, she threw it open.

A middle-aged woman with curly blonde hair wearing a tailored olive green suit stood on her step. She held up a business card.

"Jacinta Burke. I hope Fiona's told you to expect me."

Susan frowned. "No."

Fiona appeared behind her. "Sorry Suze, haven't had the chance. Jacinta's your solicitor."

"I don't need a solicitor."

Jacinta ignored that. "The police have told me they want to interview you. You're a witness, they'll do it in a special interview room with what they think of as comfortable furniture."

"Why not here?" Susan asked.

"They want to show you some photographs," Jacinta said. "They said it would be better at the station."

"But Millie..."

"I'll look after her." Fiona squeezed her shoulder. "Best to get it over with."

Susan stared at the lawyer. She should have answered their questions yesterday. "One of them is already here."

"That'll be the FLO," Jacinta said as she stepped inside the house. "Bloody FLOs. Don't say anything to her."

"I've got nothing to hide."

"Who's up for a brew?"

The three women turned to see the policewoman in the doorway to the kitchen, teapot in hand. Jacinta muttered under her breath.

"I can do that," Susan said.

"It's OK. You take it easy. I'm here to look after you."

"She's not," Jacinta whispered.

The living room door opened. "Mummy, where's my breakfast?"

"I can do that, love," the FLO said.

Millie's face creased. "Who are you?" She turned to Susan. "Mum?"

Susan glared at the FLO, wishing the woman wasn't so damn chirpy. "I'll have a cup of tea, please. Milk, no sugar. And my daughter will have a bowl of Weetabix."

She ushered Millie into the living room and sat next to her on the sofa. Watching Millie's face, she reached out for her hand. Millie stared blankly at the TV.

Susan resisted an urge to squeeze her daughter's hand tighter. She wanted to wrap Millie up in her love, to shield her from the outside world. But for now, all she could do was hide with her in a darkened room.

CHAPTER THIRTY-NINE

A SQUAD CAR was waiting for Lesley at Bournemouth Station. She'd planned to get a cab home and change her clothes before going into the office, but the message she'd picked up from Mike on leaving the interview with West Midlands Professional Standards Department had put paid to that.

She sat in the back of the car, aware that she smelled musty. Her suit had got damp in last night's rain and never fully recovered, and her shoes had lost all shape. Zoe had tried to help her pad them out with newspaper, but it had only made things worse. When she'd walked into that interview room with Superintendent Rogers watching, the man must have thought she was already turning into a country bumpkin.

The car pulled up outside the office and Lesley jumped out. She ducked into the ladies to straighten up her appearance. At least her blouse, safely protected by the overnight bag, was safe. And Zoe had lent her a hairdryer, so she didn't look too much like she'd been dragged through one of Dorset's many hedgerows.

After a long moment staring at herself in the mirror and trying not to think about Terry and that woman, she marched up to her office.

Her team were at their desks, all on their phones. She gestured for them to wind up their calls and join her in her office.

The board had been added to. Crime scene photos of poor Laila Ford that made Lesley shudder. The girl's face was a mess, her features barely recognisable. Lesley didn't envy the next of kin having to confirm identification.

Mike came in first, followed by Dennis, then Johnny. They were all subdued.

"Close the door," she said. Johnny obliged. Lesley leaned against her desk and nodded for her team to sit down. They did so, reluctantly in Dennis's case.

"Bring me up to speed," she said.

"A couple out walking found Laila's body under the mast on Rollington Hill at eight thirty this morning," said Dennis.

"Where's that?"

"The hills between Corfe Castle and Swanage," Johnny said. "Just east of the village."

"When did she die?" Lesley asked.

"Pathologist reckons late last night," Dennis replied.

"Any clues as to who might have been up there with her? Anything left behind, defensive wounds?"

"A couple of her fingernails have split," Dennis told her. "Nothing else left behind as far as we're aware. No sign of a weapon."

"Could it have been the same one?"

"It was blunt. We can't say much more right now. But pathology and forensics will—"

"Yeah, yeah. Gail's got it covered." Pathology, she wasn't so sure.

"Has anyone spoken to the other two? "she asked. "Find out when she left the cottage. Or if she was taken."

"I went to the dig site, boss," Johnny said. "They were both there working. Didn't seem too bothered when I told them."

Lesley frowned at him. "Either of those two, or both for all we know, could be the prime suspect. Please tell me you took a verbatim note of your conversation."

"I did, boss." He pulled out his notepad.

"Well that's something, I suppose. Did you tell both of them together?"

"I did. Crystal wanted to know why Laila hadn't turned up for work, and Patrick..."

Lesley gripped the edge of the desk behind her. "Next time you inform two potential suspects of a murder, how about separating them first? At the very least, they're witnesses. Now they'll be chatting to each other, getting their stories straight."

"I doubt it," said Dennis.

"You do?"

"That pair don't strike me as particularly friendly. Crystal seems to—"

"OK. However friendly they may or may not be, we need to talk to them before they have much longer to confer. And I want to keep an eye on them. Hell, one of them might be in danger. We need to appoint an FLO."

"There's a couple of girls from Poole nick who normally do that," Johnny said.

Lesley folded her arms. "How old are these officers, Johnny?"

"I don't know. I..."

"Adults, anyway. Kindly refer to them as women."

"If they were blokes, I'd call them lads."

Lesley wasn't in the mood for this. "Refer to your colleagues with respect, please Constable."

"Boss."

"But anyway, I want someone closer to home." She pushed herself away from the desk and went to the door. She opened it and leaned out. Thankfully her target was at her desk.

"PC Abbott, can you spare a moment?"

"I'm doing more paperwork, Ma'am. I..." The PC looked from Lesley to her computer screen and back again. "Of course, Ma'am."

"Good. I've got a job for you." Lesley retreated into her office. PC Abbott followed.

Lesley turned to the detectives. "PC Abbott will be stationed in the cottage. She'll be our FLO."

"I will?" the PC asked.

Lesley nodded. "You've already been there, you clearly know the village. I want you to keep an eye on Crystal Spiers and Patrick Donnelly. We'll be interviewing them, but I want to know if either of them does anything odd."

"Like what, Ma'am?"

"You'll know it when you see it."

PC Abbott looked very much as if she had no confidence that she would. "Ma'am," she muttered.

"Should Johnny or Mike accompany her?" Dennis said. "This is a job for a detective."

"The FLO job is well established," Lesley reminded him. "She doesn't need babysitting."

He grunted.

"So." Lesley clasped her hands together. "Anything else to report?"

"Not yet." Dennis's expression was tight.

"Fair enough. We've got a lot to do. Two witnesses to interview. Have we got a statement from the couple who found her?"

"Uniform took it," Johnny said.

"Good. There's forensics, and the post-mortem. Do we have a time for that?"

"Tomorrow morning," Dennis said.

"Tomorrow?"

"Doctor Whittaker has private practice on Wednesday afternoons."

"And he couldn't do it this morning?"

"No."

"God give me strength."

Dennis straightened. A ripple ran through the room.

"What?" Lesley said. "What aren't you telling me?"

Johnny was watching the DS. He cleaned his throat. "It's not that, boss."

"Well what then?"

"The Sarge. He finds blasphemy offensive."

Lesley eyed Dennis. "What did I say wrong this time?"

"It's alright, Ma'am. Let's just leave it." He was ma'aming her again. But they had a murder to investigate.

"And we still have the Weatherton investigation to pursue," she said. "I'm going to put back the interview with his wife. Maybe we'll squeeze it in later. But for now, we have to get what information we can on Laila's last hours. Ask around in the village. Find anyone who saw her last night. Check bars, cash points, bus routes. Knock on doors. We have a good chance of piecing this together, but only if we get a bloody move on."

She clapped her hands and people started to move. "Dennis, you take Johnny and Mike," she said. "I'll go with PC Abbott."

"But boss..."

"I'll see you in Corfe Castle."

CHAPTER FORTY

LESLEY'S CAR was still parked outside Dorset Police HQ where she'd left it before catching the train the previous day. It seemed like a lifetime ago.

"I'll drive," she told PC Abbott as she pinged the remote locking. "You need to tell anyone where you'll be?"

"Already done it, ma'am."

"Course you have."

They got in the car. "I still haven't figured out this satnav," Lesley said. "Tell me if I go the wrong way."

But the route between Winfrith and Corfe Castle had imprinted itself in Lesley's mind. As they approached Wareham, she relaxed into the driving. Sure, she missed Birmingham's bustle and energy. But it was nice not to get caught in a traffic jam every five minutes.

"Hope you don't mind me dragging you along," she said to the PC as they left the roundabout for the Wareham bypass. "I couldn't face being cooped up with a bunch of men."

"Not a problem, Ma'am. Just tell me what you need from me."

Lesley glanced over at the other woman. "How long have you been on the force?"

PC Abbott frowned. "Six years, Ma'am. Since I left school."

"So that makes you what, twenty-two? Or twenty-four?"

"Twenty-four, Ma'am." PC Abbott twisted her hands in her lap.

"Sorry. I'm being nosey. Remind me, what's your name?"

"Err..."

"I mean your first name."

"Tina, Ma'am."

"Pleased to meet you, Tina. And you can relax, you know. I don't need you to call me Ma'am every time you address me."

Tina nodded. They drove in silence, through Stoborough and past the turning for Arne.

"If you don't mind me asking, Ma'am, is everything alright?"

"Why wouldn't it be?" Lesley tapped the brake. The Nissan up ahead kept slowing and then speeding up. She looked in her rearview mirror, wondering where the others were.

"It's nothing," said Tina. "Sorry."

"If my behaviour worries you, I want to know. I'm sure Dennis reckons I'm off my rocker." She turned to the other woman. "I'm not, you know."

Tina smiled. "That's obvious enough."

"But still you think there's something wrong."

"I'm sorry. I spoke out of turn."

Lesley tapped out a rhythm on the steering wheel.

There was a *lot* wrong. Her husband was sleeping with another woman, she was stuck in this dead-end county, and she'd realised overnight that she didn't want to save her marriage.

But none of that should affect her work.

She stilled her fingers on the wheel. "I had a difficult meeting in Birmingham. I'm frustrated to be behind the curve on the Laila Ford murder. That's all." She smiled at Tina. "Normal service will be resumed shortly."

Tina gave a nervous laugh. They were approaching Corfe Castle.

"Where will I need to go for the crime scene?" Lesley asked.

"Turn left under the railway bridge then drive up to the walkers' car park. You can't miss it. Could you drop me in The Square?"

"OK." Lesley pulled up outside the National Trust shop, ignoring the man in the blue Audi behind her beeping his horn. Tina climbed out.

"Report back if there's anything important. We'll be over later for interviews, and I'll send a forensics team to you as fast as I can. In the meantime, make sure they don't go into Laila and Archie's room and keep an eye out for them moving any potential evidence."

"They'll probably both be at the dig site, Ma'am." Tina leaned in through the door. Another honk from the Audi. Lesley took a breath. *Ignore it.*

"True. Stick close to them. Pretend to be looking after them. You know the drill."

"Yes, Ma'am."

Lesley rounded the monument in the centre of The Square. She had to brake to avoid a young child dashing out in front of her car. His dad ran after him and scooped him up, waving an apology to Lesley.

"Will you bloody watch your children?" she muttered through gritted teeth.

At last she was heading out of the village. She was starting to find its uniform grey stone buildings and the ever-present looming bulk of the castle claustrophobic.

She followed Tina's directions along a narrow lane under the railway bridge and to a walkers' car park that Uniform had cordoned off for police vehicles. Two squad cars were there, along with a forensics van and two unmarked cars.

Dennis, Johnny and Mike got out of the brown Vauxhall Astra just in front of her.

"Body's still up there, boss," Dennis said. "No hurry, what with the pathologist being unavailable."

Every cloud had a silver lining, thought Lesley. "Show me."

He pointed towards a muddy path running up the hill.

Lesley sighed, thinking of her shoes. First last night's downpour, then this. They would be fit for nothing but the bin. "That's the only way?"

"There's another path up from the village. But this is more direct. Go round the other way and it'll take an extra half hour." He looked down at her feet. "Depending on your footwear."

He had a point. The uniformed officers all had regulation heavy boots. Her team, she realised, wore shoes with sturdy soles. And Gail had stonking great things under her protective overshoes.

"Just show me the way." She would find a shoe shop at the weekend. Heavy boots wouldn't coordinate with her skirt suits, but she'd find something more practical.

"Boss." Dennis started up the hill, his strides quick and purposeful. Lesley struggled up, occasionally bending to grab a tuft of grass and keep herself from sliding back down.

At last they reached the top. Lesley raised her hand to her eyes, trying to ignore the headache that was forming.

"Ready, boss? "The three men were ahead of her, watching. Waiting.

Don't let them see a stupid bloody hill stop you from doing your job.

She balled a fist and thumped her thigh, willing herself on. Up here, the wind was blustery and the air damp. She could swear they were walking inside a cloud.

"Jesus Christ," she muttered to herself. "Give me a canal tunnel. Give me a rundown bloody industrial estate."

She reached the tent. Her team had slowed, not walking at full pace in deference to her. She pretended not to notice. Gail stood outside the tent, protected from the damp by her forensic suit. Beyond her and the tent was a loose herd of cows, which looked as if they might be about to show interest in the crime scene.

"Lesley, good to see you. Sorry you're missing the view."

"There's a view?"

"Glorious, on a clear day." Gail swept her arm across the grey landscape. "Poole Harbour that way. The castle behind us."

"I'll save that for another day, thanks." Lesley indicated the cows. "Are they going to give us trouble?"

Gail turned to look at them. "They'll be fine. Just ignore them."

"I'll trust you on that. Let's take a look at her."

"Of course." Gail gestured for Lesley to go ahead. "Make sure you keep to the plates."

Lesley had already spotted them. She could imagine the damp seeping into the ground, making it soft. "Any footprints?"

"Plenty," the CSM replied. "Too many to be of any use. This is a popular footpath, this time of year."

Not today, Lesley thought. "Have you put cordons on the entrances?"

"We've taped it off at the path up from the village and put a sign at the fork where it goes down to Woolgarston."

"That's all?"

"People are pretty obedient around here, when it comes to footpaths. Too many landslides down on the coast for them to risk it."

"Fair enough." Lesley pulled aside the fabric of the tent. Laila's body was alone inside. The solitude made the sight of the young woman even more unsettling.

She lay twisted, her face to one side and her arms bent the other way. It didn't look deliberate. Just the way she'd landed. Her left leg was bent beneath her and a shoe was missing.

Lesley pointed. "Have you found that shoe?"

"Fifty metres away. It's in an evidence bag."

Lesley turned her head to get a better look at Laila. She crouched down beside her, wobbling slightly on the plate. *Bloody shoes*.

"Single blow?"

"Two or three, I reckon. Of course, the post-mortem will confirm."

"Was she attacked here, or brought here afterwards?"

"The blood on the grass is consistent with a sudden assault in this location." Gail pointed to staining. She raised a torch to illuminate it. "There's no clear spatter, being in such an exposed spot. But there's enough blood here to match the effects of a head wound."

"Did she die instantly?"

"Again, Dr Whittaker will know more about that."

Lesley nodded; she wasn't so sure.

"But," Gail continued, "the blood is mostly pooled on the ground. It's seeped into the grass but it looks like she bled out after hitting the ground. There's very little evidence of arterial spray."

"So the bleeding was post-mortem."

"Most likely."

This was some comfort. Being attacked up here at night, miles from help, would be bad enough. But lying here dying, heart pumping out blood, didn't bear thinking about.

"How long before she can be moved?"

"As far as I'm concerned, any time. We're just waiting for the Pathology guys to come and get her."

"Surely they aren't waiting for Doctor Whittaker to finish his private appointments?"

Gail's face darkened. "They tend to dance to his tune."

"Hmm." Lesley put her head out of the tent. Dennis was talking to one of Gail's CSIs, the one who looked like he was auditioning for the part of the Honey Monster. "Dennis, get onto Pathology. Tell them we want this body moved sharpish."

"Boss." He nodded at the CSI and pulled out his phone.

"And why are Johnny and Mike hanging around up here? Go back to the village, all of you. There are witnesses to question."

"I thought you'd want to do that, boss."

She bit down on her bottom lip. Gail chuckled behind her.

"There's door-to-door to be done. We need to build a timeline for our victim. Get down there, and get on with it."

"Right." Dennis ushered the two DCs back onto the path.

Lesley ducked into the tent. "Are they always like this?"

"I couldn't possibly comment." Gail was stifling a smile.

"What was my predecessor like? DCI Mackie?"

"Oh, the sun shone out of his arse. Until it suddenly didn't."

"How so?"

Gail tensed. "I don't like to gossip. I'll finish preparing Laila for transport, and then Pathology can have her."

She turned away, leaving Lesley to wonder what the big secret was.

CHAPTER FORTY-ONE

TINA ABBOTT WALKED DOWN to the dig site. As expected, there had been no one at the cottage when she'd knocked. Crystal Spiers stood outside the tent where they'd found Archie, talking to a group of students.

"Not you again."

"I've been assigned as your Family Liaison Officer."

"We're not family."

"It can't be easy for you. First Archie, then Laila."

Crystal raised a hand to shield her eyes. The day wasn't sunny but it was bright, the sun threatening to burn through a layer of cloud.

"We're busy. We don't need you hanging around."

"You're both back at work."

"Yes, we're both back at work. You going to judge us for it?"

Tina shrugged. She wasn't keen on FLO jobs at the best of times. "I'm sure the university would understand if you needed to take some time off."

"The university have already been onto me about that. I told them we were short-staffed, and we needed to get cracking. The woman from HR pretended she didn't want us to, but not very convincingly."

Tina nodded. It wasn't her place to tell Crystal how she should react to two of her colleagues being murdered.

But it was her place to observe, and report back. "Mr Donnelly wasn't at the cottage."

Crystal pointed towards the second, smaller, tent. "He's in there."

Tina nodded. "CID will be down later on. They'll need to interview you both. Establish Laila's movements in the hours leading up to her death."

Crystal was speaking to the students again. She paused and turned to Tina. "D'you mind? I've got work to do."

"I just wanted to warn you."

"Well, you have. Now you can leave us."

"I'll stick around and watch, if it's alright with you."

Crystal shoved her hand through her short dark hair. There was no law saying families or housemates had to accept the FLO into their house. But both women knew this field was a public right of way.

"Do what you want." Crystal turned her back to Tina and continued talking to the students. After a few moments the group dispersed, individuals peeling off to work on specific parts of the site. Crystal gave Tina a dark look then disappeared into the larger tent.

Tina's gaze flicked over to the other tent: still no sign of Patrick. Should she check?

No. No reason to suspect Crystal had been lying.

She found a relatively smooth rock and lowered herself

onto it, trying in vain to get comfortable. For the first time since the DCI had called her away from her desk, she wished she hadn't been so keen to get involved.

CHAPTER FORTY-TWO

LESLEY PARKED her car in the West Street car park again. Dennis was right: she needed to get a parking permit.

She bought a ticket and displayed it on her windscreen then hurried towards the cottage. She'd phoned ahead to Tina, who was bringing Crystal up from the dig site. How Crystal would feel about being paraded through Corfe Castle by a uniformed PC, Lesley could only guess.

As she approached the cottage, she saw Mike crossing the road. She waved him over.

"You on door-to-door?"

"Yes, boss. No joy yet."

"How many houses have you tried?"

"Me and PC Mullins have covered the cottages from the end of the road to here." He pointed past the car park. "No one recalls seeing Laila last night, or this morning."

"What about Dennis and Johnny?"

"The sarge is doing the houses closer to the path up to Rollington Hill Down. Johnny's doing the pubs."

"Good. I'm on my way to the cottage. I'll need someone to sit in while I interview Crystal and Patrick."

"Happy to help."

"That's what I was hoping to hear. Let PC Mullins know what you're up to."

Mike hurried to where PC Mullins stood at a front door, talking to a young woman with a toddler on her hip. She was shaking her head.

These cottages butted right up to the road, but it meant people kept their curtains shut at night. It seemed Laila had gone unnoticed.

PC Abbott was approaching the cottage from the opposite direction, Crystal Spiers walking next to her. The woman was keeping as much distance from the constable as she could on such a narrow walkway.

Lesley caught up with them as Crystal put her key in the lock, Mike behind her.

"She says you want to talk to me," Crystal said.

"We need to build a picture of Laila's movements yesterday evening. I'm hoping you can help."

"I'll try." Crystal shoved the door open. Lesley gestured to Tina who went on ahead to the kitchen. Crystal threw herself into the easy chair, which left the sofa for Lesley and Mike. She sat on the end closest to their interviewee.

Tina stuck her head round the kitchen door. "Can I get anyone a brew?"

"White coffee, for me," Lesley replied.

"Strong tea please, Tina," Mike said.

Lesley raised an eyebrow at Crystal. "Same as him," she grunted.

"Coming right up."

Tina disappeared and Lesley heard cupboards being opened and closed. Crystal twitched in her chair.

"Talk us through yesterday evening, please," Lesley said. "Did Laila come home to the cottage, after work?"

"She spent most the evening up in her room. She's been doing a lot of that lately." Crystal shrugged, not meeting Lesley's eye. "Can't blame her, I suppose."

"Can you be more specific? What time did she get home, did she go out, did you see much of her?"

A sigh. "She came home first. About five, I reckon. Patrick left the site not long after that, he was on cooking duty. I had to pack everything up and debrief the students. I got back around half six."

"Do you find it difficult to work there after what happened to Archie?"

"I try not to think about it. The whole thing's put us behind, your forensics people keeping us from working... I'm under pressure."

PC Abbott appeared with two mugs. She handed one to Lesley and the other to Crystal. Mike gave her a questioning look.

"You're next." She disappeared into the kitchen.

"So," said Lesley after sipping her coffee. "When you got home, who was here?"

"Patrick was cooking." Crystal grimaced. "Laila was upstairs."

"Did you see her?"

"Patrick told me she was up there."

Lesley nodded. "Did you see her at all?"

"She came down for dinner. Just before seven. Scurried back up to her room straight after. I tried to talk to her, to be friendly. She's just a kid. I figured... Anyway, I didn't see her again for an hour or so."

"You say she scurried. What was her mood like?"

"Subdued. Scared." Crystal looked at Lesley across the rim of her mug. "She kept giving Patrick funny looks."

"What kind of funny looks?" Lesley glanced behind her to see Mike scribbling furiously in his pad.

"Wary, I suppose. Like she thought he might bite."

"Had you witnessed any tension between Patrick and Laila before this?"

Tina reappeared and handed Mike a mug. She drew back with her own, standing in the doorway to the kitchen. "Am I alright here, Ma'am?"

"You're fine." Lesley was focused on Crystal. "Any tension between them?"

Crystal screwed up her lips. "You'd have to ask Patrick about that."

"I'm asking you."

Crystal scratched her chin. "I don't know the full facts. I'd rather..."

"Tell me what you know. I'll be speaking to him next."

Crystal cocked her head. "I think he tried it on with her. When she first arrived, before she and Archie became a thing."

"Just to confirm, you're alleging that Patrick 'tried it on' with Laila?"

A nod. Crystal slurped her tea. For someone whose two housemates had been brutally killed, and with a third she suspected of assault, she was remarkably calm.

"When you say 'tried it on', what exactly do you mean?" Lesley asked.

"Do I have to spell it out? He wanted to get into her

knickers. Common enough on these digs. But the man's old enough to be her father. Grandfather, even."

"Did Patrick sexually assault Laila?"

"I'm his boss. I can't go bandying around accusations like that."

"This is confidential, Ms Spiers. Did Patrick assault Laila?"

"I can't prove anything. But he was alone with her, a couple of times. I heard…"

"What did you hear?"

"A struggle. Him shouting at her, I didn't hear the words. Her crying herself to sleep, the nights it happened."

"This happened a few times?"

"It stopped, when she and Archie got together. She moved up to his room. She made sure she was alone up there as little as possible."

"Were there any incidents between Laila and Patrick after Archie's death?"

Crystal licked her lips. She gripped her mug. "I heard him go into her room, yesterday evening."

"After dinner?"

A nod. "She went up there after I'd tried to talk to her. He was in here, listening to the cricket." She indicated a small radio on the chest of drawers next to her. "When I finished cleaning up, he went upstairs. His room's up there, with Laila and Archie's. I'm down here."

She gestured behind her, towards the door leading to the stairs.

"You heard him go into her room?"

"I heard them talking." Crystal glanced upwards. "It's not hard with the way these houses are built."

"What did they say?"

Crystal's hand rested on her cheek. Lesley felt the sofa shift; Mike was shuffling towards her. In the kitchen doorway, Tina was motionless.

"I heard him say 'you and me'. Then it was muffled. All I heard after that was her telling him to get out."

Lesley nodded. "And then what happened?"

"Doors opening and closing. Footsteps. It sounded like Patrick went to his room. Then Laila came downstairs. She almost fell down, she was in such a rush."

"Did she speak to you?"

Crystal shook her head. "All she said was she was going for a walk." She looked up, her eyes glistening. "That was the last I saw of her."

Tina was holding her breath. Mike flipped to a fresh page in his pad.

"You didn't go out to find her?" Lesley asked.

Crystal looked down. "I wish I had."

"And what about Patrick?"

Crystal lifted her head. "What about him?"

"Did he stay in his room? Did he come downstairs? Did he speak to you?" Lesley knew she shouldn't fire so many questions off at once, but she was impatient.

Crystal took a shaky breath. "About quarter of an hour after Laila left, he went out too."

Tina drew in a breath. *Shush*, thought Lesley. "Did he speak to you on his way out?"

"Only to say he was going to the pub. He's a regular at the Greyhound."

Lesley eyed Mike: something for Johnny to check out.

"When did he return?" she asked.

"I went to bed at ten. I was knackered after everything

that... Then I heard him come in at about half eleven. The stairs are right over my room, it's a bloody nuisance."

"OK." Lesley rubbed her eyes. A familiar pain was brewing at the back of her neck. "Ms Spiers, can you tell me if there were any tensions between Patrick and Archie? Or between you and Archie?"

Crystal frowned at her. "Me and Archie have been mates for years. We had a bit of a fling, before his daughter was born. Just for a couple of months. We were friends, Detective. No tension."

"No disagreements about the way the dig project was being managed? No arguments about funding?"

Crystal leaned back. "No. Nothing."

"Very well. And what about Archie and Patrick?"

"They... well they managed to rub along OK. Patrick clearly resented Archie, with him being older but less senior. But they had an amicable working relationship, I guess."

"No tensions over Laila?"

"Archie wasn't that sort of man."

"And Patrick?"

Crystal looked away. "He was a bit jealous at first. But he soon saw sense. A kid like Laila would never have gone for him."

"You call her a kid."

"She was nineteen. She'd dropped out of university. She pretended she was twenty-three and a graduate. I was the only one who knew."

"Laila was lying about her age?"

"It wasn't that big a deal. She was still an adult."

"Was there anything else she was lying about?"

Lesley thought of Dennis and his mistrust of the young woman. She imagined his face when she told him about this.

"Not that I know of."

"OK." Lesley checked her watch: mid-afternoon, already. "We'll need to do a full search of this cottage, with your consent."

"Of course."

"Thank you." Lesley stood up. She wanted to process what Crystal had told her before they moved on to Patrick.

CHAPTER FORTY-THREE

THE FOUR DETECTIVES sat in Lesley's car in the West Street car park, Lesley and Mike in the front, Dennis and Johnny behind them. Dennis had pulled a face when Lesley had told him to get in the back. But she and Mike had already been waiting, having finished their interview with Crystal before Dennis and Johnny returned from the door-to-door.

"So," she said. "Anybody see Laila before she went up to the hills?"

"Nobody," said Dennis. "We knocked on all the doors along West Street, as well as the houses around the path leading up to the Downs."

"And I went into the pubs," said Johnny.

Mike laughed. "Bet you enjoyed that, mate."

Johnny gave him a flick on the back of the neck. Mike put a hand up to it and winced, but said nothing.

Lesley ignored them.

"So nobody in the whole village saw her?" she asked Dennis. "Makes no sense. She left that house at about nine o'clock. It would've been light. She would've been clearly visible."

"And she stood out," said Johnny. "With that blonde hair."

Lesley nodded. She wasn't exactly easy to miss.

Dennis shrugged. "Well, I guess if she'd had an argument with Patrick... I mean, she was heading up onto the hills when it was getting dark. It's not sensible, for a woman to do that on her own."

Lesley clenched a fist. "She had an argument with Patrick, at least that's what Crystal told us."

Dennis raised an eyebrow. "What about?"

"Crystal heard her tell him to get out. Raised voices."

"So she had an argument with Patrick, stormed out of the house and ran up onto Rollington Hill," said Dennis. "Do you think she was planning to hurt herself?"

"She didn't take anything with her," replied Lesley.

"We don't know that," interrupted Johnny. "The killer might have removed whatever she was carrying."

Lesley wasn't so sure. "We've got no evidence that she took anything with her."

"She went because she wanted time to herself," said Mike.

Lesley frowned. "Somebody knew she was up there. That somebody followed her."

"You think someone saw her go past their house?" suggested Dennis.

"Possibly," replied Lesley. "But both Crystal and Patrick knew she'd gone out. And Patrick left fifteen minutes after her."

"He was going to the pub, boss," said Mike.

"That's what he claimed. We need to check the Greyhound again, Johnny."

"I didn't ask about him. I was just looking for Laila."

"That's fine. But I do need you to go back there and ask them if Patrick was in last night and if so, what time."

Johnny opened his door. "I'll head back over there."

Lesley nodded. "Dennis. I want you to come with me to the house, we've still got to interview Patrick."

"We can hear his side of the story."

Lesley sighed. "I thought you'd see it like that."

"Well, it is her word against his. She *claims* he argued with Laila. She *claims* he assaulted her. She *claims* he went out to the pub straight after Laila left the house. But she's the only other person who was there. Maybe *she's* the one who went out straight after Laila. Maybe *she* followed her up to Rollington Hill."

Lesley pushed back her irritation. Dennis seemed to think the sun shone out of Patrick Donnelly's arse, or maybe it was just he didn't like Crystal.

"I'm not going to come to any conclusions," she said. "Let's just interview Patrick, see what he says, find out how much of it matches what Crystal told us."

"Makes sense to me."

"What d'you want me to do?" asked Mike.

"We still don't know where those sleeping pills came from. They're all denying that anybody in the house even took sleeping pills. But if Archie was drugged, somebody drugged him. And there's a chance those pills were on a prescription for one of the archaeologists."

"You want me to ring around the GPs?" asked Mike.

"Not just yet," said Lesley. "Is there a pharmacy in Corfe Castle?"

"The only one is at the surgery on West Street."

"Jeez. Everything's on West Street in this place."

"It's not a big village, boss."

"No. OK, then. Two birds with one stone. Go in there, find out if there was a prescription for sleeping pills at that address. If it wasn't made out by one of their doctors, they might have dispensed them."

"Boss." Mike opened his car door. "Anything else?"

"When you and Johnny are done in the village, go back up to the crime scene. Find out what's happening with Laila's body. I want to be sure that she's been moved. That poor girl up there on the hills just feels wrong."

"Shall we speak to the CSIs as well?" asked Johnny. "Find out if there are any updates?"

"No," said Lesley. "I suggest you ignore them."

She turned to see Johnny's frown. "Yes, Johnny. Get an update. Call me if there's anything significant. Go!"

Johnny and Mike left the car.

Lesley watched them, shaking her head. "Come on then Dennis. Time to interview your mate Patrick Donnelly."

CHAPTER FORTY-FOUR

PATRICK HAD REPLACED Crystal in the cottage's living room. He sat upright at the end of the sofa closest to the door, picking dirt out of his fingernails.

He turned as he saw the detectives enter, his gaze cold on Lesley, then warming as he spotted Dennis.

"My turn in the hot seat, eh?"

"Thanks for talking to us." Dennis said. "We know you're all busy."

Stop it, Lesley thought. She put a hand on Tina's arm. Tina retreated to the kitchen doorway once again.

Lesley took the seat next to Patrick, leaving the thread-bare armchair for Dennis. She turned to Patrick and gave him a brief smile.

"Can you tell us about your relationship with Laila Ford?"

"Blimey." He wiped his forehead, then checked his hand. His fingers were grubby. "You don't mess around, do you?"

She smiled, waiting for an answer to her question.

"Alright then... let me see. Well, she joined the dig team

five weeks ago. Crystal recruited her, not sure where. Archae-ology graduate, we were told. Hadn't managed to get herself a proper job, so Crystal took her on. I'm not sure if she was a volunteer, or if Crystal was paying her. Either way, the girl never showed any sign of having money."

"That's all very helpful," said Lesley. "But we'd really like to know about your relationship with Laila. Did you get along? Did you work well together? I gather the two of you worked in the same tent."

"The little one. The one where we've found bugger all so far."

Dennis shifted in his seat. Maybe the rose-tinted specta-cles would drop a little, Lesley thought.

"You're not happy about working in that tent?" she asked.

"The other trench, the one where – you know – that's the big one. Crystal reckons it's the great hall of a second build-ing. Another, castle even. I'm sceptical. But if it pays my wages..."

"Were you and Laila assigned to work together from the start?"

He shook his head. "She was with Archie, at first. I was with Crystal and a bunch o' kids, in the proper tent. That trench is bloody magnificent, you know."

A tut from Dennis. Lesley suppressed a chuckle. "Why did Archie move?"

"Crystal thought it was too cosy. What with them shag-ging, and that."

Lesley longed to turn and see Dennis's reaction. She kept her focus on their interviewee. "Did you and Laila work well together?"

"She was lazy, and inexperienced. It was me that did all the work."

"So you resented her."

"Just cos I didn't like the lass, doesn't mean I killed her."

"Mr Donnelly, did you—"

"Call me Patrick. Paddy, if you want to be really friendly." He gave her a wink.

"Patrick. Was there an incident between you and Laila shortly after she joined the team?"

"Incident?"

"Did you sexually assault her?"

His eyes widened in surprise. "What rubbish! I told her she was pretty, that's all. Can a fella not pay a compliment to a young woman these days?"

Patrick peered around Lesley at Dennis, expecting agreement. He got none.

"So you deny that you assaulted her," Lesley said.

"This is Crystal, isn't it? She's never liked me. Come on, let's hear it. What other tall tales has she told about me?"

"Patrick, can you describe any interaction you had with Laila yesterday evening?"

"You're making out like I killed her."

"We're trying to establish what she did and who she spoke to in the hours before her death."

His face crumpled. "Poor wee girl. So young..." He composed himself and looked into Lesley's eyes. "She came home first from the dig site. Tired, can't blame her after finding Archie like that. I was next, it was my turn to cook dinner. Pork chops. He licked his lips. "Not for Laila though, she had some vegan thing."

"Did you all eat dinner together?"

"Yeah. Crystal turned up just in time. About seven. We ate, I listened to the cricket, then I went out to the pub."

Lesley heard Dennis draw a breath. "Where was Laila when you left the house?" he asked.

A shrug. "No idea. In her room, I guess. She's been hiding there a lot lately." He shook his head, his brow creased. "Poor kid."

"What time did you return home from the pub?" Lesley asked.

"Which pub?" Dennis added.

"The Greyhound, mate, like always. I stayed till closing time, got back about half eleven."

All of this tallied with Crystal's account. "Who was here when you arrived home?" Lesley asked.

"Not sure about Laila. I assumed she was in bed. Crystal was in, cos I heard her going out about ten minutes later."

"Crystal went out?" Dennis asked.

Patrick turned to him. "I was in the kitchen, making meself a cup o' hot milk. Helps me sleep. I saw someone cross the living room, heard the front door open and close."

"You're sure it was Crystal?" said Lesley.

"When I went to the stairs, her bedroom door was open. Room was empty. You've seen how cramped this place is, nowhere else she could have been."

"Did you hear her return?" Dennis asked.

"Sorry, mate. I was asleep before me head hit the pillow."

He looked between the two detectives. "That's the kind of information you're after, is it? I'd hate to think I'd got her into trouble."

CHAPTER FORTY-FIVE

THE LANDLORD WAS confident that Patrick had been in the pub the previous night.

"Yeah, mate," he told Johnny. "He was here. Came in, oh, about quarter past nine, half past nine, something like that. Left at closing time. He's always one of the last out. Likes his Guinness."

"Was he here the whole time or did he leave at all?"

"I couldn't tell you. Too busy serving other punters. But he did have three pints in total. So, I guess that means he was probably here all that time."

"Thanks," said Johnny. He turned away from the bar to find a young woman with dark hair pulled back into a ponytail standing in front of him.

"Are you investigating Laila's murder?" she asked.

"I am," he replied. He got out his ID. "DC Chiles. Who are you?"

"Karen Dawes. I'm her friend."

"OK. Should we grab a table?"

She nodded. He led her to a spot in a quiet corner. As she sat down, he noticed her hands shaking against the table.

"You've got something you want to tell us?" he asked.

She nodded.

"Did you see her last night? Did she come to your house?"

"No." She shook her head. "I haven't seen her since... since the morning Archie died. Haven't seen her since then. Poor Laila."

He watched her. There wasn't much you could say to a young woman who'd just lost her best friend.

"Have you got something you want to tell me?" he asked, trying to keep his tone gentle.

She looked around the pub, and then leaned towards him. Her breathing was shallow.

"That Patrick," she said.

"Patrick Donnelly?"

She took a deep breath, glancing at the bar once again. "He's bad news."

"In what way?"

"He tried it on with her. He, well, he thought he could get her to sleep with him."

"When did this happen?"

She wrinkled her nose. "About four weeks ago. No, a bit more than that. Three days after she came to the village. Me and Laila, we knew each other before uni. She hunted me down as soon as she got here, found me in the cafe. Not quite sure how she managed that. It was good to see her, though. But anyway, she told me there was this guy on the dig, lived in the same cottage as her. Kept looking at her funny. She reckoned he fancied her. He was ancient!" She grimaced.

"Old enough to be her dad, her granddad even. She couldn't stand him."

"Did she do anything about it?" Johnny asked.

Karen shrugged. "I know she kept her distance from him as much as she could. That's why she took to Archie. Archie spotted there was something off. She felt like he'd stop Patrick, like he'd protect her from him. That was before she and Archie became a thing."

"So when *did* she and Archie become a thing?"

"About a week after she got here."

Johnny looked at her. "That was quick."

She laughed. "That was Laila."

"So did anything happen between Laila and Patrick? Or was it just funny looks?"

She breathed in, her nostrils flaring. "She told me not to tell anyone."

She's dead, Johnny thought. It wasn't like it mattered now. "This is confidential," he said.

The woman's voice was low. "She said he came into her room one night."

"The room she shared with Archie?"

She shook her head. "No, she was sharing with Crystal at the beginning. The two of them had the downstairs bedroom. And the two guys had the two rooms upstairs. Crystal preferred it that way." She leaned back and gripped the table. Her knuckles were white.

She looked at Johnny, her expression dark. "There was a morning when Crystal had gone out early, set something up at the dig site or something. Laila said there were no locks on the door. Patrick just came barging into her room. She was half naked, getting dressed. He grabbed her."

"Grabbed her?" Johnny asked.

"Yeah, on her..." Karen looked down. She brushed her breast lightly.

"He grabbed her boob?"

"And more. He pinned her to the wall. Tried to pull her dressing gown off."

"Then what?"

"Crystal got back. Patrick heard her coming through the front door, jumped off Laila like she was on fire. She shoved him out of the room, slammed the door behind him. Next day, she and Archie got together."

"So you reckon she got into a relationship with Archie to keep herself safe from Patrick?"

"There was more to it than that. Eventually, anyway. She loved Archie. That's what she told me. He was a good guy. Even if he was married."

"She told you he was married?"

"Last week, Thursday. She'd just found out."

"How did she feel about that?"

"How would you feel if you found out your boyfriend was married?"

Johnny smiled sadly at her. "Not brilliant, I guess."

"She was distraught. Couldn't stop crying. Laila was only nineteen, you know? She made out like she was twenty-three, told him she was a graduate. She'd dropped out of uni."

Johnny nodded. The boss had said something about this.

"This is helpful, Karen, thanks. So, after Patrick assaulted her, did she make a complaint? Did she go to the police? Did she speak to Crystal?"

Karen shook her head. "Who are you going to believe? Nineteen-year-old Laila, just turned up in Corfe Castle, nobody knows her from Adam? Or Patrick Donnelly, old bloke, respected, known Crystal for years?" She looked down into her lap. "She didn't tell anybody. She just stuck close to Archie and made sure she was never alone in that house with Patrick."

Johnny handed her his card. "If you think of anything else, you'll let me know, won't you?"

She nodded.

He remembered something. "Was Laila on any kind of medication? Sleeping pills, maybe?"

"Oh God, no. Laila could sleep for Britain. She'd never need sleeping pills."

"Not even after the trauma of Patrick assaulting her?"

"She had Archie to help her get to sleep." Karen grinned, then her face dropped as she remembered her friend was dead.

"Well, thanks for letting me know."

He hurried out of the pub. The DCI needed to know about this.

CHAPTER FORTY-SIX

Patrick had gone up to his bedroom. Lesley faced Dennis in the living room, both of them uneasy.

"Let's not talk about this here," she said.

She'd forgotten that Tina Abbott was still standing in the doorway of the kitchen. "What do you want me to do, boss?" The PC asked.

"Keep an eye on him," Lesley told her. "Keep an eye on both of them."

"One of them's lying," said Dennis.

"Straight to the top of the class, Dennis," Lesley shot back.

"There's no need to..."

"You're right," said Lesley. "I've had a rough day. And that pair don't make it any easier."

He shrugged.

"So," she continued, her voice low. "We've got two stories now. Both of them are trying to pin it on the other one. We need independent witnesses. Failing that, we need some decent forensics, and why don't you have any bloody CCTV in these villages?"

Dennis smiled at her. "It's not the big city you know, boss."

"No, it is not."

She turned to Tina. "PC Abbott, you stay here."

"What d'you need me to do?"

"The usual FLO routine. Look after them, get them cups of tea, cook their dinner if you need to."

"Ma'am?"

"OK, maybe not cook their dinner. Help them out. Pretend you're here to look after their wellbeing. I'll let you know if there's anything they need updating on. And that's a big if. I don't want this pair knowing any more than they absolutely need to."

She lowered her voice and took a step closer to the PC. "But what I really need you to do is watch them. I want to know if the two of them talk about Laila, or Archie. I want to know if either of them accuses the other of anything. I want to know if they argue, I want to know if they scratch their bloody nose. I'm convinced one of this pair is hiding something, and I want to know why."

"Have we got a motive for either of them, boss?" Dennis asked.

She glanced towards the stairs. "We've got Patrick allegedly assaulting Laila, and who knows what impact that had on his relationship with Archie. And then there's what the woman at Bristol University told us about the finances."

Dennis nodded. "We need financial forensics."

"We certainly do," Lesley replied. "Let's hope we can get something useful from Bournemouth University."

She heard footsteps rattling down the staircase: Patrick.

Lesley glanced at the other two officers. "Quiet."

Patrick opened the door from the stairs. "You still here?"

"PC Abbott is going to stay a while," said Lesley. "She's going to take care of you both. Make sure everything's OK."

"We don't need looking after."

"Two members of this household have lost their lives, in three days, in violent circumstances. I want to make sure you're safe. In fact, I might put a uniformed officer outside the front door."

"Oh, for God's sake," Patrick said. "That's bloody ridiculous."

Dennis cleared his throat.

"It's not ridiculous," Lesley said. "There could be somebody targeting this house."

Patrick eyed her. "That's not what you think. And we both know it."

"I'm sorry, Mr Donnelly, but I can't share with you the details of my thinking right now. If I have anything I need to speak to you about, I'll be in touch."

She left the house, anxious not to tell him any more. She wondered how much of their conversation he'd overheard.

Outside, she gestured to Dennis, "You go on ahead to the car, I've got a call to make."

He nodded and headed for the car park.

She dialled her daughter's mobile number: voicemail.

"Hey, sweetie, it's me again. It'd be good to chat to you. I hope you got on OK at your friend's house last night. Give me a call, yeah?"

This was the third time she'd called Sharon. It was four pm now, school was finished for the day. She'd deliberately called at times she knew Sharon had breaks. The girl always turned her phone on.

What had Terry said to her?

Lesley shook herself out. She didn't have time to worry about this right now. She hurried along West Street, her mind buzzing.

CHAPTER FORTY-SEVEN

LESLEY YAWNED as she took a seat behind her desk. Zoe's spare bed had been far from comfortable. It was lumpy and narrow. She didn't think she'd slept more than five hours and she was knackered.

"OK," she sighed. "Let's have a quick recap, and then we'll go home."

Dennis had pulled the board out, aligning it at ninety degrees from her desk. Johnny and Mike sat in the chairs they'd dragged in. Johnny was slouching, his jacket almost hanging off him.

"Where's Gail?" Lesley asked.

"She's on her way," Dennis said. He didn't look too pleased about it.

"In that case, let's get started with the witness statements. Patrick and Crystal. Both of them reckons the other one went out and could have attacked Laila."

"I went to the Greyhound," said Johnny. "I spoke to the landlord. He said Patrick drank three pints of Guinness. He was there till closing time. It's possible he left and came back, but with the time it'd take to down three pints, it's not likely. Fits with his story."

Lesley nodded. "So his alibi seems to hold up."

"Patrick said she went out after he came home," said Dennis.

"I know he said that," said Lesley. "But it's just his word against hers."

Dennis muttered to himself.

"What?" Lesley snapped. "Tell us what you're thinking."

"Crystal was hiding something about the financials on that dig. There was something Archie knew, that she didn't want getting out. So she had a motive to kill him."

"Yeah, but what about Laila?" said Mike. "What was Crystal's motive to kill her?"

"Perhaps Laila discovered what Archie knew about Crystal. Maybe she had to shut her up too."

"Feels a bit excessive," Lesley said. "I mean, it's a university archaeological dig. It's hardly the Crown Jewels."

"As far as these archaeologists are concerned," Dennis said, "What they're looking for is the Crown Jewels. Given that's allegedly King Stephen's castle, maybe there could even be some Crown Jewels there."

Lesley smirked. "It's just a field filled with mounds of earth."

Dennis raised an eyebrow. "Don't knock it, boss. Archaeological digs are important around here. The stuff they discovered in Corfe Castle in 2014..."

She raised her hand. "I don't need to know the details." She gazed at the board. It wasn't much help.

"So, we think Crystal might have had a motive for both murders." Dennis grabbed a marker pen and circled Crystal's name on the board. "And Patrick says she went out on the night of Laila's murder. She doesn't have an alibi for Archie's murder."

"Not too hasty," Lesley said, "We've still got Patrick to think about."

Mike raised a hand. "Don't forget Laila didn't have an alibi for Archie's murder."

Lesley turned to him. "You think she could have killed him?"

He shrugged.

"None of that makes any difference now," Dennis said.

"Not necessarily," said Lesley. "Just because Laila's dead, doesn't mean she couldn't have killed Archie. Whoever killed Laila could have done it *because* she killed Archie."

"This is Corfe Castle, boss," Dennis said. "That kind of thing doesn't happen here."

She raised an eyebrow. "No assumptions, Dennis. Remember what I told you right at the beginning? We follow the evidence. We build a case. We need more than just those witness statements, more than our own hunches and assumptions about these people."

Johnny cleared his throat. "Can I...?"

"Sorry, Johnny," Lesley said.

"When I was in the pub, I spoke to a friend of Laila's. Karen Dawes. She told me that Patrick assaulted Laila. Back when she started on the dig, about a month ago. He sexually assaulted her in her bedroom."

"Raped her?" Mike asked.

"Didn't manage to," said Johnny. "Crystal got home in time. That was when Laila took up with Archie."

Lesley tapped her teeth. "Crystal said she'd overheard something."

"So Laila started sleeping with Archie just to get protection from Patrick." Dennis whistled.

"Not the first time a vulnerable woman has had to hook up with a man to keep herself safe," Lesley said. "Let's not judge the girl, eh?"

"The other thing," Johnny said, "is that Laila was definitely lying about her age. She wasn't a graduate, she dropped out of university. That's how Karen knew her. Crystal did say she was young."

"Crystal told us she was nineteen," Lesley said. "But I don't see what difference it makes."

"It makes a big difference when we're looking at her character," Dennis interrupted. "Laila lied about her age. She lied about her relationship with Archie. She lied about Patrick."

"When did she lie about Patrick?" Lesley asked.

"She didn't exactly tell us the whole truth, did she?"

"Would *you* tell the whole truth if one of your colleagues had tried to rape you?"

Dennis reddened.

"Hmm." Lesley drummed a finger into the board. "So, we've got Patrick and Crystal, purely based on supposition and on their witness statements with each of them trying to pin this on the other one. But what about the evidence? What about the forensics? Where's this bloody weapon?"

"Boss," muttered Dennis.

Lesley waved him aside. "I need to know what the weapon was in Laila's murder."

Mike perked up. "I went back up to the crime scene, boss. Gail says she found remnants of iron again, just like with Archie's murder."

"She thinks it was the same weapon?"

"She can't be sure right now. She's going to do some tests in the lab. But it's looking likely."

"OK," said Lesley. "Well, if that is the case, and that is an 'if', it means that both Archie and Laila were possibly killed by the same person using this weapon. Which may, or may not, be an archaeological artefact."

"Have we checked if there's anything missing?" asked Dennis.

She sighed. "We've been so busy out at Corfe Castle we haven't had a chance to speak to Bournemouth University. Someone needs to get over there first thing in the morning."

"Fine," said Dennis. "I'll make a call."

"We need to know about the finances, and we need the inventory. We also need to go back to Bristol and talk to Susan again. With everything we now know about Archie, I want a proper statement from her."

"You're not going to get that without a lawyer present," said Dennis.

Lesley rolled her eyes. "Don't I flippin' well know it."

Dennis's lips tightened.

"Oh, come on Dennis. *Flippin'*, that's got to be OK?" She sighed. "You need to give me a list, you know. Tell me what words you'll tolerate me saying."

He gave her a surprised look.

She laughed. "Moving on. How did you get on with the GP's practice, Mike?"

"The sleeping pills were Archie's," Mike said.

"Well, that's something," Lesley replied. "At least we know they were from that house."

"Yeah, but it doesn't really help us," Mike said.

Lesley yawned again. He had a point. Still, she would check with Gail whether the pills had been found in the search of the house, and if they had been, whose fingerprints were on them.

"It's getting on," she said. "Let's all go home, fresh heads for the morning. Dennis, you and Mike head over to Bournemouth University tomorrow. I'll go to Bristol with Johnny again."

"Boss."

He wasn't objecting, thank God. Lesley shooed them away and they scuttled out of the office, leaving her alone with her thoughts and the unhelpful board.

CHAPTER FORTY-EIGHT

Fiona sighed and put the phone down. "Looks like they're not going to be able to see you today, Suze."

Susan stared at her. To be honest, she was relieved. She hadn't much liked the idea of going into the police station and making a statement. She had no idea what she would say to them, how she felt...

Her priority now was Millie. Millie, who was upstairs, cleaning her teeth. Susan had left her in the bathroom, after the girl had shouted at her to leave her alone. She was snappy today. Susan was worried about her.

She'd tried fussing over her, sitting with her in the living room, keeping an eye on her. Jumping every time the girl spoke. Could it be that she just needed space to herself? Maybe tomorrow, Susan would see if one of her friends might come around. A bit of normality. Would that help?

"So," said Fiona. "They'll be here tomorrow morning. That DCI will be at the local station. I'll take you if you want?"

"Please," said Susan. "What about Millie?"

"I'll look after her." The Family Liaison Officer stood in the doorway to the kitchen. How long had she been there?

Susan grunted. "I'd rather have a family member."

Fiona looked at her. "What about Archie's mum?"

"You've got to be kidding."

"She's not that bad."

"She's never liked me. And now she's going to like me even less."

"I don't see why she'd do that," said Fiona.

"You don't understand the woman," replied Susan.

Millie rattled down the stairs, "Where's my nightie, Mummy?"

"You haven't got a nightie, love. I put some pyjamas out on your bed for you, remember? You told me you were too big for a nightie now."

"Oh..." The girl looked like Susan had just slapped her.

Susan's stomach clenched. "I need to go up with her, Fi. I'll see you in the morning, yeah? Maybe I'll bring her along with me to the station."

"You can't do that," said Fiona.

"No," Susan sighed. "You're right. OK. Will you have her, while I give them my statement?"

Fiona looked at her. "Of course. You'll have Jacinta with you, she'll make sure they don't cross the line."

Susan shrugged. "Thanks."

Fiona leaned in and gave her a kiss on the cheek. "You'll be OK here on your own?"

"I'm not on my own," Susan said. She nodded towards the kitchen where the Family Liaison Officer had disappeared. She lowered her voice. "She never leaves. She's spying on me, isn't she?"

Fiona nodded. "But there's nothing for you to worry about."

"Guess not."

Fiona smiled. "That's something. See you in the morning."

Susan stood in the hallway as Fiona closed the front door. Her body felt numb. OK, so Archie had been a crappy husband. He'd had affairs with God knew how many women, he was sleeping with that Laila girl who'd called her last Thursday. But he was Millie's dad. And he did at least turn up most weekends and pretend to be a devoted husband. What were she and Millie going to do now?

The doorbell rang.

Millie called down the stairs, "Found them Mum, can you come up?"

"Hang on a moment, sweetie."

Susan went to the door. Fiona would have forgotten something, or maybe there was something she needed to tell her.

Tony stood on the front step. Susan looked behind her, checking for the FLO.

"What are you doing here? I told you..."

"I'm sorry, Susie," he said. "I just couldn't... I couldn't stop thinking about you. I'm worried. I want to help."

"You can help by staying away," she hissed. "They don't know."

He looked over her shoulder. "Is Millie home?"

"Of course she's home, where else would she be?"

"Mummy." Millie appeared behind her.

Susan reached out and her daughter huddled into her embrace.

"Hey, lovey," Tony said.

"Hi, Tony." Millie burrowed further into Susan's sweater.

Susan leaned over and kissed the top of her daughter's head. "Let's get you ready for bed."

"Will you sleep in my room tonight, please?"

"Of course."

She turned back to Tony. "I'm sorry, but you have to go."

"Are you sure there's nothing I can do to help?"

She shook her head. "Keep a low profile, is what I need you to do. I don't want them thinking..."

"They're not going to think anything. It's not as if he was faithful to you, is it?"

"*Tony.*" She looked down at Millie.

"Sorry, love." Tony kissed his hand and placed it on Susan's cheek. She felt the warmth light up her skin.

"I'll call you. I promise."

"I know."

Millie gave Tony a smile. "Bye, Tony."

"Bye, kiddo." He gave her a mock punch on the ear.

She grinned. Millie liked Tony. It was one of the things Susan loved about him. In the lead-up to the weekends Archie was home, she'd spent hours panicking that Millie would tell her dad about Tony, but Archie had never been around long enough for the subject to arise. And they'd been careful never to let the girl see them behaving like anything other than friends.

Susan closed the door.

The FLO was coming out of the kitchen, a question in her eyes. "Who was that?"

"Nobody."

"It was Tony," said Millie. "Our friend."

Susan put a hand over her daughter's mouth. "He was worried about me."

The FLO raised an eyebrow. "It's good to have friends' support. You taking your daughter up to bed now?"

"I am," said Susan. "I'll stay up there."

The FLO nodded. "That's fine."

Susan trudged up the stairs, all but dragging Millie up with her. As she did so, she heard the FLO in the kitchen, speaking to someone on her phone.

CHAPTER FORTY-NINE

LESLEY TAPPED her fingertips on her knee as she waited for the phone to be picked up.

After three rings, Zoe answered. "Evening, Ma'am."

"Zoe," Lesley said, "I already told you, I'm not your boss anymore."

"Sorry." Zoe cleared her throat. "Lesley."

Lesley laughed. "That's better."

"What can I do for you?" Zoe asked.

"I just wanted to say thanks for your hospitality last night."

"It was the least I could do. You looked..."

"I looked like a drowned rat, didn't I?"

"I didn't want to say."

"Anyway, thanks. And thanks for not asking any questions, either."

There was an awkward pause.

"No problem," Zoe said in a small voice. "Anything else I can do for you?"

Lesley considered. She had a new team, she was supposed to be loyal to them. But...

"Zoe," she said. "Can I run something past you?"

"Always."

"So, my predecessor down here, DCI Mackie, they told me he'd retired before I took the job."

"OK," said Zoe. "So far, so normal."

"Thing is," Lesley said, "he hadn't retired. Well, he had, but then he died."

Zoe sucked her teeth. "Ill health retirement?"

"Not as far as I've heard. And people are being weird about it."

"How so?"

"Whenever I ask about him, they clam up. I'm wondering if there's something dodgy."

"Oh, God," said Zoe. "Not another Randle?"

Lesley grimaced. "Heaven save us from David Randle and his like."

"You can say that again," Zoe replied. "So, d'you want me to do a bit of digging for you?"

Lesley gazed out of the window of her temporary house. It was starting to get dark, traffic dying down in the sleepy town. She wondered how long she'd have to live here. Maybe she should find her own place, pick somewhere a bit more alive.

"I'm not sure," she said to Zoe. "I don't want to cause trouble."

"I'll be discreet," Zoe said. "You know me."

Lesley smiled. Zoe was right. She'd spent six months investigating Detective Superintendent David Randle and nobody had known about it apart from Lesley. Not even Zoe's friend DS Uddin.

"Go on then," Lesley said. "Just see what you can find out about him. How did he die? Is there an official record?"

"You sure you can't get all this?" Zoe asked.

"I could," said Lesley. "But I don't want anybody knowing that I'm poking around where I'm not wanted."

"Fair enough," said Zoe. "Leave it with me."

"Just a bit of investigation," Lesley said. "I know you've got work to do, and I don't want to cause any trouble."

"You can trust me," Zoe replied. She hung up.

Lesley rubbed her forehead. The pain in the back of her neck was returning, from her injury after the bomb in Birmingham. She'd told her doctor she was feeling fine, that she didn't need physio. She'd told the psychologist that she was fully recovered. She'd been lying to both of them.

At night she found it hard to close her eyes. The last thing she saw before going to sleep each night was the memory of Inspector Jameson coming towards her. The doors to the shopping mall exploding, the inspector's body flying out through the shattered glass.

Lesley took a deep breath. She should eat, but she wasn't hungry. Another Mars Bar, maybe. Or she'd go to the pub. She needed people, distraction.

"Right," she told herself and pulled her coat on.

Five minutes later, she stood at the bar of the Duke of Wellington. The woman was behind the bar again, the attractive one with the long dark hair. She whistled to herself. Lesley smiled as she held out a tenner for her drink.

"You seem happy."

The woman nodded. "I've been offered a promotion. Named partner."

Lesley raised an eyebrow. "Sorry? In this pub?"

The woman laughed. "Oh, no. I'm just helping my brother out, while he finds someone permanent."

"Partner in what?" Lesley asked.

The woman mopped the bar. "A law firm, in Bournemouth."

"You're a lawyer?"

"Criminal law."

"Then our paths might cross one day," Lesley said. "I'm a detective."

"Oh, OK," the woman replied. "Are you the new DCI, in the MCIT?"

Lesley put down her glass. "How did you know?"

"News travels fast around here. Anyway, welcome."

"So you'll be defending the people that I'm arresting," Lesley said.

The woman chuckled. "I'm sure we'll face each other across an interview table sometime."

Lesley picked up her drink and walked away. As she turned, the woman spoke. "I hope you don't mind me asking, but you don't seem very happy yourself. I mean, new job and all that?"

Lesley stiffened. There was something liberating about confiding in a stranger. But this woman might not be a stranger for long. She turned back to her.

"Family problem," she said.

The woman's brow furrowed. "Sorry to hear that, can't be easy."

Lesley shrugged. "Yeah, men, you know."

The woman shook her head. "Not really."

"Well, you're lucky," said Lesley. "You don't have to put up with a rat like my husband."

"Sorry to hear that." The woman held out her hand. "I'm Elsa, by the way. Elsa Short."

Lesley shook it. "Lesley Clarke, pleased to meet you."

"You want to tell me about your husband?"

"Oh, the usual," Lesley replied. "I caught him shagging another woman."

Elsa grimaced. "A rat, indeed."

Lesley gave her a sad smile. "Yeah."

She turned towards her table. She didn't feel like confiding any more.

CHAPTER FIFTY

LESLEY RUBBED at the back of her neck as they crossed the Clifton Suspension Bridge, heading towards Susan Weatherton's house. She'd called ahead and told them not to make Susan go to the local station. It was hard enough for the woman already, without dragging her out of her home and forcing her to find childcare for her daughter. And Lesley wanted to put her at ease, as well as seeing more of Archie's home situation.

"Here we are," Lesley said to Johnny, who was driving. The route had become familiar more quickly than the rural ones, and it felt good to drive through a city again.

As they pulled up outside Susan's broad Victorian house, the curtain next door twitched. Lesley wondered what it must be like to live next door to someone like that.

"You noticed that?" she asked Johnny.

"The old guy next door?"

"Maybe we should knock on his door. Find out what there is to know."

"You reckon he'd know anything useful about Archie?"

"He might know something useful about Susan," she replied. "You go and talk to him while I talk to Susan."

He nodded and walked up the next door path.

Lesley had no sooner lifted her finger to Susan's doorbell, when the door was flung open. A slim woman with curly blonde hair and an expensive suit stood in front of her.

"You must be DCI Clarke."

Lesley held up her ID. "And you are?"

"Jacinta Burke, Susan's solicitor."

"She doesn't need a solicitor," Lesley said. "She's just a witness. Barely even a witness."

The solicitor shrugged. "Never does any harm to be thorough."

Lesley liked thoroughness herself. Building a case. Compiling evidence. Except she wasn't expecting to build a case against Susan. Should the fact the woman had hired a lawyer make her suspicious?

The solicitor led her through to a generous dining room towards the back of the house. Lesley could hear voices in the next room: the Family Liaison Officer talking to a child. The child didn't sound happy.

Susan was already sitting at the dining table. Her sister, the one who'd been here last time, sat next to her. The two women held hands.

Lesley gave Susan a kind smile. "Sorry to have to do this again, Mrs Weatherton. But we just need to get whatever background we can on your husband. It might help us find the person who killed him."

Susan sniffed. "I know."

Fiona's grip on her sister's hand tightened. "Do you need me to stay with you?"

"I'll be fine," Susan said. "You go. Stay with Millie. I don't like her on her own with…"

Lesley wondered what the FLO was like. Being from a different force, she wouldn't have met the woman. Although to be fair, she hadn't met many members of the Dorset force yet. She settled herself into a chair opposite Susan. Jacinta sat next to her client, pulling out a file.

Lesley folded her hands on the table and sat back, trying not to intimidate the other woman. "Can you tell me when you last saw your husband?"

Susan nodded. "Just over two weeks ago. He came home for the weekend. Millie had a netball tournament, he wanted to see it. It was nice, family time." Her face clouded over.

"And when did he head back to Dorset?"

"The Sunday night about seven or eight o'clock. We had tea here, the three of us. And then he had to get back to the dig site."

"I'm sorry again to have to ask this. But did you see him at all after that?"

"He was supposed to be coming home this weekend. But…"

"Did he tell you he wouldn't be coming home?"

"No." Susan looked into Lesley's eyes. "Nothing."

"Was it common for Archie not to come home when he said he would?"

"There were odd occasions when he didn't make it, but generally, he'd be home every fortnight. Sometimes more often, sometimes a bit less. But he normally rang me on the Thursday if he wasn't going to make it."

"OK." Lesley made a note in her pad. The solicitor was doing the same thing.

She took a breath. "Susan, can you tell me if there was

anything troubling Archie? Anything giving him problems at work?"

Susan shook her head. "Nothing I know of. Why? Do you think somebody at work..."

"We're not jumping to any conclusions yet. But I need to know if he'd fallen out with any of his colleagues. Particularly the colleagues on the dig, the people he was living with in Corfe Castle."

Susan sneered. "You're talking about that girl, Laila."

"I'm not talking about anybody in particular," Lesley replied. "I just need to know if there were any problems."

"You think one of those people might have killed him? You think *Laila* might have killed him?"

Lesley took a deep breath. "What did Laila say to you when she phoned you on Thursday?"

The solicitor brushed her hand over her client's arm. Susan frowned. "I don't have to answer that."

"You're not under caution, Mrs Weatherton."

"Susan, please."

"You're not under caution, Susan. And you're not a suspect. But it would really help if you could answer my questions. I'm just trying to get background information. Are you aware that Laila has also died?"

Susan looked horrified. "The girl?"

Lesley nodded. "She was found yesterday morning, on a hilltop not far from the cottage."

Susan paled. "Was she... murdered too?"

"We believe so, yes."

"Do you think the same person did it? The same person who..." Susan couldn't finish the sentence.

"We don't know that yet," said Lesley. She felt desperately sorry for Susan, but at the same time had to remember the woman might be somehow responsible for her husband's death. "We just need to get as much information as we can before we can draw any conclusions."

"You want to know if she was suicidal, don't you?" Susan asked.

"I just want to know how she sounded when she called you. Was she angry? Upset?"

"She was calm. She was *too* calm."

"Can you remember what she said to you?"

Susan sniffed. She was wearing a blue cardigan, threadbare at the elbows and damp at the cuffs. "She told me she was in love with him. Well, first she asked me if I was Archie's wife. I said yes. She told me her name. She told me he loved her. She loved him. She told me she was sorry."

"Anything else?"

"Then she hung up. I didn't know whether to believe her or not. Not about the affair. About him loving her."

"Did you speak to Archie about it?"

"I called him. But he wasn't picking up."

"So you didn't manage to speak to your husband, between the time when Laila called you and the time that he died?"

Susan stared back at her, her face stiff. "No," she whispered.

Lesley felt her heart dip. It occurred to her that Terry still hadn't tried to contact her. It had been two days since she'd arrived home and encountered him with Julieta, but not once had he tried to make contact.

Bastard.

Stop it, she told herself. *Focus.*

"Susan, can you tell me what your movements have been since Saturday?"

"Yes, I can." Susan turned to her solicitor, who withdrew a sheet of paper from under her notepad. The lawyer pushed it across the table. It contained a list of dates, times and locations. Places that Susan had been since Thursday night when Laila had called her. It ended on yesterday morning, when the police had turned up. It listed shopping trips, another netball game, the school run and work on Friday.

"Is there someone who can corroborate these?" Lesley asked.

"Yes," Susan replied, her voice tight. "My manager can vouch for the fact I was at work on Friday. There will be other mums who can say I was at the netball game on Saturday afternoon."

"What about Saturday morning?" Lesley asked.

"I've already told you I was on a shopping trip with Millie. I can't provide evidence for that. But there's no way I could have got to Corfe Castle and back in time for the netball game in the afternoon."

Lesley nodded. "Thank you for this."

There was a knock at the front door, and then voices.

That would be Johnny coming back. Lesley wondered if he had anything useful from the neighbour.

She gave Susan another smile. "I know this will be difficult, but can you tell me about the nature of Archie's relationship with Crystal Spiers?"

A shadow passed across Susan's face. "I never liked that woman."

Lesley waited.

"It's OK," Susan said, seeing the look on Lesley's face. "I know she slept with him. It was back when I was pregnant with Millie."

Lesley noticed the solicitor wincing. She was learning

more about Archie, and the more she learned, the more she disliked him. Were all men like that, if they got the chance?

"But it ended before Millie was born," Susan said. "It was only a couple of months, they were on a dig together and, well, that's what Archie did."

Lesley raised an eyebrow. "He did that a lot?"

Susan shrugged. "You already know that. Archie liked to meet women at work. Young women. Never students, he was always careful. And I never had enough evidence to actually confront him with it. I'm not sure if I even wanted to. I mean, there's Millie to think about. But then when Laila called me…"

"How did that make you feel?" Lesley said.

"I've already told you, I couldn't have got to Corfe Castle in time to…"

"I'm not asking you if you killed your husband, Susan. I'm just asking you how you felt when you discovered that he was having an affair with Laila Ford."

"How do you think I felt? Shocked, betrayed, hurt, angry. Protective of our daughter. What do you expect?"

Lesley nodded. She heard a knock at the dining room door.

Johnny poked his head around. "Er, boss."

She turned back to Susan. "Thanks for this. Obviously, we'll check out all these locations. I'll come back to you if we have any more questions. But thank you. I understand this was hard for you."

Lesley joined the DC in the hallway, closing the door behind her. Johnny was about to speak, but she put her hand up and checked for open doors. None.

"Go on then," she muttered, when she was certain that the coast was clear.

"The next door neighbour, boss," he said. "He told me Susan's having an affair as well."

"She is?"

"Guy called Tony, comes here all the time. Friendly with the little girl, practically lives here."

"How did we not know about this?"

"Presumably Archie didn't know, he was away all the time."

"Right," Lesley said. "So who is this man she was having an affair with?"

"All I know is that his name's Tony."

"Thanks," she said. "I need to speak to her."

She opened the dining room door. Susan was huddled with her solicitor, muttering between themselves.

Lesley approached the table. "Can I ask you about a man called Tony?"

Susan pulled away from the solicitor, her cheeks inflamed. "Tony?"

"We've heard that you have a friend called Tony, who comes here a lot."

Susan looked back at her, her gaze steady. "He's more than a friend."

"Did Archie know about him?"

"I didn't owe him an explanation after what he did for all those years."

Lesley could understand where the other woman was coming from. "Were you and Tony planning on telling Archie about your relationship? Were you planning to leave Archie?"

Susan hesitated. She pulled in a breath, began to speak and then stopped herself.

The solicitor put her hand on her arm. "You don't have to say anything."

Susan shook her head. "It's OK. I've got nothing to hide."

She looked up at Lesley. "Yes, Detective. I was planning on telling my husband about Tony. I was planning on telling him that I wanted to leave him and that I was going to marry Tony."

CHAPTER FIFTY-ONE

LESLEY'S PHONE rang as she and Johnny left Susan's house.

"Hi Gail, any news?"

"We've done some analysis on the residue from the weapon used to kill Laila."

"And?"

"I'm confident the same one was used in both murders."

Lesley looked over at Johnny. "Same weapon," she mouthed. He nodded.

"OK," she said to Gail, "What kind of weapon was it?"

"There were metal deposits found near both victims. Fragments that broke off the weapon after it was used. It wasn't the most stable of objects. But the metals were a copper alloy, and iron. Consistent with it being an early medieval axe."

"Not something more recent?"

"If it was, it would be more robust, and it would be made from different alloys. Modern steel would be in there somewhere. The sort of steel we use now wasn't really made till the late 18th century."

"So you're confident it was something found at the dig site."

"Either that, or something brought in from another site. We've got a botanist looking at spores and seed residue on the metal, see if it was local."

"OK," said Lesley. "Anything else to report?"

"You remember the second victim had defensive wounds? Cracked fingernails?"

"Uh huh."

"We found fibres beneath her nails. Skin cells. A couple of hairs."

"Fantastic," Lesley said. "And...?"

"We'll have to wait for the DNA analysis," Gail replied.

"How long will that take?"

"Probably a couple of days."

"A couple of days? This is urgent, Gail. Can't you get them to hurry it up?"

Gail laughed. "This is Dorset, not the West Midlands."

Lesley shook her head. "I don't care if it's bloody Timbuktu. We've got two people in that house, one or both of whom could be at risk. I need to know whose DNA was under Laila's fingernails. And I need to know yesterday."

"OK." Gail sounded subdued. "I'll see if I can get it fast tracked. It'll cost more though."

"I don't care if it costs the Chief Constable's salary, I just want it done."

"No problem," Gail hung up.

Lesley turned to Johnny as they got into the car.

"So now we know we've got one killer."

He nodded. "Makes it more likely it's going to be one of those two at the house."

"I don't want to jump to any conclusions," she said. "We wait until we get the DNA results."

"That will give us our man, or woman," he said.

"Absolutely."

"What about the storage?" he asked. "Inventory?"

"You're right, I'll call Dennis." She grabbed her phone.

"Boss." Dennis didn't sound happy.

"How are you getting on?" Lesley asked him. "Have you spoken to somebody at Bournemouth University?

"They're stalling," he said. "It seems they're not all that happy at having two members of their dig team murdered, in the space of just a few days. And now they've found out that Laila wasn't qualified..."

"Hang on a minute. Two of their staff have died and they don't want to cooperate with the police?"

"I didn't say they weren't cooperating, they're just taking a while to find somebody who can talk to us."

"That sounds like not cooperating to me. You want me to make a call?" she asked.

"I'm fine as I am."

She sighed. "I'll leave you to it. Just tell me if you need anything from me, alright?"

"Wait," he said. "Before you go..."

"Mm-hmm?"

"The post-mortem report. Whittaker called me about half an hour ago."

"That's speedy, for him."

Dennis didn't respond to the sarcasm. "The damage done to her head is very similar to what was inflicted on Archie," he said. "And apparently, there were remnants of metal in her jawbone."

Lesley nodded. "I've just had Gail on the phone, she's

found the same thing at the crime scene. Looks like we've got one weapon, which means one killer."

"Sleeping pills?" Johnny muttered.

"What about the sleeping pills?" Lesley asked Dennis. "I presume there weren't any sign of them in Laila's body?"

"Nothing," he replied. "No substances, not even alcohol."

"So maybe Archie wasn't fed the sleeping pills by his killer after all," she said. "Perhaps he just took them in large quantities."

"It was four times the normal dose," said Dennis.

"Still, that doesn't prove someone else fed them to him."

"No."

Lesley turned to Johnny. "I want to interview the bloke Susan's been having an affair with."

He nodded. "I made some calls after I spoke to the neighbour. I've got a name, Tony Goodall. And you're not gonna believe this."

She raised an eyebrow.

"He's a copper," Johnny said. "Works in Fraud in Bristol."

She gestured to the steering wheel. "Even better. Let's track him down."

CHAPTER FIFTY-TWO

Tony Goodall was a Detective Inspector, working out of Avon Police headquarters in Portishead. He was at his desk when Lesley and Johnny turned up.

He stood up, a wary smile on his lips. "Ma'am, what can I do for you?"

She shook the proffered hand and sat down. "This is about a case we're investigating in Corfe Castle."

He sucked in a breath. "I've heard about it."

She smiled at him. "I believe you have a connection to the victim."

He leaned forwards. His body language was stiff, formal. "How so?"

"The victim's name was Archie Weatherton." She watched for his reaction.

Tony met her gaze, his eyes unblinking. "OK."

"Do you know his wife, Susan Weatherton?"

He stared at her for just a moment too long.

"I do."

"Good." She glanced at Johnny. At least he'd decided not

to lie to them. "Can you tell me the nature of your relationship with Mrs Weatherton?"

He stood up and rounded the desk, closing the door behind Lesley and Johnny. "I'm sure you'll understand this is confidential."

"Of course," Lesley said.

He sat down. "Susan and I have been conducting a relationship for the last eighteen months."

"Eighteen months?"

He nodded. "Archie didn't know about it."

"I'd gathered that," Lesley said.

Johnny leaned in. "Where were you on Saturday morning?"

Lesley raised a hand to stop him. "DI Goodall, tell me about the state of Susan and Archie's marriage."

He looked surprised. "Well, what do you think? He treats her like shit, you know. Another woman on every dig. God knows how many there's been over the years."

"That's what she told you?"

"That's the truth."

"So you did some investigating of your own?" Johnny asked.

He looked at the DC. "You could say that."

Lesley eyed him. They both knew the punishment for using police resources to investigate something personal. But she had a murder to focus on.

"So you've been in a relationship with Susan Weatherton for eighteen months. How serious is this relationship?"

"You don't stick around that long with a married woman, unless you're confident she's going to leave her husband."

"So you were planning on marrying her?"

"I'd already asked her."

"When?"

"Two weeks ago."

"And she'd told Archie?"

"Not yet. She was planning to."

Lesley tapped her knee. "Are you sure she wasn't stalling?"

He gritted his teeth. "I'm sure you know that Susan has a daughter. Millie. Lovely kid. I'm fond of her. Susan doesn't want to rush things, she's thinking of her little girl."

Lesley nodded. Susan didn't strike her as the kind of woman to string a man along.

"In that case," she said, "were you aware that Susan got a call from a woman called Laila Ford, last Thursday?"

"I did. She rang me immediately afterwards."

"And what did she tell you Laila had said to her?"

"Nothing new." He barked out a laugh. "Just that Archie was shagging her. Archie did that all the time. I mean, it wasn't exactly a surprise."

"Not even to Susan?" Lesley asked.

"Not that he was doing it. Getting a call from the woman, yes. None of the women in the past have admitted to it. She knew that Archie had had an affair with Crystal when she was pregnant with Millie. But Crystal never said anything."

"So you know Crystal Spiers as well?" Lesley sensed Johnny tensing beside her.

"I've never met any of them," Tony replied. "Not even Archie. But Susan told me enough about them. Nasty lot."

Lesley raised an eyebrow. "You think Crystal was nasty?"

He shrugged. "She had an affair with a bloke when his wife was pregnant. Not sure what kind of woman that makes her."

"Tony," she said, "I'm going to have to ask you this. Where were you on Saturday morning?"

He steepled his hands on the desk. "I was expecting this." He opened a desk drawer and pulled out a diary. "I was working. Here, you can see." He pushed the diary across the desk. He'd written details of meetings and interviews he'd conducted that day.

"Bit old school, isn't it?" said Lesley.

"I like to keep my own diary as well as the electronic system," he said. "Just in case."

"OK." She pushed the diary back across the desk. "Can your departmental commander confirm this?"

"Of course he can," he replied. "DCI Malcolm Browning. Call him if you need to."

"I will," Lesley said. "Thanks for your time."

CHAPTER FIFTY-THREE

Tina Abbott clattered down the stairs in the tiny cottage.

Being a family liaison officer was one thing, but being an FLO in such cramped quarters as this was entirely different. She'd spent much of the morning trying not to get too close to Patrick. Withering under the force of his glare, fully aware that the man didn't want her there. If he could have physically pushed her out of the building, he would have.

Crystal had gone down to the dig site. Tina had been torn between following Crystal down the hill, or staying here with Patrick. But she knew the FLO normally stayed in the house. So on balance, this was the best place to be. And the DCI seemed suspicious of Patrick. He'd assaulted Laila, after all. He was more likely to behave suspiciously here than his colleague was at work.

She opened the door between the staircase and the living room. The room was empty. When she'd gone upstairs, he'd been sitting in the corner in that threadbare armchair, listening to his tinny little radio set. Something about cricket, although it hadn't sounded much like cricket to her.

She went into the kitchen: empty.

She returned to the stairway and through to where Crystal's room was. Again, empty. None of these rooms had locks. She wondered why Crystal and Patrick hadn't rectified that yet.

She hurried up the stairs. Patrick's room was immediately on the left, just feet away from Laila's and Archie's room. She pushed open the door. Again, empty. Tina felt herself deflate. He'd been waiting till she'd gone up to the loo, and he'd left the cottage.

Should she follow him down the hill to the dig site, or should she take advantage of the opportunity to have a look in his room? Gail and her team had been in yesterday, searching the house as best they could. But Patrick had insisted that as an innocent bystander, he had no obligation to let them search his room. Which meant they'd only covered the communal spaces and Crystal's room, for which they had permission.

Tina looked around the room, standing on the threshold. If she went in there and searched the room, it would be an illegal search. Not only could she get herself disciplined, but any evidence she did uncover would be inadmissible in court. She closed the door and trudged down the stairs.

She went through the kitchen and out the back door. Behind the cottage was a tiny yard, a folding table and chairs propped against the wall and a shed in the far corner.

Gail and her team had searched the shed yesterday. The door was padlocked, the only locked door in this place. Gail had said there were boxes in there. Piled up in meticulous order, all labelled and numbered. Archaeological finds.

Tina wandered across the yard to the shed. The padlock wasn't bolted. They'd had permission to search this building, so she was within her rights to go inside. If the padlock had been disturbed, then maybe somebody had put something in there since Gail's search.

She pulled a pair of gloves out of her pocket and put them on before pulling the padlock open. Then she eased the door open. The hinges were rusty, and it squeaked in protest as she pulled at it. She'd been expecting a musty space, damp maybe. Cobwebs in the corners, dirt on the floor. But no, this was tidy. It looked as if it had been swept to within an inch of its life. This shed contained important materials, and it was clearly looked after.

In front of her were four piles of boxes. Each box had a unique identifier, some with photos of their contents. Tina ran her eyes up and down the stacks, trying to identify any anomalies.

There was one box in the middle of the stack furthest away from her, which wasn't labelled. It was browning, older than the others. She looked at it, thinking. Could she pull it out without disturbing the others on top of it?

She could damn well have a go.

She prised the box out from between the others. She leaned her shoulder against the boxes on top of it, making sure they didn't topple, and eased them down to rest on the box below the one she'd just pulled out.

Carefully, she placed it on the floor, straightened the remaining pile, then picked up the box and closed the door to the shed. She put the padlock back in the position she'd found it.

She approached the kitchen window and peered through, checking Patrick hadn't returned. The house was still empty. She walked into the kitchen, closed the door through to the living room and flicked on the kettle. It wouldn't do any harm to make a noise.

The box she'd pulled out was like a shoe box, but slightly larger. She lifted the lid off carefully and placed it to one side. Inside was an object wrapped in cloth.

Tina felt her breath shorten as she pried the cloth away.

She pulled back the layers, her eyes narrowing. At last the object was uncovered, the layers of linen out of the way.

It was an axe.

At least, what remained of one. The handle was rotting away and the blade was corroded and blunt. Rust covered the tip.

She felt her breath catch in her throat.

Tina stared down at it, heart racing. She pulled her phone out of her inside pocket, not sure who she should call. As she did so, she heard the front door slam. Tina shoved her phone back into her pocket, and stared down at the open box. She threw the linen back around the object, and slammed on the lid.

Footsteps in the living room next door. Her stomach clenching, she grabbed the box, opened a cupboard door and shoved it inside. Gail wouldn't be happy about this, she was contaminating evidence. But she didn't know who was on the other side of that door.

The door opened.

Tina turned towards it, her eyes wide.

CHAPTER FIFTY-FOUR

SUSAN WAS SITTING in her front room with Millie when she heard a faint tapping at the window.

She looked at Millie, who was staring at the TV, her eyes glazing over. Susan eased herself off the sofa and tiptoed to the window. Had she been imagining it?

She stood with her ear to the curtain, not wanting to pull it aside in case it was Mr Gill from next door.

There it was, again. Tapping.

Low enough not to sound through the house, but just loud enough for her to know somebody was trying to get her attention.

She heard movement beyond the wall in the kitchen. The family liaison officer was rattling around in there, making sure Susan knew she was still here. Susan hated the woman already, even though it wasn't her fault that her job had put her here.

Susan took a breath. She eased the curtain aside, just a crack.

On the other side was Tony.

She frowned at him. "What are you doing here?" she hissed.

He shook his head. He couldn't hear her. He beckoned for her to come out.

She let the curtain fall closed. "I won't be a moment, Millie love. I just need to go and talk to somebody."

Millie looked up at her, her face creasing.

Susan felt herself crumble. Millie had slept badly last night, she'd woken three times, calling for Susan to join her in her bed, to hold her while she cried. God knew how long she would be like this. Maybe Susan should get professional help, speak to the GP.

"You want to come with me, sweetie?"

Millie looked towards the window. "Who is it?"

Susan considered telling her. Millie loved Tony, but she didn't want her saying anything to that damn family liaison officer.

"It's just a friend, Mils. I won't be a minute."

Millie swallowed and nodded slowly. Susan gave her an apologetic look, and scooted out of the room.

She glided through the hall to the front door in her socks, careful not to make a sound. She eased the front door open and slid through it, pulling it closed behind her.

Tony was in front of the garage door, out of sight of the windows.

"I thought you weren't going to come back?" she whispered.

"I just wanted to tell you something."

"What?"

"The police came to see me."

"What, that DCI?"

He nodded. "It's fine. I told her where I was on Saturday, nobody suspects a thing."

"Why should they?" she asked.

He looked at her. "Well, now they know that we're planning on marrying, I guess they might think I wanted Archie out the way."

She looked at him. "But you're not that kind of man."

"I know I'm not that kind of man, and you know I'm not that kind of man." He pulled her to him.

She buried her face in his chest, wishing she could invite him inside.

"But," he said, "I know how they think. I know how I'd think if it was me. I'm just damn glad I was at work on Saturday. Although I am sorry I wasn't with you."

She pulled back and smiled at him. "We can be together more in the future."

He blinked down at her. "You're sure?"

"Yeah. I'm not saying I'm glad Archie's dead. I'll miss him. And Millie..."

"I know." He squeezed her shoulders. "Millie's lost her dad."

She nodded. "I do love you, Tony."

He smiled at her. "I love you too, Susie." He put his hand on the back of her head, and pulled her towards him.

She let him kiss her, wishing life could be simple. Why the hell hadn't she just divorced Archie years ago when she found out about the first affair? That damn Crystal Spiers. Susan was convinced she'd been the first.

Stop thinking, she told herself. *Just relax.*

She pulled away from Tony. "We don't need to hide the

fact that you and me are together now, but I don't want to make this harder on Millie. We have to take it slow. We have to go at her pace."

"I know," he said. "You call me when you're ready, yeah?

She nodded. "Thanks, love."

CHAPTER FIFTY-FIVE

Dennis and Mike had been waiting in the lobby area at Bournemouth University for two hours. Waiting to see if one of these academics would stoop so low as to speak to a couple of coppers.

Dennis was fed up. He was hungry, his skin itched and he wanted to give up. He checked his watch for the hundredth time.

"You thinking what I'm thinking, Sarge?" Mike asked.

Dennis nodded. "Maybe we should give up. The boss needs to contact them, set up something official."

"That's not like you, Sarge."

Dennis grunted. He wasn't used to dealing with these academics. The people at the dig weren't so bad, a bit odd perhaps. Patrick Donnelly seemed friendly enough. Crystal Spiers was remote, but not snooty.

But the woman he'd spoken to on reception here had looked at him like he was smut on the bottom of her shoe.

He leaned back on the stiff bench they'd been told to

wait on. "I'm going to take a walk, call the boss and find out what's going on in Bristol."

Mike nodded. "I'll wait here."

As Dennis stood up, the woman who'd been so dismissive of them earlier approached him.

"Sergeant?"

He turned to face her, expecting the inevitable rejection.

"Mr Sidhu says he will see you now."

He raised an eyebrow. "At last."

The woman sneered at him. "Follow me."

Mike scrambled up from the bench, gathering up their things. Dennis's coat, the one Pam had bought him, was on the bench beneath where he'd been sitting. Anything to get comfortable.

They followed the woman along corridors, passing lecture theatres full of students. Young, confident bodies, passing in the opposite direction, brushed against them, not stopping to get out of their way.

"Kids," Dennis muttered.

At last they arrived at a door. The nameplate said *Tim Sidhu, Administrator*. Dennis sighed. They were being palmed off with the office lackey.

The woman pushed the door open and ushered them inside. A slim Asian man sat behind a desk. He stood as they entered, gesturing for them to take a seat.

He was about Dennis's age, greying hair that was thinning on top. He smiled at them. "Come in, Detectives., I'm so sorry to have kept you waiting."

Dennis heard Mike grunt. He took the chair the man had offered and pulled out his ID.

"I'm DS Frampton, this is DC Chiles. We're here in

connection with the murders of Archie Weatherton and Laila Ford."

The man nodded. "Such a tragic business." He bowed his head, his hands clasped together as if in prayer.

Dennis watched him, wondering how much of this was genuine. "Did you ever meet either of the victims?" he asked.

The man looked up. "Never. Doctor Weatherton was seconded from Bristol University. Miss Ford... Well, she was recruited by Professor Spiers."

Dennis raised an eyebrow. He hadn't realised Crystal was a professor.

"She taught here? Professor Spiers?"

"Still does."

Dennis glanced at Mike.

"Professor Sidhu, can I ask you a few questions about the dig? About the project at Corfe Castle?"

"I'm not a professor, Sergeant. I'm just a layman. Call me Mr Sidhu. In fact, call me Tim."

"Fair enough, Mr Sidhu. Firstly, can I ask you about the artefacts that were uncovered on that dig? Whether there was anything specifically that might have been used as a weapon?"

The man's eyes widened. "They used something from the dig site? That's impossible."

"Why's that?"

"Well, everything was labelled, catalogued, and then sent back here. I can show you. We have a store for it all."

"But our forensics manager tells us she found a number of objects stored and catalogued at the cottage in Corfe Castle."

Mr Sidhu shook his head. "No, no, that's not how it works at all. They keep things for a few days, and then at the end of every week, Professor Spiers catalogues it, logs it all on the database, and then arranges for it to be sent here. Sometimes she brings it herself. Sometimes we send a member of staff down to collect it. Occasionally we'll trust the job to a couple of students."

Dennis narrowed his eyes.

It had been yesterday, a Wednesday, when Gail had found over thirty items in that shed. Surely they hadn't uncovered that much in just two days? The site had been off limits on Monday.

Mike leaned forwards. "Is there any chance that with everything that's happened, last week's finds weren't catalogued or transferred?"

Mr Sidhu frowned. "I'll check." He turned to his desk, and clicked his mouse a few times.

"No," he said. "Friday afternoon, we had a box full of items brought in by two students."

"Very well." Dennis considered. "Are you aware that there are a number of items still at the cottage? They're stored in the shed."

The administrator turned to him. "You must be mistaken. It's all here, on the system."

Dennis met his gaze. Even if the four people in that cottage had planned on stealing some of those artefacts, theft was nothing compared to a double murder.

"I think you need to go down there," he said. "It's not for me to say what those items are, and whether they should be here at the university. But you might want to follow that up."

Mr Sidhu nodded. "I will, thank you. Is there anything else I can help with? Do you need contact details for the next of kin?"

"We already have those. We've been in touch with Mrs

Weatherton, and Laila Ford's parents are coming down to identify her body."

Sidhu winced. "I saw the news reports. I don't envy them."

"No," said Dennis. Whatever kind of girl Laila Ford had been, she hadn't deserved the manner of her death.

He took a breath. "Were there any financial or budgetary issues with this dig?"

"How do you mean?"

"Were there any challenges? Had you had funding withdrawn?"

"Quite the opposite. We'd just had a big donation from a, well, that's confidential. But we'd just had a big donation, and we'd gained some international funding too."

"So the project was in a good financial condition?"

"It certainly was. It was one of the most financially healthy projects I've administered in a while. Crystal Spiers was very good at raising funds. She'd spent sixteen years doing it, after all."

Mike cleared his throat. Dennis's mind was racing.

"It's only," he said, "we've been told that there were financial issues that caused tensions between the people in the group."

Sidhu shrugged. "Well, that's certainly not backed up by our data."

Dennis could sense Mike scribbling furiously in his notepad. They'd have to report this to the boss.

"So was there anything missing, as far as you're aware, from the dig?"

"Again, I'd have to check that on the database. Give me a moment." For the second time, Mr Sidhu checked his computer.

Dennis and Mike exchanged glances. If there weren't any financial problems, why had Archie told Bristol University that there were? And why had Archie been going to London for meetings to seek extra funding?

Was that really what he'd been doing?

Sidhu turned back from his computer. "Nothing missing as far as my records are concerned. We'd have to check the storeroom, but we have a pretty robust system. It's actually modelled on the systems that you use for forensics in police inquiries."

Dennis nodded. He had a feeling that if anything was missing, it wouldn't have made it to the university in the first place.

"Thank you for your time," he said, standing up.

"Is that all?" Mr Sidhu asked.

"For now."

CHAPTER FIFTY-SIX

LESLEY HURRIED through the front entrance of Dorset Police HQ. She was anxious to find out whether Dennis and Mike had made progress at Bournemouth University. As she swiped her ID card at the turnstile, the woman on reception waved to catch her attention.

"Sorry, Ma'am! I've got an urgent message for you."

Lesley nodded. "Yes?"

"Detective Superintendent Carpenter wants to speak to you right away."

Lesley felt her stomach sink.

"Right away?" she said.

"That's what this note says."

"OK."

Lesley made for the stairs and hurried up to Carpenter's office. She knocked quietly on the door.

"Come in."

Tugging down her jacket sleeves, she slid into the room.

"DCI Clarke. You got my message?"

"Is everything alright? I was just about to brief my team on—"

"I won't keep you long. Sit down, please."

He wasn't meeting her eye. She took a seat opposite him at the desk. No comfy chairs in the corner this time.

"Sir, what do you need?"

"I'm afraid I've received a complaint."

"Complaint?"

She'd only been on the force four days. She'd barely interacted with the public. How could there have been a complaint already?

Then she thought of Crystal Spiers. The woman hadn't wanted them at her dig site. She'd been convinced they were ruining precious artefacts.

"If it's Crystal Spiers Sir, I can..."

"It's not a member of the public," he replied. "I'm afraid it's an anonymous internal complaint."

"Oh." She scratched the back of her hand.

"The complainant is concerned that your health is impacting on your ability to fulfil your duties."

"My health, Sir?"

He eyed her. "You had a head injury back in March. You were diagnosed with a form of PTSD. I'm worried that it means you can't—"

"I'm more than up to the task of managing this investigation."

"You were sent here for a slower pace."

"And that's what I'm getting," she replied.

He raised an eyebrow. "A double murder investigation in your first week? You've only been here a matter of days, and you're already in the middle of our biggest case for months."

"With respect, Sir, I've handled cases like this before, significantly more complex cases. I'm more than capable—"

He raised a hand. "You and I have hardly had a chance to get to know each other, something we should rectify. But this complainant has seen you in action. They're concerned that your health issues are impacting on your ability to manage your team, to delegate effectively."

She felt heat rise inside her. "That's untrue. Delegation is something I—"

"I'm not making any judgments. Right now this is just an informal complaint. More of a warning, if you want to put it that way."

She swallowed. She knew what a warning could mean. "Will this go on my personnel file, Sir?"

He stared at her, tapping his fingers together. He rocked in his chair.

It was an effort to keep calm. He was torturing her, deliberate or not.

"No," he said finally. "It won't go in your file. However, I want you to consider the way that you interact with your new team. They're different from what you're used to. Please take that into consideration."

"Sir. I will."

He waved a hand to dismiss her. She left the room, her heart racing. She knew damn well who'd made that complaint.

CHAPTER FIFTY-SEVEN

THE TEAM WERE all at their desks as Lesley walked towards her office.

"My office, now," she snapped. She tried not to let her gaze linger on Dennis, who wasn't meeting her eye.

Bastard, she thought to herself. All because of that bloody swear box.

Once they were all gathered inside, she nodded at Mike. "Shut the door."

Mike did so, looking nervous. He and Johnny sat down. Dennis stood behind them, shifting from foot to foot.

Oh, fucking stop looking so nervous, she thought. *At least own up to your disloyalty.*

She took a deep breath. She had no idea if the other two knew what had happened. Were the three of them discussing her? Were they speculating on the state of her health? Were they plotting to get rid of her?

She bit her bottom lip. She was their senior officer. She shouldn't let this sort of thing get to her.

She cleared her throat. "Right. Let's get the board out."

Johnny dragged the board out from behind Lesley's desk. He grabbed a whiteboard marker and looked at her, waiting.

"OK." She could hear the irritation in her voice. Dennis would be able to hear it too. "So. We've got Susan Weatherton and her fancy man, who's a copper."

Mike sucked in a breath. "Ouch."

She looked at him. "It doesn't make any difference, it gives her a possible motive. But her alibi seems sound."

Johnny lifted a hand.

Lesley rolled her eyes at him. "We're not in school, Johnny."

"Sorry, boss. I made some calls. Susan Weatherton's alibi checks out."

Lesley nodded. She pointed at the board. "Even so, stick Tony Goodall's name up there."

"His alibi checks out, too," said Johnny. "The diary printout you gave us?"

"I know that," Lesley said. "But I just want to add it for the sake of completeness."

Johnny nodded and wrote Tony Goodall's name on the board.

"What else have we got?" Lesley asked. "How did you two get on at Bournemouth?"

Dennis still wasn't meeting her eye. "It took us a while to get a meeting, but in the end we spoke to an administrator."

"And?" she snapped.

"He told us they have a system, it's modelled on the procedures used by our forensics teams. They log everything they find on that site, and then they transfer it to Bournemouth University at the end of the week."

"But," Mike interrupted, "not everything is accounted

for. The CSIs found objects in the shed when they searched the house."

Lesley nodded. "What kind of objects?"

"Piles of them, catalogued, in boxes. Looked very professional, apparently. But according to Mr Sidhu, the guy we spoke to, everything should be over at Bournemouth University. Nothing should be in that shed."

"Not even the items they found this week?" Lesley asked.

Dennis met her eye finally. "They've only been working for two days, since we opened up the site again."

"Yeah, and there was way too much stuff in that shed for it to be two days' worth of work," added Mike. "I mean, if they'd been uncovering finds at that rate, the forensics team would have been tripping over them when they were down there."

Lesley nodded. "Have you got photos? Stick them up on the board."

Mike pulled some sheets out of a folder.

"OK," she said "We need to find out why those objects aren't going over to Bournemouth University. Are they even being catalogued?"

"Doesn't sound like it," said Mike. "Not from what Tim Sidhu says."

"Is he going to be following it up?"

"He'll be the only person who knows whether they match up to what's officially there," Dennis replied. "He said he'd be over at the dig site, later today or first thing in the morning."

Lesley nodded. "Good. So we need to find out who's been hoarding items at the cottage, and whether the weapon is among them."

"It's not," said Dennis. "I checked with Gail."

"Damn." She picked at her fingernails. How was she getting so dirty, since she'd come down here? "OK, so was anything missing from the official inventory? Our potential murder weapon?"

Mike looked down at his notepad. "All accounted for, boss. The administrator went through his records, he took us down to the storeroom. There was nothing missing. I don't mind saying, that's a damn good system they've got there."

Dennis sucked his teeth.

Lesley covered a smile. "Anything else?"

Johnny coughed. "I think I might have a link between the dig team, and the DI who's having an affair with Susan Weatherton."

Lesley cocked her head. "Go on."

"Well, I checked over that diary sheet he gave us, and I looked at the investigations he's working on. I called a mate who works out of a local CID team in Bristol."

Lesley frowned at him. She wasn't sure whether this was good coppering, or over and above what he was authorised to do.

"You found something?"

"I might have done."

"What kind of something?" Dennis asked.

Johnny glanced at him. "DI Goodall works in fraud, yeah?"

Lesley nodded.

"Well, he seems to be investigating the team that manages that dig. It looks like there might be something going on at the university."

"Which university?" Lesley asked.

"I'm not sure. Bournemouth and Bristol are both sponsoring the dig. It's officially Bournemouth's, but Bristol have also been providing manpower and funding."

"Archie Weatherton, for example?" she said.

"Exactly."

"If Tony Goodall's investigating it, it must be Bristol University he's looking at."

"You'd think so," said Johnny.

"OK," Lesley said. "I need you to look into that further. If there's a link between Tony Goodall and that team, that might be why he's befriended Susan Weatherton."

Dennis shook his head. "I don't see how that's relevant."

"Nor do I," Lesley snapped. "But it's a lead, so we follow it."

"But for a detective inspector to do that to a—"

"It happens, Dennis. It's not ethical. It might not be legal. But it happens. And it might fit with what we've been told about the financial problems. The woman we spoke to at Bristol University said they were having problems with funding for the dig. But the guy you spoke to at Bournemouth University, he said everything was in order."

"Yeah," said Mike. "He said they had money coming out of their ears."

"So why would Archie have told his boss that they were short of funding?"

"Maybe that's something to do with this fraud investigation?" Johnny suggested.

Lesley nodded at him. "We need to find the connection. We've got a fraud investigation going on at Bristol. We've got a dig that's sponsored by Bournemouth University, that says there's money pouring into it. We've got a professor at Bristol University, who says they're short on cash. And in the middle, we've got Archie Weatherton and his wife."

"I can look into it," said Johnny.

"You do that," said Lesley. "Mike, you work with him. I'll follow up on the weapon."

The two DCs nodded. Lesley turned to Dennis. "And the other thing I want to follow up on is this assault on Laila by Patrick Donnelly. I want you to check Donnelly's past. Find out if he's got form. Laila told her mate that he sexually assaulted her. With Laila dead it's going to be difficult for us to prove that. But if we can find out that he's done that kind of thing before..."

Dennis had his hands planted in his pockets. "I think it's tenuous," he said. "All he did was try and kiss her."

Lesley glared at him. "I think he did a bit more than that, Dennis. The guy's a sexual predator."

Dennis laughed. "Have you *seen* him?"

"Yes, I *have* seen him, and you'd be surprised. Men like that, they present as one thing when they meet someone like you and me. But then when they're with a young, vulnerable woman... Well, I'm sure you've come across them before."

Dennis shrugged. "We're not in Birmingham now, boss."

She gritted her teeth. When were they going to stop throwing that at her?

"I just want you to investigate him, Dennis. Find out if he's got a record, if he's got form, if there have been any allegations made against him in the past. We've still got Patrick and Crystal. Crystal with the money. Patrick with the assault."

The team murmured in response.

"Go on then," she said. "Get on with it."

CHAPTER FIFTY-EIGHT

GAIL HELD her phone to her ear, Tina Abbott watching her. The PC shifted from foot to foot, looking uneasy. Gail blinked at her, waiting for the phone to be answered.

At last it was picked up.

"DCI Clarke."

"Lesley, it's Gail."

"Gail, where are you?"

"I'm at the cottage. With PC Abbott."

"Has something happened?"

"You could say that."

"Have Patrick or Crystal done something?"

"No, not that," said Gail. Tina stared at her, cheeks flushed. They were in the kitchen of the cottage. Patrick Donnelly had been here when Gail had arrived. He'd been in the living room, giving PC Abbott a look like he wanted to hit her with something. He'd scuttled away when Gail had shown up, his body language furtive.

"What is it, then?" Lesley sounded impatient.

Gail took a breath. "We think we've got the murder weapon."

Lesley sucked in a breath. "You *think*?"

Gail looked at the box, sitting on the kitchen counter. Tina had brought it out after Patrick had gone. The lid was off and she could see the cloth inside that surrounded the weapon.

"It's an axe," she said. "The handle is severely degraded and there's corrosion on the head, but I'm confident it's the same one." She'd lifted the cloth briefly, protective gloves on. The shape of the blade fitted with Laila's injuries.

"So it matches the fragments of metal you found?" Lesley asked her.

"I'd have to do a lab analysis to know that, but it's likely."

"Where did you find it?"

"PC Abbott found it in the shed out the back of the cottage."

"I thought you'd already searched that?"

"I did. This wasn't here when I searched."

"Hang on," said Lesley. "So who's had access to that shed, between you finishing your search and PC Abbott finding it?"

"Well, we know Patrick Donnelly was here. Not sure about Crystal Spiers."

"Right," said Lesley. "And why hasn't PC Abbott called me?"

Gail eyed the PC. Tina leaned against the other kitchen counter, her breathing shallow.

"There might be a problem," said Gail.

"What kind of problem?" asked Lesley.

"I'd finished the official search of that shed. It had been locked again, or at least I thought it had. PC Abbott tells me that the padlock wasn't bolted. As far as the occupants were concerned, it wasn't going to be searched again."

"So that means..." said Lesley.

Gail felt her shoulders slump. "It might have been an illegal search. Even if it wasn't, I'd say a half-decent lawyer would squash it flat."

"In which case, it's not evidential." Lesley's voice was clipped.

PC Abbott's cheeks reddened further. Gail gave her a look that was partway between reassuring and irritated.

"OK," said Lesley. "So, have you dusted it for prints yet?"

"Not yet," said Gail. "I want to get it to the lab. I want to see if it's got prints, and if there's any DNA on it. Check the materials against the fragments we found."

"Do that, as soon as you can."

"What about the legality of the search?" Gail asked.

"Let me worry about that," said Lesley. "Even if we can't use it as evidence, it'll give us what we need. We then just need to back it up with legal evidence."

Gail looked across at PC Abbott, who was twisting her hands together in front of her.

Oh, do calm down, Gail thought. At least they had the weapon.

"Will do," she said to Lesley.

"And let me know as soon as you have a result."

"Of course I will."

"Oh," said Lesley. "And tell PC Abbott to come into the briefing first thing tomorrow morning, won't you?"

Gail nodded. She hung up.

"Well," breathed Tina. "How did she react?"

Gail cocked her head. "She's already told me she's a

stickler for procedure. Find evidence, build a case by the book. She won't like this."

"Is it certain that it's not a legal search?" Tina asked.

"The DCI will know that better than me," said Gail, although she had a pretty good idea what the answer was. "Anyway, she wants you in the briefing tomorrow morning, first thing."

Tina's eyes widened. "But I'm needed here. I'm the FLO."

"I think the DCI needs you more."

CHAPTER FIFTY-NINE

There was a pile of letters waiting on the mat when Lesley got back to her house. Two of them were junk mail, straight into the bin. Another was addressed to somebody she didn't know, presumably a previous tenant. The final one had a Birmingham postmark and was handwritten.

She gripped it, recognising the writing.

She wandered into the kitchen, delaying the moment when she would have to open the letter. It couldn't be anything but bad news. She put it down on the table.

She flipped the kettle on, grabbed a mug from the top shelf and fumbled around in a cupboard for a tea bag. She had a feeling that after she'd read this letter, she'd need something stronger.

Reluctantly, she picked up the letter. She slid her fingernail into the envelope and pulled it open. Two sheets of paper were inside: lined, handwritten. So he'd decided to wax lyrical.

She took a breath as she unfolded the paper, her mouth

dry. She'd been trying to call him for the last two days. The toad didn't even dare speak to her. He was going to do this by post.

She read.

Lesley, I wanted to send you this before you receive the official documentation. I'm genuinely sorry you had to find me with Julieta the way you did. I've been meaning to tell you for weeks. But there just hasn't been the chance. You've been so busy with work, and then when you do get home, you seem too tired for us to talk properly.

Lesley licked her lips. So he was blaming her, claiming she was too busy for a proper conversation.

Too busy, my arse, she thought. Too busy to know he was shagging some Spanish woman while she was away working.

She carried on reading.

I met Julieta in October, at a university event. We hit it off immediately. You and I hadn't been talking very much at that point. I tried to address things with you. Do you remember that conversation we had early in October? It was around the time your Canary investigation ended. I thought things might calm down at that point. But then the Assistant Chief Constable was killed, and I lost you again. I always felt that you loved your work more than you loved me.

. . .

Lesley sneered. Of course she loved her bloody work. For a woman to climb the ranks to DCI was more common now than it had been when she'd started in the force, but it still wasn't easy. She'd had to put up with the likes of Bryn Jackson, with his antediluvian attitudes towards women.

And she'd proven herself. She'd worked hard, she'd kept her nose clean, and she'd succeeded.

Terry should be pleased for her. He should have been celebrating the end of the Canary case with her, commiserating with her when only one of the bastards they'd arrested had gone down.

But, no. Instead, he was blaming her for working too hard, and running into the arms of another woman.

She turned the page.

I've tried to engage you in a conversation on a few occasions. But you don't seem to want to listen to me, so I've instructed a solicitor. I think our relationship has run its course. I don't think there's anything we can do to rectify things now. We've hardly spoken since you made DCI. I don't want to drag this out.

The solicitor reckons that you were absent from our relationship, that you weren't a full participant. He says that constitutes unreasonable behaviour. He also says that your working hours mean I've got a good chance of getting custody of Sharon. Obviously that's helped by the fact that you're two hundred miles away right now, and will be for the next six months.

. . .

Lesley felt heat rise through her body. No way was he taking her daughter from her. She clenched her fists, wanting to thump something. Preferably her husband.

She couldn't read any more. She threw the sheets down, her hands shaking. She plunged her hand into her pocket and grabbed her keys. She needed a drink. She marched along Church Street, into East Street, and shoved open the door of the Duke of Wellington.

The woman she'd spoken to last night was behind the bar. Elsa. She was a lawyer. Lesley needed a lawyer right now, but Elsa was a criminal lawyer.

She'd know family lawyers, though.

Lesley slung her keys onto the bar, prodding them with her fingers.

Elsa raised an eyebrow. "You OK?"

"Fine," Lesley snapped.

"You look like you need a drink."

"You could say that."

"Whisky?"

Lesley wasn't habitually a whisky drinker. She'd been about to ask for a gin and tonic. But she needed something she could throw down her neck fast. Something to soften the jangled nerves.

"Make it a double," she said.

Elsa nodded and turned to the optics.

Lesley felt somebody behind her. She shifted her weight, willing them to go away. Some bloke about to make a smarmy comment. *Alright, love? You don't look very happy.* God, she hated men like that.

She wondered what line Terry had used to coerce Julieta into bed. How did a man like Terry get a woman like that to sleep with him in the first place? What sob story must he have told her?

Elsa placed the glass on the bar.

"Thanks." Lesley downed it in one, coughing as she placed it back on the bar. "That's better."

Elsa smiled and her eyes darkened. She had beautiful eyes, unlike Lesley whose eyes were small and blue-grey. "Want to share your problems?"

Lesley shook her head. She heard somebody clear their throat; that man was still hovering behind her.

She turned to him. She was about to tell him to bugger off when she recognised him.

"Fuck. What the hell are you doing here?"

His face paled. It wasn't the time or the place for her to be apologising for her language. If he only knew…

"Boss," Dennis said, his eyes not quite meeting hers.

"What is it, Dennis? Did I forget something in the briefing?"

"I came to your house. I saw you leave, I followed you here."

"Well, congratulations on making detective of the year."

He looked from her to Elsa. Elsa shrugged. Lesley knew what they were thinking. Mouthy old bitch from the city, come down here to throw her weight around and swear at everybody. Well, she didn't give a fuck right now.

"What do you want, Sergeant?"

"I came to apologise," he said.

"What for?"

He swallowed. "I think you know what for."

"I want you to say it."

Lesley was in a shitty mood, she knew. She also knew she shouldn't take it out on Dennis. But he'd made that complaint to Carpenter. Maybe he deserved everything he got.

"What for, Dennis?" she repeated.

"You were summoned to the Super's office, weren't you?"

Elsa was making for the other end of the bar, serving another customer. She knew when she wasn't wanted. The woman had discretion, an important trait in a lawyer.

"I *was*, Dennis," she said. "You know anything about it?"

He blinked. "I want to say I'm sorry."

"Why did you make a complaint about me? You only gave me a few days, and already you're judging me."

He paled again. "I was worried about you."

"Worried, my arse. You don't like me. You don't like the way I talk. You don't like being bossed around." She leaned in. The whisky was kicking in. "You don't like having a woman as a boss."

"That's not true," he said. "I've worked for plenty of women."

"Yeah? You worked for a bloke before me."

His face darkened. "I'd rather not..."

"What is it about Mackie?" she said. "What is it everybody's not telling me?"

"Please, boss. I don't want to talk about it."

She sighed. "Come and sit with me."

She took her empty glass and led him to a table. The table was small and round, with a slight wobble. She leaned on it, trying to steady it, and then realised she was a little unsteady herself.

"Let's hear it," she said. "Your apology."

He placed his hands on the table, holding it still. "I made a complaint. It wasn't so much a complaint, as a registration of concern. I know you had health problems up in the West

Midlands, and I know that's why you were sent here. I was worried that getting landed with a double murder case so quickly, might impact on those—"

"You thought I couldn't do my job," she said. "You thought I couldn't manage the team."

"I won't lie to you, boss. There was a bit of that, too. But you have to understand, we don't often get a case like this. We need to make sure it's done properly."

She ground her fist into the top of the table. *"Properly?* Properly is my middle bloody name. I make sure *everything's* done properly. If you knew what I'd found out tonight and I have to deal with tomorrow..."

"The weapon?" he said.

She raised an eyebrow. "You know?"

He nodded. "PC Abbott came back into the office after you'd left, with her tail between her legs. She looks like she's expecting to get sacked tomorrow."

Lesley laughed. "The Federation would have me strung up if I tried that. And besides, she uncovered a vital piece of evidence. OK, so she didn't do it by the book. But if she hadn't, we'd still be running around without anything to go on."

He nodded. "CPS won't be able to use it, though."

"That's not the important thing," she said. "If that weapon tells us who killed Archie and Laila, then we know where to look for something we *can* use."

"Crystal," he said.

"Or Patrick," she replied.

"Fair enough." He stood up. "I need to get home. Pam, my wife, she's waiting for me."

She shrugged. "You go home, enjoy your evening." She wanted to be jealous of him. But the truth was, she was glad she wasn't going home to domestic mundanity. It had been years since she'd enjoyed that sort of thing.

"Boss." He looked relived.

"And thanks," she said. "This took guts."

He nodded. She grabbed his arm as he turned away.

"Next time you've got a problem, you come to me though, eh?"

"Boss."

As Dennis left the pub, Elsa slid over to the table, taking his seat. She set a gin and tonic down in front of Lesley.

"I took the liberty," she said.

Lesley grabbed it. "Thanks, this is more me."

Elsa cocked her head. She had a dimple in her left cheek, and it deepened when she smiled. "Thought as much. You need help with your man problems?"

"I certainly bloody do. My husband's filing for divorce, and he's the one who's sleeping with another woman."

"Well, you're fine then," said Elsa. "Adultery."

"He says he's already filed," Lesley said. "Claiming unreasonable behaviour. Apparently I work too much."

Elsa laughed. "You're a detective, of course you work too much."

"He's an academic," Lesley replied. "God, I'm sick of academics at the moment."

She slumped into her chair and took a swig of her gin and tonic. It felt good to drink something cool and refreshing after the heat of the whisky.

"You can't help me," she said. "You're a criminal lawyer."

"But I've got plenty of friends who are family lawyers," Elsa replied. "You want me to make a call?"

Lesley nodded. Back in Birmingham, she'd have had half

a dozen people she could call. She would have run rings around Terry.

But here she felt untethered. She had nobody she could lean on. Maybe Elsa would be that person?

"Yes, please," she said. "And get yourself a drink while you're at it."

CHAPTER SIXTY

SUSAN LISTENED to her mother-in-law talking to the undertaker and wished she'd refused the woman's offer to come with her. Archie's body was about to be released and it needed somewhere to go.

Undertakers weren't something Susan knew anything about. So when Rowena had turned up, insisting that she could handle all this, Susan had acquiesced.

Millie was at home with Fiona. Susan wondered what Fiona's employers thought about her taking so much time off work. And what was Fiona's husband doing while she was looking after her?

Susan needed to open her eyes and take a look at the people around her. She wasn't the only one affected by Archie's death. The woman sitting next to her, as much as Susan disliked her, had lost her son.

How many people would be at his funeral? His colleagues, friends. She felt her stomach lurch: former lovers? Would Crystal Spiers have the audacity to turn up?

"Mrs Weatherton?"

Susan realised the undertaker wasn't talking to her mother-in-law anymore, but to her.

She blinked. "Sorry, I was miles away."

The undertaker smiled. She was a plump blonde woman in her mid thirties, who wore too much makeup and had a *mustn't smile properly, we're grieving* smile.

Susan swallowed. "Sorry. What is it?"

"We just need you to sign this form," the woman said.

Next to her, Rowena jabbed at a sheet of paper with a sharp pink fingernail.

Susan frowned. "What's it for?"

"It's a contract for our services."

Susan blinked back at the woman. How long had she been sitting here, not listening? They'd agreed all the details of Archie's funeral. The coffin, the hearse, the mourners' car, everything. It had all washed over her.

She should be a part of this, not just a willing bystander. But all she wanted to do now was put it all behind her. Get the funeral over with. Get on with grieving her dead husband. Start life with a new, living, one.

There would have to be a transition period, of course. Millie would need to get used to Tony, and if Susan was honest with herself, she did too. A week ago she'd been anxious to start her new life. But now she was a widow.

Susan shuddered at the word. *God, a widow.* It made her think of elderly women dressed in black, wide-brimmed hats and lacy veils. Queen Victoria, spending most of her life mourning Prince Albert.

That wasn't Susan. She wanted to live.

She nodded. "Sorry." Miles away, again.

She picked up the pen next to the contract and signed. She had no idea what she was agreeing to. But Rowena had lost her son. She didn't know her daughter-in-law was about to start a new life with another man. She didn't know her son had slept with dozens of women while he was married. She didn't need to know.

The undertaker gave her that smile again. She was being dismissed.

She followed her mother-in-law out of the building. They'd come in separate cars.

"You'll be alright on your own?" Rowena asked her.

Susan wondered if she should ask her the same thing.

"I'll be fine, I've got Fiona. Have you...?"

Rowena shrugged. "I'm used to being alone."

Susan felt a pang of guilt. She'd never got along with her mother-in-law, never sought out the woman's company. With Archie away so much, there had been little reason. High days and holidays, Millie's birthdays, Christmas.

She took a step towards her mother-in-law, and gave her a tentative hug, something she'd never done before. Something she might start doing now.

"Thank you for coming with me," she said. She meant it.

Rowena returned the hug, gave her a tight smile and walked to her car on clicking heels. Susan slid into her own car, feeling relief wash over her. At least that was done. All she needed to do now was get through the days before the funeral. Get through the funeral itself, and then decide what happened next.

She grabbed her phone and dialled: voicemail. It wasn't like him not to pick up.

"Tony, it's me. I've been to the undertakers with my mother-in-law. Call me, will you?"

This was the third message she'd left him this morning.

Had her becoming a widow scared him off? Did he

prefer her when she was unattainable, when she couldn't commit?

She shook her head. *Don't be stupid.* He'd proposed to her only two weeks ago. They were planning to start a life together. She took a shaky breath and clutched her wrist, checking her pulse. Racing.

She turned the key in the ignition, and headed for home.

CHAPTER SIXTY-ONE

Tina Abbott was already in Lesley's office when she arrived the next morning. Lesley walked around her to reach her desk. She wasn't sure how she felt about the PC waiting in here for her.

"Tina," she said as she sat down. "What can I do for you?"

Tina stood in front of the desk. Lesley didn't ask her to take a seat. She sensed that the younger woman felt more comfortable making this as uncomfortable as possible.

"I just wanted to say I'm sorry, Ma'am."

Lesley eyed her. "What for?"

Tina straightened. "Searching the shed yesterday, at the cottage."

Lesley leaned back in her chair.

She was hungry. She'd ferreted a stash of yoghurts away in her bag, they'd make a tolerable breakfast. She still hadn't found the fridge. In West Midlands, eating at her desk had been the norm. She'd sat through briefings grabbing the opportunity to refuel, and her colleagues were used to her snacking on chocolate bars, yoghurts and Pot Noodles.

But here, she hadn't seen anybody eat at their desk. They took lunch breaks, for God's sake.

She sighed. "Well, I guess there are two ways to look at it, Constable. Sit down."

Tina eased herself into a chair and pulled her feet underneath her. She sat straight, her body language stiff.

Lesley leaned across the desk. She counted on her fingers. "So first up, there's what you did. You snuck around behind the backs of the people that you were appointed FLO for. I did tell you to keep an eye on them. I did tell you to watch them. I didn't tell you to start searching the house."

"I'm sorry, Ma'am. I—"

Lesley nodded. "Was the shed door open?"

"It wasn't locked, Ma'am."

"No?"

"The padlock was loose, it was hanging off its bolt."

"That helps."

Lesley raised her second finger. "Secondly, you uncovered the murder weapon. Gail and her team had already been in there and they hadn't found it. Which means someone put it there after they searched. Figured that hiding it in plain sight would be the best way to go." She cocked her head. "If you hadn't gone back in there, we'd never have found it."

Tina relaxed a little.

"But I can't say that to the CPS," Lesley said.

Tina stiffened. "I really am sorry, Ma'am."

"Stop apologising, Constable. On balance, you did a good thing. Have we heard from Gail about fingerprints or DNA on that axe?"

Tina shrugged. "Not sure, Ma'am."

Lesley saw movement out of the corner of her eye. She looked past Tina to see Gail passing Dennis's desk. He turned to speak to her, but she ignored him, heading straight for Lesley's door.

"Looks like we're about to find out," she told PC Abbott.

PC Abbott stood as Gail entered. She shuffled away from the desk.

Lesley sighed. Tina needed a stronger backbone. She showed promise, but needed to stand up for herself.

Gail threw the door open, not pausing to knock. "I've got it."

"Got what?" Lesley asked.

Dennis and the two DC's crowded in behind Gail, almost shoving her into the room in their haste.

"What you got then, Gail?" Johnny asked.

Lesley gave him a *shush* look.

Gail approached Lesley's desk. She placed down a print-out. "The hammer's been wiped," she said. "No prints, nothing at all."

"But..." said Lesley.

"There's a small amount of blood on it. It doesn't match Laila or Archie."

Lesley blew out a breath. "Now we're talking. Do you know whose blood it is?"

"Not yet," said Gail. "But it's already at the lab. I'll update you as soon as we've got a match."

Lesley looked at Dennis. "Have we taken DNA swabs from Patrick and Crystal?"

He nodded. "CSIs took them when they searched the house."

"Good," Lesley replied. "I want to know the moment that result comes back."

"Of course," said Gail.

Mike stepped forward. "I've got some more information on the finances, boss."

"OK." Lesley lifted herself out of her chair and rounded the desk. She perched against its edge. "Make yourself comfortable, everyone. Let's hear this, Mike."

He went to the board. He wrote *University of Bristol* and *University of Bournemouth*, then drew a line between the two and from those to Crystal Spiers and Archie Weatherton's names.

"I've spoken to Tony Goodall," he said. "And to Archie Weatherton's boss at Bristol University. It looks like someone was embezzling money."

"From Bristol?" Lesley said.

"Possibly," he said. "Possibly from Bournemouth. They seem to have had a joint budget for the project. Both universities contributed and money came in from external sources as well."

"The administrator at Bournemouth said everything was in order," Dennis said.

Mike turned to him. "That's not what Tony Goodall reckons. He's been gathering evidence that a member of that team was not only embezzling money, but also falsifying records and submitting inaccurate returns to the admin team."

"Do we have any idea who this person is?" asked Lesley.

"DI Goodall isn't a hundred per cent certain yet," Mike said. "But he's working on it being Crystal Spiers. After all, it was her job to manage the budget."

"Archie had a role in it, too," Dennis said. "He was seeking funding, attending meetings."

"Only because there wasn't enough money," Mike said. "Tim Sidhu told us there was plenty of cash. But if Archie thought the budget was short, there's only one person who would have told him that, and that's Crystal Spiers. She was telling him they were short of cash and getting him to raise money from other sources. But at the same time, she was receiving money from Bournemouth University and Bristol too."

"And creaming it off for herself," Lesley added.

Mike nodded. "Tony Goodall's requested access to her bank accounts. The link with this murder case is what he reckons will get him a warrant."

Lesley chewed her nail. "Keep working on that. I want to know as soon as you find concrete evidence that Crystal was cooking the books."

"Boss?" Dennis raised a hand.

Lesley eyed him. "How many times do I have to tell you, Dennis?"

"Sorry, boss. Anyway, I checked the system. Patrick Donnelly..."

"What about him?"

"He doesn't have any convictions, but he was arrested for sexual assault twelve years ago."

"Where?" Lesley said.

"Dublin."

"Which is why we didn't know about it."

"I went back to find he'd worked at the university there. He was accused of assault by a student, but she dropped it before it went to court."

"Good work," said Lesley. "So we know he's got form."

"That doesn't mean he'd go so far as to kill somebody," Dennis said.

"Still," said Gail. "He was pretty pissed off with Laila after he assaulted her, and she managed to get away. Maybe he took that out on Archie, and then on her. Who knows what a man does when he gets jealous?"

Dennis gave Gail a look. She folded her arms across her chest and cocked her head, as if in challenge.

"OK," said Lesley. "So this makes it more credible that Patrick assaulted Laila. That doesn't necessarily give him motive to kill her, or to kill Archie. But with Crystal, we've got this embezzling. What if Archie found out, and she wanted to shut him up?"

"That doesn't explain Laila, though," said Johnny. "She was a junior member of the dig team, she was brought in just a few weeks ago. She wouldn't have known about the finances."

"She was sleeping with Archie," said Mike. "Pillow talk."

"Good point," said Lesley. "Put it on the board."

Mike wrote *embezzlement* and *fraud* on the board. He linked those words to Tony Goodall's name as well as to Crystal's, with a question mark.

Lesley looked at his notes. "I'm concerned about the link between DI Goodall and Archie Weatherton. On the one hand, we've got him investigating Crystal Spiers. Who years ago had an affair with the husband of the woman that *he's* now having an affair with. I want to speak to his boss in Bristol. Dennis, get me some contact details."

"Boss."

Tina was standing at the back, shifting from foot to foot. "What about the weapon?"

"It's not much use to us," muttered Dennis. "Not with the way it was found."

"It's a whole lot of use to us," Lesley said.

He stared at her. "If PC Abbott had just followed procedure—"

Lesley thumped the desk to stop him. "Now is not the place to discuss ifs and buts and might have been's. We have the weapon, we'll make use of it."

He grunted.

"The lab's already on it," said Gail. She checked her phone. "Nothing yet."

"Keep tugging at those threads." Lesley gave Dennis a look. "All of them. I want to know as soon as we get anything more."

CHAPTER SIXTY-TWO

THE TEAM FILED out of Lesley's office.

"Not you, Dennis," she said as he made for the door.

"Boss?"

"Just a quick chat."

"Certainly."

He exchanged glances with Johnny, who shuffled to the door. When the others had left, Dennis closed the door and approached Lesley's desk.

"Boss? I already apologised..."

She shook her head. "I think we should just forget that ever happened, don't you?"

He smiled. "Thanks. What did the Super say?"

"That's my business, Dennis. But don't worry about it. You came to see me. You found my house. You followed me to the pub. You were obviously pretty keen on apologising. I'm assuming that means you truly regret what you did."

He nodded.

"And that you won't do it again."

He looked down. "That depends."

She laughed. "Oh, on what?"

He looked at her. "If I'm worried that your health is impacting on your ability to do your job, and on your welfare, I can't ignore it."

"You're worried about me?"

"You might say that."

"Despite the fact that I'm a mardy old bitch who swears too much and refuses to work the way you want to?"

"I think you're very good at your job, no matter how much you try and hide it."

Lesley was as surprised as if he'd slapped her.

"Well, thank you, Dennis. I'll take the compliment. But I do want to talk to you about the way you addressed PC Abbott in that meeting."

His face darkened. "She did an illegal search, boss."

"She also uncovered a crucial piece of evidence. And the shed door wasn't secured."

"She's not trying to make out that she spotted the axe through the shed door when she happened to be passing it?"

"She wouldn't insult my intelligence, nor I yours. But if needs must, that's what we'll say. Or something along those lines."

"With respect, boss. I thought you were all about doing things by the book."

"I am. This is a final resort, Dennis. I don't want to use this evidence. I wish I damn well could, but I can't. It's the most important item we've got and because of the way it was found, we can't give it to the CPS. But that doesn't mean it won't help our investigation. If Gail finds DNA on that axe…"

Dennis shrugged. "Can't deny that. I just think PC

Abbott should have been told not to go poking her nose into the investigation."

"By whom?"

He reddened. "Ma'am."

She let it drop. "I see it differently. I see it as a young constable using her initiative. I see it as a woman who went over and above to help us crack this investigation."

He stared at her. "You're joking?"

"No, Sergeant. PC Abbott shows potential. She's keen, she's bright, and she's damn good with the public."

His left eye twitched.

"I said 'damn', Dennis. I could have said 'bloody', I could have said worse. But I didn't. I said 'damn'. Can we compromise on that at least?"

He shuffled his shoulders. He was itching to look back at his desk, where the swear box sat in proud isolation. She wouldn't be putting any coins in it. But at the same time, she didn't want to offend him.

"I'll try not to blaspheme," she said. "I can't promise, but I'll do my best. And I'll keep the swearing to the kind of words you might use in front of your Great Auntie Mildred."

"Not *my* Great Auntie Mildred," he muttered.

"You've got a Great Auntie Mildred?"

"I was talking figuratively," he replied.

She laughed. "Me too. Right, come on then. We've got work to do. Two suspects, one weapon. Let's narrow it down, eh?"

Lesley's phone vibrated on the desk. She glanced at the display. "That'll be all, thank you Dennis."

He looked down. Even if he could see the name upside down, he wouldn't recognise it.

He left the room and closed the door. As he approached

the bank of desks, the two DCs looked up. Johnny spoke to him. Dennis shook his head. He picked up the swear box, opened a desk drawer and placed it inside. He closed the drawer, saying something curt to Johnny.

Lesley smiled. She answered the phone. "Zoe, good to hear from you."

"I've got some information on your DCI Mackie."

Lesley crossed to the door of her office and made sure it was firmly closed. She walked back to the window and stood against it, anxious for nobody in the next room to overhear her.

She cupped her hand around the receiver. "Go on."

"OK," Zoe said. "He was a DCI in Dorset Police from September 2003 to just two months ago. He retired early, age of fifty-eight."

Lesley raised an eyebrow. "How did he manage that?"

"Not sure yet. I can keep digging if you want?"

"Don't draw attention to yourself."

"I won't."

"No idea why he retired early?"

"Not yet. But what I can tell you is that within a week of retiring, he died suddenly."

"Ill health retirement?" Lesley asked.

"No," Zoe replied. "He killed himself."

"What?"

Lesley ran over the few conversations she'd had about DCI Mackie since joining the Dorset force. Nobody had mentioned suicide.

"Maybe he was terminally ill?" Zoe suggested. "And decided to end it himself before it got too bad."

Lesley leaned against the cold glass at the window. "Poor man."

Suicide was frowned upon amongst police officers. They saw at close hand the impact it had on the people who discovered the body and those closest to the deceased. She wondered what level of desperation would have made DCI Mackie want to inflict that on the professionals who would be left to clean up the mess.

"So where was he found?" Lesley asked.

"Near Swanage, on the beach. Below the cliffs."

"He threw himself off a cliff." Lesley shuddered.

"Yeah."

She looked out through the glass separating her office from her team. DCI Mackie had only been dead for two months. She didn't know how close they'd been to him, but they would still be grieving.

Dennis was at his desk, talking on his mobile phone. He'd found it so hard to accept her. Maybe it wasn't because she was a woman, or because she was from the city. Or even because she swore.

It was because she wasn't DCI Mackie.

"Thanks for this, Zoe," she said. "I appreciate it."

"Do you need me to do any more digging?" Zoe asked.

"Not right now," Lesley replied. "Let's just leave it."

CHAPTER SIXTY-THREE

JADE FORD GOT off the bus and yanked up the hood of her hoody, wishing she'd worn something better than a denim jacket over it. Did it always rain in this godforsaken place?

She'd been warm on the bus, at least. The heating had been right underneath her seat, blasting through her legs and making her sweat. Her limbs felt stiff after being cooped up on a total of three buses. Five hours, it had taken.

She was in a square. A monument in front of her, the castle to the side.

She checked Google Maps. Laila had lived up to the left, in a row of cottages. Jade sniffed. She didn't like the country-side. Her sister loved it, yomping around in muddy boots, digging up pieces of history.

But Jade was a city girl. She'd moved to London after graduating, and hardly spoke to her family these days. But Laila had sent her the parcel that was burning a hole in her rucksack, and she needed to know why.

She hauled her way along the narrow lane, her legs stiff.

The houses were tiny, with low windows and doors made for gnomes. God knows how people lived here.

At last Jade found the right address.

A man was outside, unlocking the front door. He held a blue and white golfing umbrella which he shook out before stepping inside. He was old, older than her dad.

Was this the right house?

She double checked then walked to the house, her senses tingling. She knocked.

She pulled her shoulders back, trying not to look as if she'd spent five hours sitting on buses. Trying not to look like she'd barely slept for the last two nights.

The door opened. The man wore a threadbare grey jumper and a pair of jeans with mud on the hems.

"Who are you?" he snapped.

She stared back at him. "My name's Jade. I'm Laila's sister."

His nostrils flared. She felt a shiver run down her back. *Dirty old man.* She knew the type.

Laila had told her about him, and now here she was, turning up on his doorstep. Was this wise?

You can do this.

"Can I come in?"

He raised an eyebrow. "You're her sister?"

She nodded, slowly. "Please, let me in."

He stood back, not leaving quite enough space for her to pass him.

She shrunk away as she squeezed through. If it wasn't for her damn rucksack, she'd have turned her back to him. But she didn't want him anywhere near that.

The parcel inside it was like a beacon, itching for her to

open it again. She'd read the contents. She'd called Laila about it.

But it had been too late. And none of it made any sense.

Bringing it here might be a bad idea, but it was all she had.

CHAPTER SIXTY-FOUR

Tina Abbott sat at her desk, thanking the heavens that Lesley Clarke was the forgiving type.

The DCI had given her paperwork to run through. She hadn't kicked her off the case, despite everything. She'd been taken off the FLO assignment and she wasn't exactly a core part of the team. But here she was, still working through evidence, still involved.

She liked the DCI. The woman was abrupt, her language made DS Frampton bristle. Tina enjoyed that. It was like a breath of fresh air in the office, better than DCI Mackie. He'd looked at Tina in a way that made her flesh crawl. He'd made comments about the way her uniform fitted. She shuddered at the memory.

She opened another file, evidence that had been sent through from one of the universities, Bournemouth or Bristol. She was losing track. But DI Goodall had shared his files with her, she'd managed to win his trust.

She scanned the document in front of her and sighed. Nothing useful. She closed it down and opened another.

Three documents came and went. Nothing relevant, or at least nothing she could see. Maybe she should talk to one of the DCs. Check she wasn't missing something obvious. But they were busy, each assigned their roles. The DCI had made it clear what people were supposed to be doing.

Mike was working on some of the documents, too. She'd conferred with him before she started. But Mike was OK. He wasn't old-fashioned like DS Frampton, or standoffish like Johnny. He was a misfit too.

She opened a fifth document and ran her eyes down the screen.

She stopped. She scrolled back up again.

Tina shook her head. She put the document to one side and opened another one. They were similar. She brought the two up next to each other and flicked her gaze from side to side.

She opened a third.

This one corroborated the first two. She felt her breath catch in her throat. She looked over at Mike, who was on the phone. She glanced over towards Dennis Frampton. The DS was looking at her, a question in his eyes. Tina felt her limbs stiffen.

"Sarge," she said. "I think I've got something."

CHAPTER SIXTY-FIVE

"You've come a long way," the man said.

Jade shrugged.

"Her funeral won't be till next week, the police have still got her body."

"I didn't come for her funeral."

He sat down in an armchair. It was green and threadbare, and it sagged as he sat.

Jade stood behind the sofa. She eased the rucksack off her back and held it in front of her, like it was made of precious metal.

"So what are you here for, then?" the man asked.

"What's your name?" she asked him.

"Patrick," he said. He had an Irish accent. "And you're Jade. You don't look like her, you know."

Another shrug. She wasn't about to tell him they had different dads.

"She was pretty, your sister," he said.

I know, she thought. *She told me what you did to her.*

The man leaned back in his chair and plunged his hands into his pockets.

"You gonna tell me what you're here for, then?"

"I'm tired," she said.

"Well sit the fuck down."

She bristled at the harsh language. "I wouldn't mind a cup of tea."

He barked out a laugh. "So you turn up out of nowhere. A week early, at least, for the funeral, and you want me to make you a cup of tea?" He gestured toward the kitchen. "The kettle's through there."

Clutching the rucksack to her chest, she shuffled through to the kitchen. Making herself a drink might calm her nerves. It might steady her unease at being alone with this man.

What had she been thinking? She should have gone to the university, she should have contacted one of Laila's bosses. But they didn't know about Laila's background. Not a graduate, but an undergraduate. And one who'd dropped out, at that.

She jumped as she heard the front door to the cottage open. Voices, a man and a woman. She stepped back into the living room, the rucksack still in her arms.

A woman stood in the doorway. She had short, messed up hair and her trousers were covered in mud.

She looked at Jade. "Who the hell are you?"

CHAPTER SIXTY-SIX

THE TEAM STOOD in front of Lesley's desk, their body language itchy and impatient. They were desperate to get out there, to make an arrest.

"You've got enough, boss," Dennis said.

Lesley shook her head.

PC Abbott stood next to her, her fingers brushing the desk. She'd printed out three documents and brought them in, Dennis trotting along beside her. Lesley was pleased with the young woman. She'd messed up at the cottage, the illegal search. But now, she'd made up for it.

Lesley spread the documents out on her desk. "It's not enough," she said. "You know what I said. Dot the I's, cross the T's. We need everything. You guys know the leads you should be following. Mike, the funding. Dennis, the assault. Johnny, talk to Tony Goodall in Bristol. See what he makes of this."

Dennis sighed. "It's plenty. I admit that—"

She raised a hand. "I'll tell you when it's plenty."

"Boss?" Johnny said.

"Get on with it then," she said. "I need to talk to the Super."

CHAPTER SIXTY-SEVEN

Susan sat down on her bed as the call was picked up.

"Tony," she breathed. "I've been trying to get hold of you."

"Sorry, sweetie. Busy at work. How are you?"

"Coping," she said.

Millie was downstairs with Fiona, the two of them making pancakes together. She'd seen Millie smile for the first time since the news about her dad.

She clutched the phone closer to her ear. "I miss you."

"I know, Susie, but you asked me to stay away."

"I told them about you, remember? I don't need you to steer clear anymore."

"It's complicated, love," he said. "And besides..."

"Besides, what?" she asked him.

He took a breath. "There's something I haven't been telling you. Now isn't the time. I'll come round later, yeah? We'll talk tonight."

"No," she said. "What is it?"

"It's a case I'm working on. It involves... Nothing. You don't need all this."

"Tony." Her heart felt heavy. "If there's a problem, I want to know about it. I'm fed up with people tiptoeing around me. Fiona looks at me like I might break."

"But you might," he said.

"I was going to divorce him, wasn't I? He was unfaithful for years. Why should I be grieving for him?"

His voice softened. "You are, Susie. Despite what we have, you're allowed to grieve for him."

"Tell me about the case," she said.

"I can't, love. It's confidential."

"So why did you raise it?"

"We're nearly done with it. Once it's over, I'll tell you."

"OK." She sniffed.

She heard Millie's voice coming up the stairs. "Mummy! Pancakes!" Susan felt her heart lift.

"I'll speak to you later," she said. "Love you."

"I love you too, Susie."

CHAPTER SIXTY-EIGHT

DETECTIVE SUPERINTENDENT CARPENTER gazed at Lesley over his desk. This was the third time she'd been in here and she still didn't feel comfortable.

The man leaned back in his chair, making it swivel from side to side.

"So you want a warrant," he said.

"I'm not sure we've got enough yet. But my team is still working on it."

"What angles are they pursuing?"

"We're looking for more paperwork, more documentary evidence," she said. "Dennis is looking into the suspect's past and Mike has been liaising with the fraud team in Bristol."

"So you're still investigating both of them?"

"We can't rule out the possibility they both might be involved, Sir."

"Hmm." He looked down at the documents she'd placed on his desk. "But you've got one who you prefer?"

She nodded. "I do, Sir."

"Do you think you've got grounds for arrest?"

Her head was throbbing. She'd taken painkillers, but they'd hardly made a dent. "Not quite, Sir."

"So what are you doing here?"

"I want to be ready. If one of them killed Laila and Archie, the other one is at risk."

"They've been at risk for days," he said. "What's all the urgency now?"

"When you finally uncover the evidence you need, Sir, I believe it's prudent to act quickly."

He snorted. "Prudent to act quickly? No, Lesley. You need more. Get back to me when you've got hard evidence."

She licked her lips. "In the meantime, I'll head over to the cottage."

He raised an eyebrow. "You won't be making an arrest."

"No, Sir. But it might help if I speak to them."

"Very well. But you be careful, won't you?"

She nodded. "Of course, Sir."

CHAPTER SIXTY-NINE

"Answer the question, then," the woman snapped. She took off her coat and hung it on a hook next to the door. She frowned as it brushed Patrick's umbrella and water dripped onto her sleeve.

Jade clutched the rucksack closer to her.

"Who are you?" The woman looked angry.

"She's Laila's sister," Patrick said.

The woman's eyes narrowed. "Sister?"

Jade nodded. "I'm Jade. You must be Crystal."

"Are you here for the funeral?

Jade shook her head. "That's not until next week."

"So what are you here for? You can't get her stuff, the police still have her room cordoned off." Crystal's gaze went upwards.

Jade placed the rucksack on the floor. She bent to it and unzipped it slowly. She pulled out the envelope Laila had sent her.

"I wanted to ask you about this," she said.

The woman stared at the envelope, her face pale.

"What's that?" Patrick asked. He stood up and approached Jade.

She shrank back, holding onto the envelope. The rucksack leaned against the wall.

"Documents," she said. "Laila sent them to me."

Crystal's eyes narrowed. "Where did she get them?"

Jade shrugged. "I don't know. She told me to keep them safe. They make no sense."

Crystal stared at the envelope in Jade's arms. "Give them to me."

Jade stared back at her. She clutched the envelope tighter. "I just want to ask you..."

Patrick took a step closer. He smelled of garlic and cigarette smoke.

"Hand it over," he said. "It belongs to the dig, yeah?"

Jade looked from him to the woman. "Laila sent it to me, so it belongs to me."

Crystal's gaze was level. "I'm the manager of this project. I suggest you give it to me." She licked her lips. "I can help you understand what it means and why Laila thought it was important."

Jade loosened her grip on the envelope. The woman's eyes narrowed. She put out her hand, like she was dealing with a wild animal that might bite.

Jade grabbed the rucksack. She plunged the envelope inside and zipped it up.

"It's OK," she said. "I'll talk to the university."

CHAPTER SEVENTY

LESLEY SPED ALONG THE A351, Dennis beside her in the passenger seat.

"It's forty miles per hour along here, boss," he said, his voice thin.

"It's an emergency."

"But I thought you didn't get a warrant?"

"Not yet."

They overtook a line of traffic, Dennis shrinking back in his seat as Lesley floored the accelerator. He was breathing heavily.

Oh, calm down, she thought. It wasn't like there was much traffic along here. She might be missing Birmingham, but getting to and from a crime scene was a damn sight easier in Dorset.

"OK," she said. "When we get there, we need to present a united front."

"I don't know what we're here for anyway, boss. How can I do anything else?"

She glanced at him. "You've seen those documents. You know what my suspicions are."

He nodded. "Yes, but you said it's not enough."

"Once we have the DNA from the axe. Then we'll have enough."

"But you know that isn't evidential."

"It'll give us what we need."

They approached the castle and she slowed, along with Dennis's breathing.

"I'm damned if I'm parking in that bloody car park again," she said.

Dennis drew in a breath, but didn't say anything.

"Sorry, Dennis." She rolled her eyes. "I'd rather not park in that car park again. Is that better?"

He nodded. "There. There's a spot in The Square."

He pointed to a blue Mini pulling out of a parking space in front of the pub that Patrick Donnelly frequented.

"Perfect," she said.

As she eased into the parking spot, her phone rang. It was Mike.

"I got an email," he said.

"From Tony Goodall?"

"No boss, from Laila's sister. She sent it half an hour ago. Her name's Jade Ford."

Lesley glanced at Dennis. "I'm putting this on speakerphone."

"Boss," Mike said.

"Carry on."

"So it looks like Laila sent her some documents," Mike said. "She said Patrick Donnelly was looking for them in Archie's stuff. Laila found it the night before she died, and she posted it to her sister."

"Shit." Lesley slumped back in her seat. "And?"

"It's evidence that Crystal Spiers was embezzling money from the dig accounts."

Lesley and Dennis locked eyes. Still on the phone to Mike, she flung open the car door and hurried towards the cottage. Dennis was right behind her.

"Forward it to me," she said to Mike. "I want to check it before I go in there."

"Will do."

CHAPTER SEVENTY-ONE

JADE SLUNG her rucksack over her shoulder and made for the door.

The woman, Crystal, stood in front of her, her legs planted firmly.

"You're not going anywhere."

"I'm sorry," Jade said. "I came to the wrong place. I won't bother you any more."

Crystal put out her hand. "Give it to me."

Jade matched the woman's body language. "It's mine. Laila sent it to me."

Crystal gestured with her fingers. "Uh-uh."

Jade stepped to one side, hoping to squeeze past the woman. But Crystal moved with her, blocking her way.

Jade moved forward, pushing Crystal towards the door. The woman shoved back. Patrick advanced behind her. She was cornered.

Jade glanced at the umbrella Patrick had hung up. Crystal followed her eyes. She laughed and grabbed it.

Jade bristled. "What? You're going to hit me with that?"

Crystal lifted it.

Patrick stumbled into Jade. "Crystal, what are you doing?"

Crystal turned to him, her eyes wild. "We can't let her go! That envelope she's got in her rucksack, it's mine."

"What are you on about?" he replied.

Crystal stared at him.

Now was Jade's chance. She dived past Crystal, pushing towards the door. She grabbed the handle. She felt Crystal's hand on her arm, pulling her back.

"No, you fucking well don't, lady."

Crystal raised the umbrella and hit Jade across the head. Jade clapped her hand to her eye. She'd hit her with the tip.

There was thumping at the door. "Police! Let us in!"

Jade shoved past Crystal, half blinded, and crashed into the door. "Help! Let me out!"

CHAPTER SEVENTY-TWO

DENNIS MATCHED Lesley's pace as she sped along West Street.

"If Mike's right," she breathed, "then Patrick could be next."

He panted, struggling to keep up. His face was red, his forehead damp.

At last they reached the front door. Lesley hammered on it. "Police! Let us in!" She could hear voices inside, shouting. A scream?

She turned to Dennis. "What the...?"

He gave her a worried look. "We need to get in."

"That's a woman. That's two women!"

Dennis pushed past her and thumped on the door. "Police! Open up!"

There was another crash. The door flew open. Lesley almost fell inside. She grabbed Dennis's arm to stop herself.

A woman was sitting with her back to the doorframe. She had short red hair and she was huddled over a rucksack. Her face was bleeding.

Who?

Lesley looked past the woman. Crystal was running for the kitchen.

"Stop!" Lesley shouted.

"I'll get her." Dennis ran ahead, squeezing past Patrick Donnelly to follow Crystal. Lesley bent to the young woman.

"Are you alright? What happened to you?"

"She..." The woman pointed towards where Crystal had gone. "She killed my sister."

Dennis reappeared, Crystal in front of him. She wore handcuffs and an expression that could melt iron.

"Bitch." Patrick, standing next to the easy chair he'd sat in so many times, gave her a kick.

"Don't," Lesley warned him.

He glared at her. "You gonna stop me?"

Lesley turned back to the woman slumped against the front door. She was sitting up, her hands dabbing at the wound on her face.

"It's alright," Lesley said. "Don't touch it. Dennis, call an ambulance."

Dennis was struggling with Crystal, who was trying to get as far from Patrick as she could in the confined space.

"I've got enough on my plate here, boss."

Lesley grabbed her mobile and made the call. Then she squatted to bring herself level with the woman.

"Are you hurt?"

The woman nodded, her eyes rolling in her head. She dabbed at the skin above her eye; the bleeding had slowed. "I'm fine. Where's...?" She searched the area around them, then reached down and grabbed a red and blue rucksack. She pulled it to her.

"Who are you?" Lesley asked her.

"Jade," the woman croaked. "Jade Ford."

"Laila's sister."

Jade nodded. "Who are you?"

"DCI Clarke," Lesley replied. "We're investigating your sister's death."

The woman opened the rucksack, her fingers shaking. She pulled out a brown envelope.

"You sent this to us," Lesley said.

"Just in case."

Lesley took it from her. She pulled out a stack of papers.

"What's that, boss?" Dennis called across the room. He'd got Crystal under control with Patrick's help. Patrick sat on the sofa, panting.

Crystal stood next to Dennis, occasionally tugging at the handcuffs. He growled at her every time she did. Lesley hadn't thought him capable of growling.

"It's the evidence we need, Dennis," Lesley said.

"The email Mike told us about?"

She showed him the file. "Laila hid it, she sent it to Jade here."

"She found it in Archie's stuff," Jade said. "She was worried someone might hurt her to get it."

Lesley's heart felt heavy. "When did she send it?"

Jade shrugged. "I got it the day she died."

Lesley exchanged glances with Dennis. The last thing Laila had done before she was attacked had been to send this evidence away. To put it somewhere safe. She'd thought she was protecting herself, but it was too late.

Poor kid.

Lesley's phone rang. *Not now.*

It was Gail.

"Tell me it's the DNA."

"We don't have a match yet, but I can tell you it's a woman."

Lesley felt satisfaction wash over her. She turned to Crystal. "Crystal Spiers, I'm arresting you for murder."

CHAPTER SEVENTY-THREE

Lesley threw her bag down on the desk and sat heavily in her chair. She'd stayed at the cottage until Jade had been taken away in an ambulance and a squad car had arrived for Crystal. Patrick had been brought in in another car and was giving a statement to Dennis.

She turned in her chair to look at the board. She'd placed it back behind her desk, shielded from the road outside. Had it helped? It had been Jade's email that had done it, combined with the axe.

She heard the door open and turned.

"Sir." She stood up and smoothed down her skirt. Her hair was out of place and her blouse had come loose.

Carpenter approached her, hand extended. "I hear congratulations are in order."

She swallowed and took his hand. "Thank you, Sir."

"You did well."

"We didn't get that warrant, Sir."

He raised an eyebrow. "From what I've heard, she was in

the middle of attacking somebody when you got there. You prevented another crime, potentially another murder."

She felt a chill run down her. "Sir."

They hadn't even known about the existence of Jade Ford, let alone that the young woman had come to Dorset and put herself at risk. What kind of sisterly bond made a person do that?

The Super dropped her hand. "You've made a good start," he said. "Despite everything."

"Despite everything, Sir?"

"You're supposed to be getting some rest and recuperation." He chuckled. "Mind you, I want you to work hard while you're here."

She smiled. "I can do that, Sir."

Working hard would be her rest and recuperation. She didn't need to be mollycoddled, or taken care of. She just needed to get on with the damn job and put the memories of the bomb attack behind her.

CHAPTER SEVENTY-FOUR

"Come on Millie, we'll be late."

Susan beckoned to her daughter, who was dragging on her coat. They had a meeting with the school, aimed at helping Millie settle back in. She wouldn't be returning until next week. But in the meantime, they'd assigned her a support worker. Someone to keep an eye on her and watch out for her welfare. And they had an appointment with the woman this afternoon.

She pulled open the front door and turned to see Tony walking up the path. Her face froze.

He smiled. "Susie." His smile dropped. "I've got news."

"I already know," she said.

"Dorset Police called you?"

She nodded, then glanced at Millie. "Not here."

He reached out a hand and stroked the side of her face. She let him. Let Millie see. Just a stroke.

"I've got something I need to tell you," he said.

"You're involved, aren't you? They brought you into their investigation?"

"It's more complicated than that." He looked down. His feet shifted on the path, his body language uneasy.

"Oh my God." Susan stared at him, her body hollowing out.

He'd only been with her because of the case. She'd been a route to Crystal.

"I thought we had something," she said.

"What do you mean? We still do."

"I've read about officers like you. They groom a woman. To get closer to the case."

His jaw hung open. Tears welled in his eyes. "I can't believe you think that of me."

"You didn't?"

"No." He grabbed her hand. "Susie, I had no idea. I didn't know Crystal Spiers was working with your husband. I only found out two days ago. If I'd known, I would have told you."

"Oh."

"We're still engaged, aren't we?"

"Shh." Millie was behind her, muttering to herself. Susan beckoned to her daughter. "Come on, Mils."

She turned back to Tony. "Can this wait? We've got a meeting."

"I love you, Susie," he said. "I love Millie, too. We can be a family. I don't expect things to happen as fast as they have been. But I can wait."

She nodded. She was crying too.

"We'll be OK, Susie. Millie will be OK. I'll do whatever it takes."

She took his hand. "So will I, Tony."

CHAPTER SEVENTY-FIVE

Lesley walked into the office, feeling like it was her first day all over again.

She'd spent the weekend trying to make a home out of her cottage. She'd wanted to go back to Birmingham, but Terry hadn't answered her calls and neither had Sharon. Part of her was tempted to go anyway, to confront him and to seek her out.

But her daughter needed space. And she didn't want to face her husband right now. The letter from the solicitor hadn't arrived yet, but when it did, she'd be ready.

She walked past the bank of desks where her team sat. Dennis sat back in his chair as she passed. "Morning, boss."

"Morning, Dennis." She noticed the swear box was still gone. She looked at the space where it had been and raised an eyebrow.

He smiled. "In the drawer, boss."

"Good."

She looked across at the two constables. "Busy?"

"Paperwork, boss," said Mike. "You know how it is."

She laughed. "I damn well do."

Dennis opened his mouth to speak, but then closed it again.

She continued into her office. Dennis followed her, closing the door behind him.

"Everything alright?" she asked.

The board was still behind her desk, but it had been cleaned. The photos of Laila, Archie, Crystal and Patrick: all gone.

"Who did this?" she asked.

"PC Abbott, boss."

Lesley looked out through the glass. PC Abbott was nowhere to be seen. She would be out in her squad car, doing what uniformed constables normally did.

"I want to add her to the team," she told him.

"We've already got enough guys."

"That's exactly it, Dennis. Guys. She brings some balance to the team."

"You can't recruit her just because she's a woman."

She gave him a look. "This is not me being politically correct, Sergeant. This is me identifying an officer who can contribute something to this team. I'm not saying there's anything wrong with those two DCs out there, they're good coppers. But she can bring something else."

His face darkened. "Not my decision, I imagine."

"I've already spoken to Carpenter," she said. "Don't worry, she's not going to be a detective, not taking the exam. But she will be working with us in a support capacity."

He sniffed. "I'll tell the guys."

"You do that," she said.

He went to the door.

"What's next?" she asked him. "The board's empty."

"We need to coordinate with DI Goodall's team in Bristol, pull the two cases together. Make sure it's all tight enough for the CPS."

She nodded. "Glad to hear it." That was the stuff she liked. Building a case, stacking up evidence, making the CPS's job as easy as she could.

She sat down at her desk. She'd brought a mug from the cottage and a photo of Sharon. She could make herself at home here. The cottage showed potential. It had a damp problem and was smaller than she'd like, but there were flowers outside the front door. Weeds too, but she could dig those up. And here in this office... The building might look like a motorway service station, but at least she had plenty of light, and a new team.

She looked up at Dennis. "Let me know if anything comes up, won't you?"

He nodded. "Yes, boss."

CHAPTER SEVENTY-SIX

Lesley finished wiping down her kitchen cabinets. They'd been sticky and smelt of onions, but now they gleamed. She closed the final door and stood back to survey her work.

It had been years since Lesley had spring cleaned. And now the cupboards needed filling. She hadn't bought food yet, nothing more than some more Mars Bars and a couple of Pot Noodles. She was hungry. She'd go to the pub.

She closed her front door, turned back to survey the cottage and noticed more weeds growing out of a crack in the paving. She sighed. At least her front garden was small, it wouldn't take much effort to keep it neat.

She strolled along the narrow lane towards the pub, nodding at a couple that she passed on the way. She picked up her phone and dialled Sharon again. As she pushed open the door to the pub, her daughter picked up. Lesley swallowed, surprised and relieved.

"Mum?"

"Sharon, love." Lesley hovered by the door to the pub,

not wanting anybody to hear her conversation. "I've been trying to get you all week."

"Sorry, mum. I was a bit freaked out. Dad told me you ran off."

"I ran off for a reason."

"Yeah. I know about that."

"You know?"

"Dad told me. Julieta, her name is. She seems alright, but..."

"But," Lesley said.

"Are you coming home?"

Lesley looked further into the pub. Elsa was behind the bar, sharing a joke with a customer. The place was fuller than it had been last Monday night, and felt livelier. Sunshine slanted through the windows and the place felt cheerful.

She swallowed. "I'm sorry, Sharon. I'll come home at the weekend. But I've got to stay here for six months, it's in my contract."

A pause. "Can I come and see you at the weekend instead?"

"Haven't you got studying to do?"

"I can get the train down on Friday after school and then head back on Sunday. I can study on the train. I want to see you, Mum."

Lesley softened. "Of course. I'll check the train times."

"I've already looked. I'll be getting into Bournemouth station at six twenty."

"Perfect."

Lesley glanced at the bar. Elsa was holding up a wine glass, a question in her eyes. Lesley nodded.

"I'll see you on Friday, love," she said.

"Looking forward to it."

Lesley walked to the bar. Elsa filled the glass and handed it over. Her hand brushed Lesley's as she did so.

Lesley felt a jolt run through her body. She looked at Elsa, startled by her reaction. She'd been attracted to women before meeting Terry, but she hadn't thought about it in years.

Elsa gave Lesley a smile, her eyes dancing. Lesley returned it.

"You look happy," Elsa said. "It's the first time I've seen you like that." Elsa leaned on the bar and looked into Lesley's eyes.

Lesley leaned in. She could feel Elsa's breath on her skin. She patted her phone in her pocket.

"I think I could be, you know," she said. "I think I finally might manage it."

CHAPTER SEVENTY-SEVEN

Lesley stood at the edge of the Bristol churchyard, watching the mourners emerging from the church.

Susan Weatherton was surrounded by family. A tall blonde woman Lesley recognised as her sister, huddling over her. A little girl, the daughter, gripped her hand tightly, her face running with tears.

Lesley felt herself soften as she watched. She pulled back behind a tree, anxious for no one to see her. As she did so, she became aware of someone standing behind her.

She turned. "Dennis?"

He gave her a tight smile. "I thought you'd be here, boss."

"I just wanted to..."

He nodded. "I know."

It was common for police officers to attend funerals, or at least to lurk around the periphery. Sometimes the killer attended. Perhaps because they were a friend or family member, or perhaps because they wanted to bring themselves closer to the consequences of their crime.

But Crystal Spiers, Lesley knew, was in a police cell. She would be charged today.

She walked away from the church, keeping step with Dennis.

"So what brings you over here?" she asked.

"I've got a meeting with DI Goodall," he said. "Part of the wrap up."

She nodded. "I'll come with you."

"Boss."

They walked quietly back to her car. His was parked right behind her. The hearse was further along the road, with the black vehicle Susan had arrived in. Lesley spotted Tony Goodall standing next to a car beyond it. She gave him a small wave which he returned.

She got into her car and opened the window as Dennis bent to speak to her. "I'll see you at the Fraud Office, boss."

She nodded. "Can I ask you something?"

"You can."

"DCI Mackie," she said. "What happened to him?"

His face tightened. "He died. I don't like to talk about it."

She looked at him. "How did he die?"

"I don't like to talk about it."

"I heard he killed himself."

A shiver ran through Dennis's body. "Please."

"OK." She gave him a tight smile. "Sorry to remind you of unpleasant memories. See you shortly." She pushed the button to close the window.

DCI Mackie had supposedly thrown himself off a cliff just north of Swanage. But she'd had a call from Zoe that morning. Ever tenacious, Zoe had been hunting through records. She'd discovered that DCI Mackie had shown no signs of depression, had not been in any trouble at work, and had been looking forward to retirement. He'd even booked a cruise for the summer.

So why would a man who'd booked a cruise and hadn't been to his doctor about depression or any other illness, throw himself off a cliff?

Lesley started the car. She looked in her rear view mirror to see Dennis talking to Tony Goodall.

Susan came out of the churchyard, her daughter still gripping her hand and the other mourners behind her. She looked across the road at Tony, gave him a nod and then walked in the other direction. Lesley wondered how much Susan knew about Tony's investigation into Crystal. Would their relationship work out, or would it be forever tainted by how it had begun? It wasn't her business.

She checked her rear view mirror and pulled out. She'd sit in on this meeting, but she'd let Dennis take the lead.

After that, she wanted to talk to Zoe. She was still concerned about DCI Mackie. If her predecessor had died in suspicious circumstances, did that put her at risk?

Stop it, she told herself. *You're not in the West Midlands now.*

She'd moved here for peace and quiet. No more conspiracies, no more corruption. The quiet life. "A quiet life indeed," she muttered as she drove across the suspension bridge, wondering if she'd ever get used to it.

———

I hope you enjoyed *The Corfe Castle Murders*. Do you want to know more about DCI Mackie's death? The prequel novella, *The Ballard Down Murder*, is free from my book club at rachelmclean.com/ballard. *Thanks, Rachel McLean.*

READ A FREE PREQUEL NOVELLA, THE BALLARD DOWN MURDER

How did DCI Mackie die?

DS Dennis Frampton is getting used to life without his old boss DCI Mackie, and managing to hide how much he hates being in charge of Dorset's Major Crimes Investigation Team. Above all, he must ensure no one knows he's still seeking Mackie's advice on cases.

But then Mackie doesn't show up to a meeting, and a body is found below the cliffs a few miles away.

When Dennis discovers the body is his old friend and mentor, his world is thrown upside down. Did Mackie kill himself, or was he pushed? Is Dennis's new boss trying to hush things up? And can Dennis and the CSIs trust the evidence?

Find out by reading *The Ballard Down Murder* for FREE at rachelmclean.com/ballard.

READ THE DORSET CRIME SERIES

The Corfe Castle Murders, Dorset Crime Book 1

The Clifftop Murders, Dorset Crime Book 2

The Island Murders, Dorset Crime Book 3

The Monument Murders, Dorset Crime Book 4

The Millionaire Murders, Dorset Crime Book 5

The Fossil Beach Murders, Dorset Crime Book 6

The Blue Pool Murders, Dorset Crime Book 7

...and more to come!

Buy now in ebook, paperback or audiobook